EDGE OF
COLLAPSE

EDGE OF COLLAPSE SERIES BOOK ONE

KYLA STONE

Edge of Collapse

Printed in the United States of America

Cover design by Christian Bentulan

Book formatting by Vellum

First Printed in 2020

ISBN: 978-1-945410-67-3

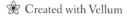 Created with Vellum

Much of this story takes place within the fabulous Manistee National Forest in Michigan. For the sake of the story, I have altered certain aspects and taken a few liberties with a real town or two. Thank you in advance for understanding an author's creative license.

Love is the voice under all silences, the hope which has no opposite in fear; the strength so strong mere force is feebleness: the truth more first than sun, more last than star...

— e.e cummings

1

HANNAH
DAY ONE

The light went out. It was the first thing that alerted her.

The single lightbulb encased in wire mesh on the ceiling glared down on her continuously—twenty-four hours a day, seven days a week, three hundred and sixty-five days a year.

The sudden darkness pressed against the backs of Hannah Sheridan's closed eyelids. Sensing the change, her body woke from her restless nightmares.

She sat up from the bare mattress on the cold concrete floor. She turned her head left and right, straining her eyes.

At first, she thought she'd been plunged into complete and utter blackness.

But no, the narrow rectangle of a window on the southwest side of the room allowed in the barest trickle of dim light. The window was located beneath the back deck. Filtering through the iron bars, very little daylight made its way down here.

She'd grown used to it.

Hannah blinked, let her eyes adjust.

Shadowy shapes appeared—the bean bag in the corner, the doorless bathroom across from her, the small fridge, the rolling cart with the microwave, the narrow counter with the sink and cabinet where she kept her dishes along the far wall.

The silence was the second thing.

She was used to quiet. But this was something else.

The rumble of the generator outside the window. The buzz of the small fridge. The cycling of air from the heating and air conditioning unit.

Everything had gone still and silent. No sound but her own breathing.

For several long minutes, she didn't move.

Was this another trick? A trap just waiting to spring its jaws?

She was used to tricks, too. She lived inside a trap.

The light didn't come back on. The fridge didn't buzz. The generator didn't rumble back to life. She glanced at the tiny camera affixed to the ceiling above the secure metal door.

The little glowing green dot no longer glowed. The camera was blind.

The power had never gone out before. He came and checked it often, made sure everything worked and remained in pristine condition—the electricity, the water, the heat, the camera, the security system.

The generator kept her alive. It also kept her trapped.

Slowly, she pushed aside her two blankets and rose from the mattress in the corner of the room. Her bare feet hit the chilly concrete floor, but she barely noticed.

Her mind spun and whirred, confused thoughts ricocheting against her skull. Nothing made sense.

Why would the power go out? Had he forgotten to refill the generator? Was it something else, like a storm or a power surge?

When would it come back on? Would it come on? Would he know it was out and return to check on her?

Sometimes, he came every seven days. Sometimes, two weeks passed. There was no rhyme or reason to his visits.

No way to tell how many days she'd need to survive before he returned—if he returned.

It was easy to lose track of time here. At first, tracking the days had been of crucial importance. Counting the hours. The days, weeks, months. Then the years.

Always hoping for rescue. Praying for it. Desperate for an escape that never came.

She looked at the calendar she'd made with chalk on the wall above the mattress. It was too dim to see them, but her mind conjured the images clear as day. She'd stared at those blunt marks hundreds, thousands of times.

She knew it was day by the dull gray light. But what day? What month? November? December? Or even later? When had she stopped keeping track?

Only a few weeks. No, it was longer. Maybe even months.

Her mind was clouded and foggy, like it had been stuffed with cotton. It was hard to think straight. Got harder with every day that passed, every day that took her further from who she used to be and sucked her deeper into this endless hell.

Fatigue gripped her and tugged at her arms and legs. Who cared what day or month it was? Nothing ever changed. Nothing ever would.

Her entire life consisted of these four concrete walls. A fifteen-by-twenty room.

She should've given up long ago.

She was close now. The despair like a sucking black hole, pulling at her, threatening to drag her under once and for all. A bottomless sea of darkness closing over her head, drowning her slowly, strangling the breath from her lungs.

For years, she'd fought it. Every day, an hour of calisthenics to keep her muscles from atrophying. Jumping jacks. Sit-ups. Squats. Every day, writing in the journal with the crayons he allowed her. Every day, mentally practicing the guitar or the piano. Composing songs in her head.

Imagining the life she would have if—when—she ever got out of this place. Imagining the life her husband and son were living right that minute. Her family and friends and co-workers—the world continuing on without her.

But the last few months, it had become harder and harder to cling to that minuscule seed of hope. Hope was the ultimate Judas. It had betrayed her hundreds, thousands of times.

In the end, it was hope that caused the most suffering.

Hannah stared across the room at the imposing metal door and the electronic key pad and lock. She stared until the shadowy shape took solid form, until her eyes ached and begged her to blink. She didn't.

Her brain filled with the buzzing static of barely restrained panic. What if he wasn't coming back? What if the water turned off next? She had MREs and enough supplies for another two weeks if she rationed, but no longer.

She had a single cup, a single bowl, and two pans she could fill with water. And the small sink built into the counter—she could fill the basin.

How long would that last? A few days? A week?

What about the heater? The chilly concrete floor felt like it was growing colder by the minute. Even the air on her face and hands felt cooler.

She thought she was still in Michigan, though she wasn't sure.

Wherever she was, the winters were brutal. Only the heater kept her from freezing to death down here.

She knew the season by the temperature drop, the coldness of the floor. If she pushed the rolling cart beneath the single window, climbed on top of it, and peered out through the bars, she could see the snow on the ground, sifted beneath the wide wooden planks of the back porch.

She would freeze to death long before she ran out of food or water.

Outside, the dog barked. He'd been quiet the last day or two. She'd never seen him, but she'd pictured him in her mind a million times. Judging by the deep menace in his bark, he was a huge German Shepherd/Wolfhound/Rottweiler mix, with vicious eyes and razor-sharp teeth.

A monster. Just like his owner.

Placed there like Cerberus guarding the gates of Hades, in case anyone was stupid enough to try to get in—or out.

She'd never heard another human voice, other than *his*.

The man who'd put her here. The man who kept her imprisoned like a rat in a cage.

No neighbors. No visitors. Only the damn barking dog and the occasional rumble of a truck or snowmobile engine when he came to see her.

Fear crept into the corners of her mind, anxiety tangling in her belly. She padded to the center of the room and turned in a slow circle, trying to push the cobwebs from her sluggish brain, trying to *think*.

She wrapped her arms around her thin ribs and hugged herself. She wore a loose hunter-green knit sweater that matched her eyes over a thin nightgown, with a pair of oversized long johns beneath it all—she had a few different outfits that she washed in the tiny sink once a week by hand.

How long would it take the temperature to drop to intolerable levels? How long for the human body to freeze to death inside an unheated concrete basement?

Maybe it was nothing. She was panicking over nothing. The electricity would switch back on in an hour or a day. Everything would return to the horrible state of normalcy she'd endured for years.

Somehow, she knew it wouldn't.

Maybe he'd finally tired of her and decided to let the generator run out. Decided to let her suffer slowly, to die in degrees by starvation and freezing to death.

That thought didn't ring true. When it was time to kill her, he would do it himself. She knew that like she knew her own name.

Something had happened. He'd been killed in a crash or struck by a train or dropped by a brain aneurysm. Anything was possible.

There were a thousand ways to die. A hundred ways to go missing, to suddenly disappear from your own life.

She knew that better than anyone.

As much as she longed to see him dead, he was her only link to the outside world. To life. She loathed him but depended on him for every single thing.

He'd used that to control her completely. To exert his indomitable will over every aspect of her pitiful life.

Grinning with that dead-eye smile as he keyed in the lock code each and every time he entered the room. *Hurt me, and you kill any chance of ever getting out of here alive.*

He wasn't stupid. He knew how lethal hope was—how powerful a weapon it could be.

To her right, she felt the door like a physical presence, looming just at the periphery of her vision.

She turned again, faced it. The cold of the floor leached through her feet. Sent chills racing up her spine. She shivered.

Nothing worked. Not the power. Not the heat. Not the little blinking light on the camera.

What if...

She lowered her hand to her stomach, nearly touched the rounded, basketball-sized belly, but didn't. Her hands dropped limply to her sides.

The door was always locked. A power outage wouldn't change that.

Hannah Sheridan was just as trapped as she'd ever been.

2

HANNAH
DAY ONE

Almost without thinking, Hannah found herself moving numbly, mechanically toward the sink. She knew every inch of this room by heart. She didn't need to see to know what she was doing.

She pulled her two pans out of the cupboard and filled them with water. She set them on the counter. Next, she filled her single cup and bowl. She plugged the small stainless-steel basin of the sink with the stopper and began to fill it.

A few days' worth of water. She wouldn't use the water for anything but drinking, conserving as much as she could until it ran out.

But the cold . . . that would kill her faster than anything. She only had the two blankets and the sweater she already wore. It wouldn't be enough.

None of it would be enough.

She would die here, in this horrible prison. There wasn't a damn thing she could do about it. Panic and dread swirled in her stomach. Nausea crawled up her throat, and she almost retched.

She tugged the hair tie from her wrist and pulled her thick, waist-length dark brown hair into a messy bun. She used to brush it every day. But lately . . . lately, she could barely muster the energy to feed herself.

He made her pay for that.

He liked her pretty. He never struck her face. Never pulled out her hair.

And he liked her clean. She always had shampoo and conditioner, body wash and deodorant, toothpaste and an electric toothbrush.

A supply of vitamin D to keep her healthy. Even a few maternity clothes as her belly expanded.

He kept the cupboards and the minifridge stocked with microwavable meals, pastas and proteins, and canned fruits and vegetables.

She'd learned what happened when she didn't eat, when she didn't keep herself clean and presentable.

She glanced at the door again. Locked. It was always locked.

Absently, she touched the mangled fingers of her left hand. They were permanently disfigured—broken one by one, again and again. Pain so excruciating, she'd passed out.

He'd woken her up with a pan of cold water dumped on her face, only to start with the next finger.

Disobedience brought pain. Defiance brought pain. Hope brought pain.

The first lessons he'd taught her.

She was stubborn. She never learned the first time.

She'd tried to use the razor for shaving her legs on him. It hadn't gone well. He was fast and strong and smart.

On her second attempt, she'd unwound the metal spiral from the notebook he'd so generously provided her. She'd waited for him to get close before lunging, striking at his eye with the wire poking from her fist.

He'd jerked away at the last second. The wire scraped a deep gouge into his cheek, drawing blood and creating a scar, but no permanent damage.

He'd broken two ribs for that.

The third time, she'd rubbed the end of a metal spoon against the rough concrete floor for hours a day, for days on end. She'd gripped the rounded spoon end in her right hand and waited. Waited until he was close but distracted. She'd gathered all her strength and courage and plunged it into his neck.

She'd missed his carotid artery. It hadn't gone in deep enough to incapacitate him.

He'd stomped her bare foot with his boot—breaking her big toe and spraining her ankle—and re-fractured two of her fingers. *Snap, snap.*

She couldn't walk for days, could barely move, curled on the mattress in a fog of agony. She would rather die than live like this. And if she was going to die, she was determined to take him with her.

On his next visit, he'd dropped a picture onto the mattress beside her crumpled form. A photo of her then three-year-old son, Milo.

In the picture, her husband, Noah, held him, his face drawn with grief and worry. Noah wore his patrolman's uniform and stood on the front porch of their two-story colonial house in Fall Creek, a small township located in southwest Michigan.

She understood instantly that this photo had been taken mere days ago. He knew her family and where they lived and could get as close as he wanted at any time.

This was a warning. A promise.

The next time she tried anything, the people she loved most would suffer.

She had crayons and chalk instead of pencils, plastic silverware instead of metal, clothbound notebooks instead of spiral. Those things mattered little, though. She still had the Bic disposable razors. She had the sharp metal edges from her canned food.

But she didn't dare use them. He'd broken her, and he knew it.

That was the day the fight to kill her captor had died.

But not the fight to survive.

Day after day, month after month, year after year, she'd managed to wake up each day, to continue to live, to continue to hope. To believe that she would get out someday, that she would see her son again. Milo. That was the seed she held onto, the thing that kept her clinging to sanity.

Hannah was incredibly stubborn. Always had been. But she was only human. Her captivity wore her down. The isolation, the confinement. The constant, never-ending cruelty and suffering.

Every day, more and more of her sanity slipped away. During the worst times, she went away in her head for hours at a time. Blank spaces full of nothing.

Each time she came back, she was still here in this prison of fear and pain and misery.

Hannah stood completely still in the darkness. The sink filled, and she turned off the faucet. The last of the water drip, drip, dripped.

Instinctively, almost against her will, she turned back toward the door.

The dog had stopped barking. Complete silence enveloped her. The power was off. The generator wasn't working. Nothing was working.

Hope was her worst enemy.

If only she could give in. Killing herself would be a mercy. She'd thought about it a million times. Let the thoughts spin round and round inside her head. Plotting and planning.

It wouldn't be hard, not compared to this. It was far easier to give up. Easier to resign herself to her fate—a future of dying slowly, broken bone by broken bone, or a death of her choosing. It was death either way.

And yet, it hadn't happened yet. Somehow, despite everything, she was still here.

That stubborn part of her always clinging to life, to hope. Even in the face of overwhelming evidence to the contrary.

Could she bear another crushing disappointment? Even just walking across the concrete floor felt like a monumental effort. All she wanted to do was lay down and go to sleep and never wake up.

The door was locked. It was always locked.

She'd beaten her fists against that immovable steel door thousands of times, struck it until her palms bled, scraped at the frame until her fingernails broke off.

She rested her hands on her belly. Felt movement. Quickly dropped them to her sides again.

She took a step forward. One, two, three. Ten steps to the door.

It's not going to open. It never does. Why do you do this to yourself?

She stood in front of it, bouncing on her heels. Fear and apprehension battling with desperation, with a crazed, terrible hope.

The concrete floor was freezing now. So was the air. Goosebumps pimpled the flesh on her arms and legs. The cold entered through the soles of her feet and radiated up through her shins, her thighs, her torso. She shuddered.

Hope or no hope, this was real. This was happening. Without heat, she was dead.

She rested her right hand on the handle. Swallowed hard, battling her despair, her own disintegrating mind.

A terrible tightness gripped her chest. Her ears rang. Her hands shook.

She turned the handle.

The door swung open.

3

HANNAH

DAY ONE

I t was too good to be true. It couldn't be real.

It *was* real. This was no dream. It was real and it was happening.

Hannah didn't know how long she stood there, hovering between two worlds. Her prison behind her and her future before her—unknown and utterly terrifying.

How had the loss of power affected the electronic lock? She had no idea. Maybe it was all connected to the generator—the camera, the security system, the access panel.

It was possible he'd finally made a mistake. After all these years, maybe he'd accidentally left the door unlocked.

And she'd been so beaten down, so despondent and resigned to her fate, she'd stopped checking.

A thought came to her—slow and fuzzy. Back in her old life, a life she could barely recall, one of her college professors had once told the story of the dog who was trapped inside a cage for months. When the cage door was finally opened, the dog remained huddled inside and refused to come out.

The dog's spirit was broken. He'd forgotten what freedom meant.

Had she forgotten too? Nausea churned in her stomach, acid burning the back of her throat. She nearly vomited.

A thousand what-ifs careened through her brain. If the power hadn't gone out . . . if she hadn't forced herself to try the lock, in complete defiance of everything experience had taught her thus far . . . if she'd given up . . .

But she hadn't given up. She'd opened the door.

And now? Now everything was different.

In a heartbeat, her entire world had changed.

She was out of the cage.

Instead of joy or triumph, it was fear that gripped her. Her constant, familiar companion. Always pressing down on her chest, a choking panic clawing at her throat.

Her breath came in sharp, shallow gasps. Her heart galloped like a jackrabbit inside her ribcage, adrenaline thrumming through her.

What now?

Now you run.

The air smelled stale and musty. She blinked in the darkness, barely able to make out the wooden basement stairs leading up to another door with a rim of light at the bottom and sides like a lighthouse beckoning her onward.

It was a normal door. A regular wooden door, like in every house she'd ever been in. No metal. No reinforced frame. No electronic keypad.

Just a door.

A door leading to the whole bright and terrifying world.

She glanced back into the room, into her tiny, cramped prison.

Was there anything she wanted to take with her? Her journals? Her notebooks filled with poetry and song lyrics? No. Not even those.

She would leave everything behind, shedding her past self like a caterpillar shed its skin.

It won't be that easy, a voice in her head whispered.

She ignored it. There would be time for all those thoughts later. Now, she just had to get out.

With her good hand, she gripped the railing. With her bad hand, she cradled her swollen belly, as if that could hold her up.

She began to climb. One step at a time. Counting with each step. *One, two, three.* Breathe in, breathe out. *Six, seven, eight.*

At the top of the stairs, she hesitated. Fear thrummed through her. What waited for her on the other side? Freedom or just another trap?

He could be there, sitting at his kitchen table waiting for her, grinning his Cheshire Cat grin. A cruel trick. Playing with her the way a bored cat played with its dinner.

Hannah wouldn't go back down those stairs again. She couldn't. Her mind would crack and shatter into a thousand pieces and she would go away and never come back again. She would shrivel into dust and nothingness.

She wasn't going back. There was only forward.

She twisted the handle and pushed open the door.

Harsh whiteness struck her eyeballs. It felt like a huge spotlight shining directly into her face, like needles piercing her brain.

With a muffled cry, Hannah crumpled to the stairs, nearly falling backward. She barely kept her grasp on the railing. Her knees struck the edge of the stairs. Pain stung her kneecaps.

She flung her left hand over her face and squeezed her eyelids shut. Her eyes stung and prickled. Hot tears leaked down her cheeks.

Long minutes passed before she could even think past the blinding pain, the shock and confusion.

Daylight. The thought trickled in slowly. Her eyes were used to artificial light but hadn't seen the sun in years. Her retinas couldn't take the harsh bright light.

Panic threatened to overtake her again. How was she going to escape if she couldn't see? She was already weak, crippled, and defenseless. How could she possibly do this blind?

It wouldn't work. This couldn't work. He would find her. And when he did, he'd be angrier than ever before.

He would break her fingers again, then her toes, her hands, her wrists. He would take his knives to her. Cut off her fingers one by one and watch her bleed . . .

Stop it! she screamed at herself. *Just stop!*

She fought back the fog of frantic, jumbled thoughts careening inside her head. She had to think clearly or she would never get out of here alive. She would never reach her son or hold him in her arms again.

She wasn't blind. Her eyes would adjust. It would just take time.

Time being the one thing she didn't have.

She had no idea when he would come back. In a week? In a day? In the next hour?

She didn't even know for certain that he wasn't already here. Waiting for her, lurking just out of her reach, watching. Or maybe he was out in the yard, and as soon as she stumbled or made a noise, he'd come racing in to haul her back down to that prison.

She stilled, forced herself to inhale a deep breath. The mustiness of the basement was gone. The air smelled fresh—if a bit dusty, cool but not freezing, the temperature inside the house somewhere near sixty degrees.

She strained her ears for any noise, any shuffle of footsteps or muffled breathing to alert her to the fact she wasn't alone, that he was right there with her, watching her every move, just waiting for the right moment to pounce.

Only the roar of her own pulse in her ears. The utter silence pressed against her eardrums. She held her breath, listening, listening.

Nothing. She had to believe that he was gone. If he was here, she was dead anyway. But if he wasn't . . .

Every minute that passed was a minute closer to getting caught. She couldn't stay here. She had to get as far away as possible. She had to get the hell out of here—wherever here was.

Her eyes still closed, she touched her belly with her good hand. He would come after her. She had no doubt of that. He would need to find her before she found help, before she told everyone all about him.

She needed a head start. She needed every hour and every mile she could put between herself and this place.

Think! Take it one step at a time. Don't get overwhelmed. Don't think of the time slipping by, every second, every minute wasted. First things first.

She had to find a way to be able to see. She needed something to deflect the brightness, to shield her eyes. She needed sunglasses. But how to find those when she had no idea where to look—and couldn't actually look at all?

Her hand was still on her belly, touching the cotton fabric of her sweater. If she could figure out how to wrap it around her head, the dark green fabric would block light.

It was also the only thing keeping her warm. She dreaded taking it off. The thick, unwieldy arms would be hard to tie around her head and remain in place.

Plan B. She needed a pair of scissors. Most people kept a pair in a kitchen drawer. Maybe he did too. She just needed to find the kitchen and could feel her way from there.

She could do this. She could figure it out.

It meant moving into the house blindly, unable to see where she was going, making her way by touch alone. Her temporary blindness made her even more vulnerable and helpless than she already was.

Fresh panic clawed at her, closing her throat. She could hardly breathe, couldn't move, her arms and legs rooted to the spot. Blackness swirled in her mind and threatened to take her away again. But she couldn't let herself go away.

Every minute counted. Everything mattered.

She fought to stay present, to push down the mind-numbing fear paralyzing her.

It was either move or die.

Hannah refused to die.

Keeping her eyes squeezed tightly shut, she flailed ahead, pushed the door out of the way. She crawled on her hands and knees further into the house. Felt cool linoleum beneath her.

The dog barked, startling her.

Her heart bucked in her chest. She collapsed, cowering beneath the onslaught of overwhelming terror.

He was here. He'd unleashed the monstrous dog, sicced it on her, brought it inside to tear out her throat. The monster of her nightmares took over. The yellow eyes and red slash of a mouth. The claws closing around her throat and cutting off her breath.

Her mind threatened to go away. Blank darkness tugged at her frantic thoughts, stealing them away. *No!* She couldn't disappear now. She had to stay present, to fight through it, no matter how terrifying.

She forced herself to count inside her head, to calm down. *One, two, three . . . thirty, thirty-one, thirty-two . . . fifty-five, fifty-six, fifty-seven . . .*

Think! some small part of her brain cried. That deep booming bark came from outside of the house. The dog was outside, not in here. It couldn't hurt her. Nothing was hurting her.

She sucked in several ragged breaths until she'd regained control of herself. Focus. Focus on escape. That was all that mattered.

She shut out the barking and listened for noises inside. No signs of life. Nothing, not the soft buzz of the fridge or the ticking of a clock.

More importantly, no squeak of a boot on a floorboard, no sigh of a body shifting, or low, steady breathing.

It didn't mean she was alone.

And it certainly didn't mean she was safe.

4

HANNAH
DAY ONE

Heart banging in her chest, Hannah crept across the floor, her right hand splayed in front of her to feel whatever lay ahead, her damaged left hand balanced on the heel of her palm.

Her knees still hurt. Her lower back ached. The dull pain in her ruined hand never went away.

She ignored it all. She was used to pain, to the agony of broken bones and the tenderness of slowly healing bruises. This was no different.

Her fingers found the thin spindle of a chair leg, then the thicker leg of a table. She moved around the table and kept going several more feet until she reached a smooth, warm surface.

Wood, not the cool sleek surface of a stainless-steel appliance. A cabinet door.

She reached for the knob of the cabinet, felt higher and found the first drawer. She explored each object with her fingers, her muddled brain formulating the correct objects with painstaking slowness—cold metal spoons, forks, and bread knives.

She pulled each object out and tossed it on the floor, not bothering to put it back nice and neat for him.

In the next drawer—the smooth cylinders of spices and herbs. In the next, round rolling pins and wide thin cutting boards. And in the fourth drawer, measuring spoons and cups and a can opener.

Her fingers closed over something sleek, cool, and pointed. Scissors.

Relief shot through her veins. She sank to her butt and leaned back against the cabinet, legs stretched out in front of her. She fumbled for the bottom hem of her shirt, feeling for the starting point and fitting the scissors in place.

Eyes still squeezed shut, cautiously feeling her way, she cut a strip of cloth about four inches wide and a couple of feet long.

She dropped the scissors, folded the strip in on itself once, then placed it over her eyes like a blindfold. Once she'd tied and knotted the ends around the back of her head, she adjusted the blindfold so that there was a bit of space to peek through at the bottom.

Slowly, she opened her smarting eyes. The darkness offered sweet relief. When she glanced down, she could make out the black and white checks of the linoleum floor through the glaring white light.

It was enough. And it would get better.

With every minute she spent outside the cramped hellhole of her prison, the fog in her brain cleared a little more. She was free.

She was *free*.

She could scarcely wrap her mind around it. But that didn't matter. All that mattered was that she was getting the hell out of here.

Hannah grabbed the scissors and pulled herself to her feet. What was next? Her eyes couldn't take looking out the window, not yet.

She went still and listened. The dog barked, the sound closer and much louder now.

She still heard nothing else. No rumbling car engines. No sounds of neighbors.

She was somewhere far from civilization. It only made sense. He would want her somewhere that no one could hear her scream.

And no one ever had.

The nearest town might be fifty miles away. It was the middle of winter. She couldn't go out in a sweater and long johns and expect to last more than a few hours.

She had to gather as many supplies as she could before she set out.

Using her narrow strip of vision, she made her way gingerly through the kitchen and onto a wooden plank floor. She stumbled into a brown leather sofa, almost knocked over an end table covered in books, found a fireplace and a wood-burning stove, and finally reached the hallway.

It was dark inside the first bedroom. The blinds over the windows were drawn and the curtains were closed, shielding her from the painful daylight.

She closed her eyes, folded the lower lip of the blindfold, and slowly opened them. It only took a minute to adjust as she took everything in.

Log cabin walls. Nubby gray carpet. A double bed with a blue and navy-striped comforter, nightstands on either side, a dresser along the far wall beside the double accordion doors of the closet.

Everything clean and neat and orderly.

She checked the nightstands first, hoping for a gun tucked in a drawer. No such luck. She headed for the closet.

Her gut roiled in revulsion at the thought of wearing his clothes, but it lasted for only a moment. She wanted to live. The knowledge that she was going to steal his own things to escape held a certain satisfying appeal.

Within minutes, she'd found a fresh T-shirt, two long-sleeved waffle-knit shirts, two hooded sweatshirts, a windbreaker jacket, and a heavy, hooded, insulated brown coat that reached her knees.

She put it all on, dressing in layer after layer. The men's clothes were large on her short, slight frame, but they would also fit over her distended stomach.

The pants were harder. In one of the drawers, she found some long johns and cut off the excess length where her ankles ended.

She put on a pair of men's insulated winter hiking pants over them. They were too big for her legs and hips, but too snug to fit around the fullest part of her belly. She wasn't sure what to do about that yet.

She added several pairs of warm wool socks, then went back to the closet, knelt down, and rummaged around the stuff stored on a couple of shelves stacked on the floor. She needed a backpack to carry supplies.

She didn't find a pack, but she did uncover a heavy, down-lined sleeping bag rated for winter temperatures. She tossed it on the bed, along with two extra pairs of wool socks.

There had to be a place he stored his winter gear. But wherever it was, it wasn't here. Time to keep looking.

She replaced the blindfold over her eyes and cautiously and painstakingly searched the rest of the house. With every minute that passed, the watery glare lessened, and she could make out more details of her surroundings.

She searched the bathroom, and then headed back to the living room and kitchen. She opened the pantry. It was stocked with at least a month's worth of food. Perfect.

Her stomach rumbled. She grabbed a package of beef jerky, ripped it open with shaking fingers, and crammed a leathery piece into her mouth.

She stuffed the bag in her coat pocket. Her fingers brushed something hard, smooth, and plastic. She pulled out a pair of men's sunglasses.

Relief washed through her. She put them on but kept the blindfold partially in place. Her vision cleared, the pain lessening.

She kept moving.

Across from the basement was another door, which opened to a mudroom with a washer and dryer. Winter gear and outdoor supplies hung from every hook.

Two pairs of boots and some tennis shoes were stacked neatly beneath the hook. A set of men's skis against the wall beside a tall cabinet.

She had to sit on the floor to pull on a pair of the boots. They were loose, but the several pairs of wool socks she wore helped. She tied the laces as tight as she possibly could. There was still room at the toes and heels, but they would have to do.

Using the wall, she pulled herself back to her feet. Out of the corner of her eye, she glimpsed a small wooden porch outside the rectangular window inset in the back door.

Recognition jolted through her. She'd stared at that back porch a hundred thousand times. But always from below.

She was standing directly above her mattress and the barred window.

She closed her eyes, opened them, forced away the dark sucking panic.

She wasn't stuck down there anymore. She wasn't a trapped, helpless thing. She was free, and she had to do whatever she needed to in order to stay that way.

The dog kept barking, loud and deep and booming.

She dared to look out the back window. With the sunglasses and the partial blindfold, it was bearable. Slowly, the blurry images in all that whiteness shimmered into shapes and objects her brain recognized.

A thick blanket of snow covered the yard. Past the yard, thick forest rimmed the small clearing on all sides as far as she could see. Trees and more trees, branches bare and blanketed in snow.

It took a minute for the names to come back to her, but they did. Her lips formed each word: maple, hemlock, yellow birch. White ash. Beech.

The most beautiful trees she'd ever seen.

It didn't matter how beautiful they were—like a postcard picture with their naked limbs blanketed in pristine snow, the vibrant green pines against all that white.

She was stuck in the middle of nowhere.

Twenty yards directly in front of her stood two sheds. The first was smaller with an opening cut out of the bottom. The second was larger with a padlock and chains wrapping the double doors.

To the left stood a carport with stacks of firewood covered by a tarp beneath it.

Her gaze returned to the large shed. Maybe there was something inside she could use—

Movement in the snow ahead of her.

Hannah froze.

5

PIKE
DAY ONE

Thirty-four-year-old Gavin Pike picked out flowers for his mother. White lilies, her favorite. He always brought her flowers and chocolate for their family's Christmas Eve dinner at her home.

It made her happy. And when she was happy, things went easier for him.

He grabbed the bouquet from the refrigerated case at the florist's shop without checking the price and got into line. The overwhelming scents of greenery, potpourri, and the sickly fragrance of everything floral filled his nostrils and almost made him choke.

"Baby, It's Cold Outside" played over the shop's radio. The whole place was lit up with lights strung everywhere and Christmas trees in every corner.

He looked forward to Christmas only because it meant a few days off in the middle of the week. Let the lemmings consume themselves with festooning their homes with garish decor and slaving over gifts and home-cooked turkeys their whiny brats wouldn't even appreciate.

Once he made the requisite holiday visit to his mother and brother tonight, he'd have Christmas day, Thursday, Friday, and the entire weekend off to play. And to hunt.

The lights flickered off. The song cut off abruptly right before the hideous chorus.

The woman ahead of him clutched a vase of red and white roses. She turned and looked up at the fluorescent overhead lights with a frown. "What happened? It's not even snowing out."

"Maybe a squirrel got in the transformer again," the cashier said. "But the computers are down. Cash only until they come back online."

Pike sighed and shifted, adjusting the collar of his uniform shirt impatiently. He'd just finished his night shift as a correctional officer at the Berrien County Correctional Facility in Baroda, Michigan. He enjoyed working nights. Less oversight and B.S.

He also served as a volunteer reserve officer with the Fall Creek Township police department. Not because he enjoyed volunteering. The job entailed other perks.

This morning, he was tired and grumpy and just wanted to get away from the fragrant stink already giving him a headache. He needed a cigarette.

Several horns blared outside. Tires squealed.

He glanced at the clock hanging on the wall behind the counter. It was battery-operated and still working. 12:22 p.m. Maybe he should just leave—

Behind him, someone screamed.

Pike whipped around and glanced through the picture glass windows of the florist's shop to the busy street. His heart jolted in his chest.

A massive blue Suburban careened through the intersection just outside the shop. It was headed straight toward them. The Suburban jolted over the curb as pedestrians scattered in its wake, shrieking and shouting.

No time to think. Only react. He threw himself sideways, lunging for the refrigerated cases along the left wall. He stumbled over a decorative row of potted poinsettias, knocking over several and stepping on plants and flowers in his haste.

The Suburban slammed through the shop's front window and brick façade exterior. Glass shattered. Fragments of mortar exploded. Splinters of stone, brick, glass, and pottery flew through the air like knives.

Pike cowered, his hands shielding his head, his body half-shielded by the tall cases.

The other shoppers darted deeper into the store, searching desperately for safety, but they were out of time. The woman with the red and white roses froze in the center of the store, her mouth opened in a frozen O of terror, still clutching that damn vase.

The Suburban plowed into the building, crushing anything in its path. It smashed through tables and stands and dozens of vases, pots, and terrariums, wreaths and bouquets, grinding roses, lilies, chrysanthemums, tulips, and sprays of greenery beneath its wheels.

The huge grille mowed into the woman with the roses with a dull thud. The Suburban crashed into the register counter and finally came to a stop against the rear brick wall. The entire front was crumpled like a pop can.

A middle-aged Caucasian man in glasses and a plaid coat stumbled out of the driver's side. He half-bent and retched, vomiting all over the dust, glass, and petal-strewn floor. "Oh no! Oh no, no, no!"

"You killed that woman!" another woman shrieked. "Someone call the police!"

"I couldn't stop!" the driver wailed. "My car—it just stopped working! The anti-lock brakes. The engine. The power steering. I just —I lost control on the ice . . ."

He glanced at the bloody body tangled beneath the wheels of his Suburban and vomited again. He wiped at his mouth with a shaking hand. "I'm sorry. I'm so sorry . . ."

Pike rose cautiously to his feet. He brushed shards of glass and pottery and shredded flower petals from his uniform. He was unharmed. The adrenaline dump made his legs shaky. He needed a damn cigarette.

He didn't bother to check on the woman beneath the Suburban. She was clearly dead. If others were hurt, it wasn't his problem.

He picked his way gingerly through the wreckage of the store. There was no door anymore. No window. Just a wide gaping hole spiked with jagged glass shards. Still holding the lilies, he stepped through the hole and out into the street.

The traffic lights were dark. Dozens of cars were still stopped at the intersection, unmoving. Several had rolled onto the curb or crashed into light poles. There were dozens of fender-benders. Two blocks south, a serious pile-up of at least ten vehicles snarled the intersection.

Along the median, leafless trees were wrapped in Christmas lights, their bulbs dead, the streetlight poles wound with pine, holly, and ribbons.

The sidewalks weren't crammed with holiday shoppers like the big cities, but there were still several dozen people out and about, hurrying to finish last-minute tasks before Christmas.

"My phone won't work!" a man shouted. "I can't call 911!"

"Mine either," a shaken shopper said.

"What's happening?"

"What's going on?"

"It's just a power outage. A really bad one."

The fools started talking about power outages they'd experienced or heard of. The Polar Vortex of '18. Snowmageddon '22, when a blizzard dumped four feet of powder and electricity was out for a week.

They didn't get it. They never did. They always looked for the simplest explanation and clung to it. That tendency allowed many an unseen, unsuspected evil to have its way in the shadows.

He was still holding the bouquet of lilies in one hand. The petals were crushed and bruised from where he'd pressed them against his chest. With his free hand, he pulled his iPhone out of his pocket. It was as he expected: dead.

Pike wasn't stupid. The power grid had nothing to do with cars or phones. This was something different. Something more.

It might be some solar flare thing. Or maybe a cyberattack by a rogue country. Or the US government had finally turned on its own people.

It didn't matter. He didn't care about any of it.

He was thinking about his hunting cabin.

Thinking about the nice setup he'd rigged for the place. The new, top-of-the-line generator running the lights, the heat, the security system—all regulated by a self-contained computerized system.

Including the camera that he accessed on his secret phone so he could watch her anytime he wished. In the middle of a staff meeting. At dinner with his mother. Working the job.

It always gave him a little thrill. A buzz better than a hit of crack cocaine.

He pulled out the second phone, the secret one. It was just as dead as his iPhone.

Maybe everything was fine. The generator still whirring away. The locks still in place. The only way to know for sure was to verify with his own eyes. He had no choice.

Pike dropped the bouquet to the glass-littered street. He needed to get to the cabin.

6

HANNAH
DAY ONE

The snow moved.

No, it was something white moving through the snow.

Hannah sucked in her breath, her heart hammering against her sore ribs.

All this time, she'd pictured that deep, savage bark belonging to a mangy German Shepherd or giant slobbering Rottweiler or even the demon-dog Cerberus himself. The reality wasn't anything like she'd imagined.

An enormous white dog strained at the chain linking his collar to a steel ring attached to the smaller shed—a doghouse, she realized. His fur was thick and shaggy. He was huge—at least up to her waist, with a massive head easily twice as large as her own. He might weigh one hundred and fifty pounds or more.

He was beautiful. Scary as hell, but beautiful.

The dog saw her in the window and lunged against his collar, barking fiercely. The dog's domain was clearly marked by muddy tracks worn into the snow.

She recognized the breed, though it took her brain a long time to conjure the correct title. A Great Pyrenees Mountain Dog.

Against her better judgment, she opened the back door. Cold slammed into her like a physical force. Icy fingers slid down the back of her neck and stung her cheeks. She wrapped her scarf tighter around her neck and slipped the jacket's furred hood over her head.

The hairs on the back of her neck prickled like she was being watched.

Blood rushed to her head and she swayed, dizzy. She held herself up with one hand pressed against the door. She had to remember to take it slow in her condition.

Her condition. Her mind shied away from the truth. She didn't want to think about it. She'd ignored it as much as she could the last seven or eight months.

She could keep ignoring it for a while longer, at least.

With her balance restored, she turned slowly, squinting, struggling to distinguish the shadows from the trees from the white snowbanks.

White powder spilled from the branch of a pine tree and fell into the snow with a soft *pfft*. She flinched, wildly scanning the yard and the trees for movement, for any signs of *him*.

There was nothing. Just trees and snow. Her and the dog.

Her eyes hurt. A deep aching in the back of her head. But if she squinted behind her sunglasses, she could see well enough. The day was heavily overcast, the sun hidden behind a bank of dark clouds swollen with the promise of an approaching snowstorm.

The storm was coming. She needed to hurry.

Instead of heading back inside for the skis and her new pack, she moved toward the dog. She knew better, knew she should get the hell out as fast as she could, the dog be damned.

But she couldn't help herself. She was drawn to him almost

against her will.

Her boots sank deep into the snow and her nostrils stung. The cold air burned raw in her throat with every breath. It was fresh and clean and smelled of pine and earth and things wild and alive and *outside*.

She opened her mouth, closed it. Inhaled sharply, the brittle air stinging her throat. She hadn't spoken aloud in so long. She didn't speak to him. She had nothing to say to him.

The first few years, she used to sing. Would sing for hours every day, memorizing the songs she'd written, creating tunes and rhythms and harmonies. She'd loved music. Majored in music education in college.

She didn't sing anymore. Hadn't for a long, long time.

The only sounds he ever wanted to hear from her were screams and whimpers of pain and acquiescence. He had no use for her voice. Maybe she'd started to believe the same thing.

She took a step closer. Didn't take her eyes off the dog.

He stood, staring back at her. He didn't bark. He didn't growl. He just watched her.

All this time, she'd thought of him as an enemy, *his* minion. A savage guard to make sure she remained trapped here for the rest of her miserable life. She'd despised this dog almost as much as she'd hated her captor.

Maybe she had been wrong.

She made her way hesitantly closer.

The dog didn't move.

She took another step. It was so cold, she could see the white puffs of her breath.

He raised his head, ears cocked, his muzzle tilted. Studying her, just like she was studying him.

His paws and legs were splattered with mud. His fur was matted in places. Even as big as he was, he was far too thin. The outline of his ribs jutted beneath his thick coat.

The thick metal chain looked so ugly and *wrong* on a dog so regal.

It didn't matter how dirty and ragged he was. He looked like he belonged next to one of the great kings of myth. King Arthur, or maybe a great Viking warlord.

This dog wasn't the enemy.

He was a prisoner. Same as she was.

Would he die if she left? He must have food and a source of water that didn't freeze inside that shed that served as his doghouse. But how long would it last?

Would her captor bother to feed him if she wasn't here anymore? If the guard dog had nothing to guard?

She took another step.

A low growl started in his throat. A deep rumble of warning. His black lips curled over long sharp teeth.

Those jaws could clamp down on a grown man's throat and shred it to pieces in seconds. She was sure of it. He looked like he could take down a ten-point buck without a second thought.

She was nothing to him.

It was a risk—a risk she shouldn't take.

Every second she remained here was a second closer to being found again, being dragged back and thrown into the basement to rot. Or being skinned alive, or some other torture whose horrors she couldn't even imagine.

She should go. She needed to go.

But something held her in place, something that wouldn't let her abandon this dog.

He was still trapped. Still a prisoner of the same man who'd tortured them both.

She couldn't just leave him.

7

HANNAH
DAY ONE

Hannah pulled the package of beef jerky out of her coat pocket and took out a slice. She tossed it at the dog. It landed in the trampled snow a few feet from him.

His big brown eyes never leaving her, he padded over to the dried meat and inhaled it in one gulp.

She tossed him another one. He ate it just as fast.

He was hungry, maybe starving. She'd suspected as much. Her captor wouldn't value dogs any more than he valued women.

She moved closer until she was less than three feet away, just outside the reach of his chain.

The dog stiffened. He lowered his head, growling louder.

"Don't be afraid," she said. The sound came out like a rough, nonsensical grunt. Alien to her own ears. Her throat was raw, her voice box unused.

She tried again. "I won't hurt you."

This time, the words were clearly words, though they were hoarse and rough. She cleared her throat, swallowed what felt like rocks in her mouth. "Don't be afraid."

She took a third piece of jerky. She needed this food for herself, though she'd packed as much as she could carry. But she couldn't stop herself. She couldn't bring herself to leave him behind.

She stood close enough that if he lunged, he might be able to reach her. Escape would be that much harder if he bit her. She'd found some bandages, Advil, and Neosporin in the bottom cabinet of the bathroom, but not much else.

Anxiety twisted her stomach. Apprehension sent her heart racing. Her palms were damp beneath her gloves. She held out the strip of jerky.

The dog watched it hungrily, his gaze jumping from the food to her face to the food again. His tail stood out stiffly behind him, the long plume barely moving. His hackles were raised.

She could almost reach his collar. This close, she could see the raw skin beneath the collar, the rusty red of dried blood staining his fur. She'd need to get that off too.

"It's okay," she murmured. "You're okay. You're going to be free now. I know you're scared, but it's going to be okay. I promise."

A foot separated her from the animal's powerful jaws and slobbering fangs. He could do more than hurt her if he wanted. He could snap her neck as easily as a toothpick.

She dropped the jerky in front of him. He darted down to get it.

This was her chance. Her blood rushed in her ears. Adrenaline surging through her veins. She leaned in and reached for the chain hook. She got one hand on it, tried to jam open the hook with her gloved fingers, her bad hand utterly useless.

The dog lunged sideways with a snarl. She didn't let go. She should have, but she didn't.

The hook was open. She just needed to angle it and slip it off the ring of his collar. She just needed—

His heavy, muscled body slammed into her legs, knocking her over. She fell on her butt.

She kept her grip on the collar, felt the hook slide free, and let go as the chain clanked to the ground.

Startled, the dog lunged at her.

She jerked back, lost her equilibrium, and landed flat on her back in the snow.

He pounced on top of her, huge paws pressing down on her chest. He loomed over her. Hot animal breath blasting her face, spittle splattering her cheeks.

Instinctively, she tried to raise her arms to protect her face, but the dog's giant head and torso crouched above her kept her from moving. He had her pinned. Helpless.

"Go!" she screamed at him, her voice scraping her throat. "Get out of here! You're free!"

As if he'd understood her, the dog leaped up. Still growling, he released his hold on her and turned and snuffled at the chain looped and inert in the snow.

Hannah lay still, unmoving.

His head lifted, sniffing the air. And then he ran.

The dog galloped away, his long legs kicking up snow as he ran between a row of pine trees at the edge of the yard. He never looked back.

Just like that, he disappeared.

Hannah expelled rapid puffs of white smoke. Her cheeks were cold. Her heartbeat thudded loud in her ears. Slowly, she raised one arm and wiped the dog spittle from her face with her coat sleeve.

Disappointment settled in her gut like a block of ice. She hadn't managed to get the collar off, but she'd done it. The dog was free.

She didn't know what she'd expected. That he would follow her dutifully, licking her hand in gratitude?

He wasn't tame or trained like a golden retriever. He'd been hurt and abused just like she had. Was it any wonder his instinct was to run as far and as fast as he could?

"Good for you." She pulled herself awkwardly into a sitting position. Her belly only got in the way as she climbed laboriously to her feet, breathing hard.

She didn't begrudge the dog his freedom. She knew how desperately they'd both longed for it.

Whether he could survive out there on his own, that was the critical question.

The same question facing her.

She would find a way to survive, just like the dog would.

"I hope I see you again," she whispered.

She'd made it this far. She wasn't going to let him win. Whatever gift of fate or accident had offered her this chance, she wouldn't waste it.

The thought of heading out into the great unknown all alone was almost unbearable.

She was weak. Her hand was crippled. And she was pregnant.

Fear gripped her. The evil she feared wasn't a demon, a ghost, or the imaginary monsters of books and movie screens and childhood closets. Her monster was very real and very dangerous.

But she wasn't his anymore. She wasn't a prisoner. She was free.

And if she wanted to stay free, Hannah Sheridan had to run.

8

HANNAH
DAY ONE

Hannah watched the woods for another minute, but the dog was gone. No time to keep waiting or hoping.

Anxiety twisted in her gut. She didn't know what time it was. Probably sometime after noon by the light filtering through the clouds.

The seconds and minutes were slipping by. She needed to move.

Before she turned back to the cabin, her gaze snagged on the half-cut pile of firewood and chopping block beside the large shed. An axe was stuck in the wood, a fine silt of snow covering the axe head and the handle.

She might need something like that out in the woods. She shuffled through the snow to the chopping block and tugged on the axe. It was stuck.

She brushed off the snow and grabbed it with two gloved hands. The broken fingers of her left hand wouldn't curl around the handle, but she got the thumb around and braced it so that both hands were working together.

She yanked again, harder this time. The axe came free.

Holding her pants up with her deformed hand and dragging the axe with the other, she trudged through the snow back to the house. She stood inside the back door and forced herself to scan the mudroom again.

The seconds were ticking away inside her head, but she didn't want to miss something crucial she might need later.

Inside the cabinet next to the washer and dryer, she found scarves, a thick fur winter cap, and a pair of gloves and mittens. The second shelf contained a compass, a bunch of paracord, a canteen, a flashlight, a neatly folded, unused brown tarp, and a folding knife.

And nestled far back at the bottom, a black backpack.

She took it all. For the next thirty minutes, she packed her supplies.

She used a length of the paracord to tie a belt beneath her belly to hold her pants up. A further search of the kitchen revealed several Zippo lighters, waterproof matches, and a can opener.

After she'd packed MREs, granola bars, canned tuna, canned peaches, two packages of beef jerky, a canister of mixed nuts, a bag of Doritos, and a camping pan, she filled her canteen with the remaining water in the tap.

Her gaze landed on the skis. She knew how to ski. Once upon a time, she'd been good at it.

Cross-country skiing would be much faster than walking, especially in this thick snow. His skis were much too big for her, but she'd make it work. She didn't have much of a choice.

Hannah hauled the skis, poles, and boots into her arms, barely able to carry them with her useless ruined hand. She stepped outside onto the porch and used her back to close the door behind her.

Part of her wanted to burn the cabin to the ground. But that would take extra time, and time was a luxury she didn't have.

It was enough that she was leaving forever.

She had her pack ready, the sleeping bag rolled up in the tarp and attached to the bottom of the pack via paracord. Her coat pockets were filled with beef jerky, nuts, and granola bars.

The folding knife was nestled in her pants pocket, a long kitchen knife slid through a knot in the paracord she'd created at her hip as a makeshift sheath, the axe attached to the side of the pack with a creative bit of webbing and knot-tying.

She was sure her captor owned guns, but he'd kept none in the cabin. She'd grown up around guns, shot a hunting rifle a few times, but had never really gotten into hunting—to her father's disappointment.

It was strange, the things you remembered. She couldn't recall his facial features or even whether he was blond or brown-haired, the sound of his voice or how old he was—but she remembered the feeling of disappointing him, that curdling guilt in her belly.

She would remember when she saw him again. She would hug her father and say all the things she'd never bothered to say when he was just a phone call or a days' drive away. She had a lot of things to make up for to a lot of people.

She bent to take off her oversized winter boots and put the ski boots on instead. She attached the regular boots to her pack by the laces. She lugged the skis and poles and her pack down the porch steps.

She hesitated, staring down at the skis and chewing on her lower lip. What was she missing?

She'd been raised in a rugged, small town in the UP, the Upper Peninsula. She and Oliver, her older brother, had grown up skiing, snowmobiling, and ice fishing.

Her parents weren't survivalists or preppers, but they'd taught her how to stay alive in the harsh northern winters.

Once upon a time, she'd known the basics. If only she could remember all the things she used to know, used to believe, used to be.

That was another life. Another world. She'd been another person then. A person she barely even remembered. Brave. Stubborn. Daring, maybe a little reckless. Confident and capable.

Where had that girl gone? How had she been beaten and battered into something else? Was it too late to ever find her way back?

She didn't know the answer to that. All she knew was that she'd never find out if she didn't leave this place as soon as possible. If she didn't push back the confusion and fear and panic gnawing at her brain.

She needed to think clearly, make a plan, and execute it.

No one was coming to rescue her. The whole world probably believed she was dead. Including her husband and son. Including her parents. Whoever had once looked for her had stopped long ago.

This was up to her and no one else. If she didn't want to die here, she would have to reach down deep, find some former thread of herself, and hold on for dear life.

9

PIKE
DAY ONE

Pike pulled his Zippo lighter out of his coat pocket along with a pack of his favorite Djarum Black clove cigarettes he'd purchased online from a store in Indonesia.

With one hand still on the wheel, he snapped the Zippo lid a few times to steady his nerves and lit the cigarette. He drew in a deep breath, inhaling the sweet, calming scent of cloves.

He unrolled the driver's window a few inches and squinted into the dirty windshield of the ancient dung-brown 1979 Chevy Blazer. It was a piece of junk, but at least it had snow tires—and was still running. Which was more than could be said for the wrecks of vehicles cramming the roads.

Including his own 2016 black Ford F350 with the shiny grille, bull bar, and hunting spotlights set atop the roof. It was still stalled in the parking lot of the florist shop.

He'd known it wouldn't start but checked it anyway, then grabbed the stash he always kept in the back, just in case—a backpack of emergency supplies, a tent and winter camping gear in a large black duffle bag, and his favorite scoped hunting rifle.

It had been easier than expected to find a working vehicle. Whatever this event was, it only affected newer vehicles with computerized systems. Within thirty minutes of hiking north along the side of the road, the decrepit old Blazer had rumbled past.

He'd dashed to the middle of the road and waved it down, holding his Corrections Officer badge high in the air. It had served him well many times in the past. It served him now.

The driver—a sixty-something fat fool in a trucker's hat, with a trucker's belly—had stopped. Pike looked professional enough in his CO uniform. Almost like a real police officer. Maybe the guy would've stopped for anyone. It didn't matter.

As soon as the guy manually rolled down the driver's side window, Pike rested his hand on the Sig Sauer P320 pistol at his open-carry side holster and gave his usual fake-cop spiel. "Toss me the keys and get out of the truck."

The man had complied immediately. It had been easy. It was all so easy. He never even had to draw his gun.

Pike had considered shooting him in the head anyway, but decided not to. He only resorted to violence when he had a low likelihood of detection.

He wasn't a man who left anything to chance. He was careful, precise, meticulous. A professional who took care to avoid unneeded complications and potential exposure.

The thrill of hunting was in the kill. The thrill of killing was in the hunt. A symbiotic relationship—and Pike's motto, the absolute, primal truth by which he lived.

The world was divided into predator and prey. The rules society erected for itself were shams, civilization only a mask meant to hide the violent, brutal truth—men were made to kill.

Gavin Pike was made to kill.

Every other animal on the planet instinctively understood the hierarchy of the ecosystem in which they lived. The mouse knew the hawk, the fox, and the wolf were his betters, that the only way of surviving another day was to run or to hide.

The hawk, the fox, and the wolf knew their role was to rule, to hunt and kill at their pleasure, to show no mercy to the creatures whose sole purpose was to nourish the food chain, rung after rung, all the way to the top—to the supreme ruler, the most cunning, intelligent, and skilled predator—man himself.

Animals were stupid. They didn't share the talents of man. Their cunning was simple and predictable. For the apex hunter, the only true thrill came from stalking and defeating an adversary who could think and strategize and counterplan—a creature equal to himself.

Or at least, a creature capable of equality.

Pike had yet to discover prey who equaled him in any way. And he'd been trying.

He flicked ash out the window as he drove past a sign for the town of Newaygo. He continued north on M-37 toward Baldwin.

This time, he'd avoided driving through Kalamazoo and Grand Rapids. The snarl of broken cars, trucks, and buses in the cities likely made the roads impassable.

Thankfully, the former owner of the Blazer had recently filled the tank. The detours had added more mileage and extra time to the trip.

Plus, he'd been forced to weave around several hundred stalled vehicles and dozens of people stranded on the side of the road with no way home.

They should've walked to the nearest town. Instead, most of them sat in cars that grew colder by the minute or stood shivering outside, waving desperately at the rare working vehicle roaring past. Waiting to be rescued.

He ignored them all. A few tried to run into the road to flag him down. He gunned past them with a spray of snow and grit and a malicious smile.

The traffic thinned out as he entered the Manistee National Forest. Dense hardwood forest crowded both sides of the road. Towering red pine, maple and oak, their branches and boughs heavy with snow.

Less than forty miles away now.

His hunting cabin sat on a twenty-acre lot nestled in the middle of the Manistee National Forest, along an unused dirt road that spurred off an old, unused logging road.

Manistee National Forest covered over five hundred and forty thousand acres of rivers, streams, and lakes, rolling forest hills, valleys, and marshlands. It was a mosaic broken up by private property and small towns and crisscrossed by highways and hundreds of miles of hiking, biking, and snowmobile trails.

The cabin was located east of Manistee, just south of 55, and as far from the hiking and snowmobile trails, campsites, and popular rivers as possible. It was a wilderness oasis, cut off from civilization, exactly how he wanted it.

He didn't mind the long, almost two-hundred-mile drive he took nearly every weekend. After endless days surrounded by sheep and fools and morons, he needed the solitude to get his head straight again, to remember who and what he was.

And if he was lucky, to hunt.

Pike knew how to divide his false life from his real one, to keep his genuine self carefully and neatly hidden behind a mask. He knew how to blend in, how to camouflage himself.

His very appearance was camouflage. Dishwater blond hair, medium height, neither fat nor thin, pleasant smile. Bland and unassuming. He looked like anyone and no one. Completely forgettable.

He'd spent his life studying other people, learning to imitate their facial expressions, their tone, their body language. It was an art form he had perfected in his teens. He was an expert at copying the facsimile of emotion. Had learned how to manipulate others for his own advantage from a young age.

He was careful to cover his tracks. Always. Leave no trace behind. No evidence. No victims who could I.D. him. He was meticulous about that. None ever would.

Except for one.

The one still at his cabin. The one he'd kept.

He gripped the wheel, negotiating the rutted logging road. The old Blazer juddered across frozen potholes and corrugated icy tracks. He slowed as the studded tires began to slide across the ridges of ice and snow.

Pike didn't feel fear. He didn't feel much of anything unless he was hunting. Feeling the blood of his prey slick on his bare hands. Feeding on the panic and terror in their eyes.

Then he felt many things—triumph, pride, delight. Power.

The only emotions that mattered.

He felt something now, a foreign, discomforting feeling turning his guts inside out—dread. He tossed the cigarette stub out the window and gripped the steering wheel with barely restrained rage.

She was the only person on Earth who could out him.

He cursed his mistake. He wasn't a man who made mistakes. It'd been stupid to leave a victim alive for so long. What the hell had he been thinking?

He needed to correct that error.

He had his KA-BAR combat knife on him. His Sig Sauer. And his Winchester Model 70 Featherweight in .270 with a Nightforce SHV 3–10x42 mm scope that cost more than the rifle, and plenty of .270 Win cartridges in his emergency pack.

He would finish this today.

10

HANNAH

DAY ONE

Cross-country skiing while pregnant was not a joke.

Hannah was immensely grateful that she'd kept up her calisthenics. Her lower back ached. A weight pressed constantly against her bladder and spread up into her chest, squeezing her lungs until she couldn't inhale a full breath.

At least she was well-nourished and hydrated—for now.

It had been years since she'd skied, but she'd grown up cross-country skiing with her family. Her mother had skied competitively in college. They spent weekends snow camping and skiing miles of trails in the gorgeous UP wilderness surrounding the Porcupine Mountains.

Slowly, painfully, her muscle memory returned. It was awkward and difficult, especially with her belly altering her sense of balance. She tried to keep the skis parallel to each other, her torso straight as she bent forward at her ankles and slightly at her knees.

She scooted one ski forward, then the other, using the poles to help her remain upright. It took a while, and several hard falls, but she finally found a gliding rhythm that worked.

She had a hard time wrapping her left hand around the pole's handle. She'd tied her hand to the pole with a short length of paracord and used her undamaged thumb to grip as well as she could. Her whole hand ached from the strain.

She'd followed the cabin's long, winding driveway to a narrow road that was probably gravel or dirt beneath the snow. Only a few tire tracks marred the blanket of deep white snow.

Hannah skied along the middle of the road, heading south by her compass.

She still didn't know where she was. She'd found no maps or information inside the cabin. She'd decided to head south until she found a road or town sign and could orient herself.

She could be anywhere in the whole state of Michigan. She was pretty sure she was still in Michigan. Her captor visited her often enough that he couldn't be too far from his work and the fake life he'd built for himself.

She was going by instinct. Southern Michigan contained little to no wilderness. The larger cities of Detroit, Grand Rapids, Kalamazoo, Lansing, and Ann Arbor were all in the lower half of the state, along with hundreds of smaller townships and villages dotting the many lakes and rivers.

Pushing further north, Michigan grew wilder and more remote. The Upper Peninsula north of Mackinac's five-mile-long suspension bridge was almost an entirely different state. A different country.

The land of endless, dense pine forests. Rugged coastlines. The Porcupine Mountains. The UP looked different; it tasted and smelled and felt different.

No matter where she was, if she headed south, she should eventually hit a village, township, or city. Still, it unnerved her that she hadn't seen another homestead or cabin yet.

She was desperate to see another human being other than *him*.

Her left pole snagged a snow-covered bush on the side of the road and nearly ripped itself out of her left hand. Pain seared her misshapen fingers. Her hand muscles cramped.

Frustration bubbled up so hard and fast she nearly cried. She needed the support, but with her worthless hand, the stupid thing was worse than useless.

It had only been an hour or two, and already, her leg muscles ached in protest. Her back hurt and her lungs burned from the cold and exhaustion.

She tore the pole free, her gloved fingers fumbling with the paracord twisted and knotted at her wrist. She hurled the pole as far as she could into the woods.

It struck a birch tree a few yards in and landed in a snowbank, the pointed end sticking out at a forty-five-degree angle.

Hot tears stung her eyes. Furious, she screamed. In the quiet, the sound exploded in her eardrums.

As if in answer, a branch snapped across the road.

She whipped around, her heart beating hard. She nearly lost her balance but managed to lean on her pole and remain upright.

The hairs on her neck stood on end. Her skin crawled, like something or someone was watching her. Peering between the tree trunks, lurking in the shadows.

She heard nothing else. Saw nothing. Must be an animal, a squirrel or a raccoon. Still, it took several minutes for her heart rate to return to normal.

She paused for a protein bar and several sips of water from the canteen to settle her nerves. Hydration was just as important in cold weather as the heat, even if she didn't feel as thirsty.

She'd been careful not to break a sweat beneath her layers. She'd unzipped her coat, loosened her scarf, and removed her coat hood, even taken her mittens off for a while, leaving on the thin gloves underneath.

Even though it was bitterly cold, she was expending considerable calories and exertion. If she allowed herself to sweat and her clothing absorbed the moisture, the dampness would decrease the insulation of her clothing. And as sweat evaporated, her body would cool even further.

The thought entered her head: COLD. The four basic principles to keeping warm. C—Keep clothing clean. O—Avoid overheating. L —Wear clothes loose and in layers. D—Keep clothing dry.

Her father had taught her that. She hadn't thought of it in how long? Since long before the basement prison. She would depend on it now. It might just save her life.

She pressed on, traversing hills and ridges and crossing a wooden suspension bridge over a frozen, windswept river she didn't know the name of. Great hardwood and coniferous forest towered on either side of her.

Occasional breaks in the trees offered sweeping overlooks of snow-studded valleys and distant hills. Pristine white snow blanketed everything.

It was beautiful, but in her fear, she barely noticed her surroundings.

Hours later, the daylight began to dim. She could just barely see the sun through the thick clouds. They were low and dark and rolling in fast. It would snow tonight.

She'd had to stop twice to pee. The immense pressure against her bladder had made it impossible not to. She did her business squatting, using a tree for balance—and realized in her frantic rush to escape the cabin, she'd forgotten to grab toilet paper.

At least there was snow.

She grabbed a handful, did what she needed to, and yanked up her pairs of pants, retying the paracord belt. She'd forgotten soap as well, so she found another clean patch of snow and cleaned her hands as best she could.

A while later, she reached a clearing in the trees. She leaned her remaining ski pole against her chest and raised three fingers above the horizon line: a trick her father had taught her. Each three-finger segment represented approximately an hour. Still three hours until sundown.

Exhaustion pulled at her. Her thighs ached. Her lower back hurt. Every muscle in her body was sore. Even with her regular calisthenics, jogging around a fifteen-by-twenty room didn't replace actual exercise and exertion. Her condition tired her out even faster.

A clump of snow collapsed behind her.

Fear shot through her. She turned awkwardly, her boots and skis still pointed forward, and frantically scanned the trees.

A twig cracked to her right.

She stopped breathing.

Something—or someone—was out there.

11

HANNAH
DAY ONE

Hannah went completely still.

Pine and maple and oak towered all around her. Spruce boughs rustled against each other as the breeze picked up. Naked branches like claws scraping at the iron-gray sky.

A flash of white. Something moving fast between a cluster of birch trees.

She squinted, straining to make out details. Heavy shadows crouched deep in the woods. Tree trunks and underbrush conspired into the ominous shapes of claws and teeth and hunched monsters.

A whitish blur as something knocked more snow from a waist-high tangle of bushes several yards into the forest. A white plumed tail. A black snout.

The dog.

She didn't smile. She hadn't smiled in five years. She didn't remember how.

She did let out an icy breath. Something released inside her chest. She wasn't alone after all. The dog was following her.

"I thought you'd be long gone by now." Her voice was impossibly loud in the dense quiet. The snow muted everything. It felt like they were the only two beings alive in the entire universe.

She fished around in her pocket and tossed another piece of jerky onto the snow behind her. His ancestors were bred as sheep-herding dogs in the Pyrenees Mountains of France. A Great Pyrenees was born to the snow and cold and the wilderness.

He could feed himself better than she could, but she gave him the jerky anyway.

"I'm glad you're not gone. I'm glad you're here."

Silence. No more twigs cracking or snowy footfalls.

She knew he was still out there. Moving as silent and invisible as a ghost. She could feel him, circling, studying her, trying to make up his mind.

"You can trust me. I think we need to trust each other."

She turned back around and left the jerky. He could smell it. He would come for it when he felt it was safe. Maybe the food would help him make up his mind and decide to stay with her.

She felt better just knowing he was there. Less afraid. Less alone.

He hadn't attacked her back at the cabin. He wouldn't attack her now. He might be a friend—if she could convince him to trust her. Trust was a thing neither one of them would give easily.

She'd have to earn it.

"You need a name." She chewed thoughtfully on her bottom lip. "I think I'm going to call you . . . Ghost."

There was no answer from the woods. She didn't expect one. Not yet.

Hannah continued on, pushing each ski with legs that grew more and more tired. She picked her way gingerly over the ice and snow, falling hard several times.

Thirty minutes passed, then an hour. It felt like days.

Snow started to fall. It spiraled down from the sky in thick wet clumps. Snowflakes gathered on her shoulders, her thick fur hood, her nose, and collected on her scarf beneath her chin.

The cold bit into her skin, burrowed into her bones. She shivered and blew into her gloved hands frequently to warm her exposed cheeks.

She needed to rest, and soon.

If she couldn't find shelter under a roof, she'd have to make one. That wasn't her plan when she'd brought the tarp and the sleeping bag, but the possibility had lurked in the back of her mind.

She'd hoped to find another cabin, a small town, or a vehicle on the road, but she'd passed no signs of humanity.

Everywhere she looked was dense wilderness, thick snow, and miles and miles of trees.

She kept pushing herself. A little further. Just a little more.

Her mind wandered. Bad memories kept invading her thoughts—pain, terror, darkness.

She tried desperately to push them away. They were like chains around her neck, dragging her down, threatening to pull her under.

She counted the trees. She hummed the chorus of songs she could barely remember. As the music came back to her, so did the memories, jagged and fragmented, but they came back.

She focused on the songs she used to sing to Milo every night before bed, not the traditional lullabies but slowed down, a cappella versions of her favorite classics: Guns N Roses' "Sweet Child of Mine", Elton John's "Your Song", Leonard Cohen's "Hallelujah", U2's "One."

And the one she and Milo had both loved: "Blackbird" by the Beatles. *Blackbird fly, blackbird fly . . . Into the light of a dark black night . . .*

She thought of her son. His chubby face. His beautiful smile. She would get home, wrap her arms around him, and never let go.

A faint sound snapped her back to the present.

She stopped, heart thudding, and strained her ears.

The distant rumble of an engine.

Someone was coming.

12

HANNAH
DAY ONE

Relief flooded her veins.

Someone to help her. To stop and pick her up and get her out of this endless freezing wilderness. After five brutal years, someone was finally here to save her.

The engine grew louder, closer. It was definitely coming her way. The vehicle would round the bend in the trees thirty yards ahead of her in only a few moments.

A tiny warning niggled at the back of her mind. What was a car even doing out here on this isolated road without a single home other than *his*? What was at the end of this road, other than the cabin?

The hairs on the back of her neck lifted. Her heart went cold in her chest. What if it was him? What if he was on his way to the cabin right now to check on her? How else would he get there but on this very road?

Here she was, just standing in the middle of the road like a rabbit waiting to be snared.

The engine roared loud in her ears. Fear clamped down on her.

The monster came for her—yellow eyes and a red slash of mouth, thin bony claws wrapping around her throat and squeezing, squeezing—

Panic overtook her. *Run! Hide!* Her only thought in her fogged and frantic brain was escape.

She scrambled awkwardly for the snowbank on the right side of the road closest to her. Her skis nearly crossed, nearly sent her sprawling. Her heart in her throat, her pulse a roar in her ears. She could barely hear the vehicle bearing down on her.

She hurled herself sideways over the snowbank and rolled into the snowy ditch between the forest and the road. As she fell, she glimpsed a flash of an old brown truck's grille nosing around a cluster of black spruce beyond the bend in the road.

She lay on her back, panting and terrified. Her stupid skis stuck straight up.

They'd give her away.

Grunting in frustration, she tried to twist her skis to lay them down, but the back ends stuck in the snow. She reached for the buckle clasps on the boots, her distended belly keeping her fingers from getting anywhere near them.

The truck was coming. She could hear it, could feel it vibrating through the ground straight into her throbbing heart.

She managed to wrench her body onto her side, the skis scraping with her, finally twisting sideways and clanking one on top of the other.

Her cheek pressed against cold snow. Her whole body shaking, trembling in a heart-banging, palm-sweating delirium.

The rumbling engine drew alongside her. She didn't breathe. Forgot how to breathe.

It stopped. The truck stopped in the road, level with the snowbank. Idling right on top of her. Only the hump of snow and the ditch between her and him. If he got out of the vehicle and peered over the side, he would see her.

She had no idea what his car looked like. She didn't need to know.

Who else would stop in the middle of nowhere? Waiting for something. Searching for something—for someone.

A muffled squeak above her. A sound she couldn't place for a moment. The window rolling down. Then a terrible *click, click, click*. The scratch of the strike wheel. The drifting scent of cigarette smoke stinging her nostrils.

Not just any cigarette smoke. The distinctive, sweetly sickening smell of clove.

The familiar smell on his clothes. His thick fingers closing over her mouth.

The *click, click, click* of his Zippo lighter, snapping the lid open and closed, open and closed, a repetitive, habitual gesture like other people cracked their knuckles.

It was *him*.

An electric shock of fear shot through her. A wild bird's wings beat frantically against the cage of her ribs.

Her vision went dim. If he opened the door and got out of the car, she was dead. *He'll catch you, he'll kill you. It's over, it's over, it's over. You got so close, but now it's all over . . .*

The blank terror came, the blackness closing over her mind, and she was fading, fading, fading. She went away inside her head.

She came back. Didn't know how much time had passed, seconds or minutes. She was freezing cold. Face wet with snow and tears and snot, her heart still a trembling thing inside her chest.

Lying on her side, her left arm stuck beneath her ribs, knees pushed up to her belly. The smell of ice and pine needles and dirt strong in her raw, irritated nostrils.

And something else. The stink of car exhaust.

The truck.

She blinked. Everything was black. The blindfold had slipped down beneath her sunglasses. With trembling fingers, she raised her right hand and scrunched up the fabric.

The white world returned. Hard-packed snow inches from her face, the rise of the snowbank, her hunched knees and the skis folded one over the other. Gray sky above her, the naked branches spreading like claws.

It came back to her in bits and starts. The sound of the engine. The panic. The *click, click, click* that twisted her stomach in revulsion and horror.

He was still there. Still right above her.

She waited, trembling and shaking, her mind screaming inside her skull. Not breathing. Blood a roar in her ears.

Her right hand reached for the kitchen knife tied to her paracord belt. *I won't go back. I'd rather die than go back . . .*

The truck shifted into drive. The wheels spat snow and gravel and dirt as the vehicle rolled slowly down the road. The growl of the engine slowly faded into silence.

Hannah didn't move for a long, long time. She didn't know how long. She drifted in swells of fear and pain and grief and terror. Her thoughts frenzied and incoherent, her body rigid and freezing and far, far away.

Only one clear thought churned in her brain.

This is only the beginning.

13

HANNAH
DAY ONE

Dusk blanketed everything in dim light, the shadows lengthening and deepening, taking on strange unfamiliar shapes that shifted and prowled and skulked like demons, like monsters.

The snow fell heavier and heavier. The harsh and bitter wind battered her, stinging her cheeks, driving the snow down her scarf and the back of her neck.

Hannah constantly strained her ears for any sound over the *swishing* of her skis but heard nothing. Not a single car or sign of human life. She wasn't sure if she was relieved or even more terrified.

It had taken every ounce of courage within her to pry herself out of that snowy ditch, brush herself off, and clamber back onto the road. She'd just kept going, pushing one ski in front of the other, for as long as she could. It was the only thing she could think to do.

Except now night was coming. The temperature was dropping rapidly. Snow began to fall, thick and heavy.

She could barely feel her fingers inside her gloves. Her teeth were chattering. She couldn't stop shivering, which was only using up her precious energy stores.

She should have found shelter over an hour ago. Everything would be that much more difficult in the dark and the snow. But her terror had driven her onward.

Hannah glided off the road into the woods, making sure wherever she built her shelter, it couldn't be seen from the road. She scanned the trees on either side of her, searching for a good spot.

After a few minutes, she spotted a huge felled pine lying parallel to the road about twenty-five yards into the tree line. She paused for a moment, staring at it, considering.

Hardly any snow had fallen beneath it. The log itself was wider than her arms could stretch around, and would provide a break from the wind and snow.

It'd been years since she'd gone winter camping with her father and brothers. Another lifetime ago. Another Hannah had done those things with such confidence and expertise, her laughter ringing in the cold air.

Not her. Not *this* Hannah—whatever broken, scared, cowering thing she'd become.

But it was this Hannah who'd have to act now. Who'd have to remember if she wanted to stay alive in this beautiful but inhospitable wilderness.

And she did. It was the one thing she clung to without doubt or hesitation. She wanted to live. Needed to live.

She blinked and forced herself to focus on the log again. This was it. She wouldn't find anything better. It would have to work. She'd make it work.

She unsnapped her ski boots, stepped out of the skis, and gathered them into her arms along with the pole. She trudged awkwardly deeper into the woods.

It was hard going at first, her boots sinking into shin-deep snow-drifts. She almost fell twice. Once she'd reached the fallen pine tree, she leaned her ski equipment against the log and searched for a good place to set up.

Several yards down, a cluster of towering pines growing near the fallen log offered some shelter from the wind and falling snow. The log lay a few feet off the ground here. Very little snow lay beneath it.

She used the axe to chop off thin branches covered in brown pine needles and placed them beneath the log. The branches and needles were mostly dry, protected by the pine canopy above.

She was lucky. The pine branches would soften the ground and keep some of the cold from leaching through. It was important not to lose body warmth to the freezing ground.

Using the tarp, she set up a makeshift tent over the log to protect her from falling snow. She slipped the lower half of the tarp beneath the log over the pine needles. She secured it with paracord tied to a couple of branches.

She pulled off her pack, removed the sleeping bag, and stretched it out over the bottom layer of the tarp. For better insulation, she found several long, thick pine boughs and layered and packed them across the back of the tarp and along the sides of the front.

On second thought, she went back for more and covered the sides of the tarp as best she could to camouflage it. The tarp itself was brown and should blend into the forest. At least, she hoped it would.

By the time it was fully dark, she'd made a decent shelter for herself.

Now for a fire. The knowledge came back to her in fits and starts. Things she hadn't thought of in years but had done a hundred times. It came slow and halting, but it came.

She'd known once how to take care of herself. She could figure it out again.

She lowered the tarp "door" of her shelter and shuffled along the fallen tree to the crown. Dozens of twigs and dead boughs littered the ground. After gathering a large armful of different sizes—pencil and finger-width, she headed back to the shelter.

She cleared a small area of snow and dug a shallow pit with her axe, shaping snow walls in a C-shape to block the wind. She set up her kindling.

Her thoughts were slow, her hands stiff. The cold stung her cheeks and forehead, tunneled its way between her gloves and her coat sleeves, snuck chilled fingers between the folds of her scarf.

She dug one of the lighters out of a side pocket, but with a sinking stomach, she realized that she didn't have anything for tinder. Panic rising, she searched the backpack for anything useful.

She needed a fire. It wasn't optional.

Her gaze snagged on the bright red bag of Doritos. Her father had used them once in a pinch. The chemicals, powdered flavors, and oil in the chips would burn for several minutes. They were perfect for combustion.

Using a handful of Doritos as a fire starter, she finally coaxed tiny flames to life. Once the small fire was steady, she thought about her other needs.

She placed a few fist-sized rocks near the fire to warm them. She could place them inside her shelter with her as a makeshift heat source once they were hot.

The water in her canteen was nearly gone. She was surrounded by frozen water, but she couldn't use it.

She knew snow should never be eaten for hydration. The energy required by the body to heat and liquefy the snow caused further dehydration and increased the chance of hypothermia.

She needed to melt the snow first, both for drinking water tonight and for tomorrow. She couldn't go another day drinking so little. She dug inside her pack, pulled out the small camping pan, and set it over the fire.

She poured in the last of her water and heated it, slowly scooping new snow into the pan. The water helped it melt faster and kept the snow from burning the pan. She refilled the canteen plus a few of the extra Ziploc sandwich bags she'd raided from the cabin's kitchen.

Too tired to cook an actual meal, she ate two granola bars and several handfuls of nuts. She chewed a few pieces of beef jerky and tossed another one into the snow, hoping Ghost would find it.

Something moved inside her belly. What was once the faint flutter of butterfly wings was now hard knobby elbows and knees poking her ribs, her stomach, her bladder.

She closed her eyes and tried to ignore it, but it was a constant worry at the back of her mind.

How far along was she? Eight months? Further? How long did she have? How long until this . . . thing . . . was out of her?

She hated herself for even thinking it, but she couldn't change her feelings. A monster had put this thing inside her. She loathed it as much as she loathed him.

The sooner she was rid of it, the better.

Exhaustion pulled at her. She wanted to do nothing but sleep, but she forced herself to unlatch her ski boots, strip off her damp socks, and replace them with dry ones from her pack.

The damp, worn ones she stuffed into an unused sandwich bag. She needed to be careful. Trench foot was a real threat.

Once she entered her shelter, she laid awake for a long time. She stared up at the log only inches above her face, felt the rough pine needles against her back and legs beneath the sleeping bag. It was still cold, but she was shielded from the wind and the snow.

The night closed in, freezing and dark and as wide as the

universe. She wished she could see the stars. She wished the fear thumping in her chest would go away.

Her ears strained for every sound. She flinched at every thud and bump as tiny creatures scurried through the night, went stiff every time a clump of snow toppled onto the tarp and slid off, nearly wept when the wind started a low mournful howl through the trees.

She hoped the noises were Ghost patrolling between the trees, keeping watch. She prayed it was him out there and not something else.

She slipped the kitchen knife out of the knotted slip at her hips and held it in her right hand at her side. Not that a knife would do much against the monster after her. Not that she had the first clue how to defend herself.

The last five years had proven that, hadn't they? The fact that she'd been naïve and stupid enough to let herself be taken in the first place. She hadn't even tried to fight. Hadn't seen the trap. Hadn't known she was doomed until it was far too late.

The evil she feared wasn't a demon, a ghost, or the imaginary monsters of books and movie screens and childhood closets. Her monster was very real, very alive.

She knew it in the deepest marrow of her bones. She'd known it the second she smelled the familiar clove cigarettes, heard that terrible *click, click, click.*

He would come for her.

What would she do when he found her?

14

PIKE

DAY ONE

Fury burned through Pike's veins.

He roared into the driveway, plunging through a foot of fresh powder. The old Blazer grumbled in complaint, but Pike didn't care. He just pushed it harder.

With a curse, Pike parked and kicked open the driver's side door. He jumped out and slammed the door behind him.

The cold hit him like a shock. The frigid air stung his exposed face around his eyes and mouth. He wore his heavy insulated coat, balaclava covering his neck and most of his head and face, and thick gloves, but it was still freezing.

Temperature and wind chill records had been broken almost daily this winter. Minus twenty or colder every night. Wind chill in the negative thirties. He didn't know the temperature today. Other than a canned emergency response message repeated over and over, most of the radio stations were pure static.

He usually listened to classical music on his trips to the cabin.

Today, he left the static cranked high. The harsh noise grated his nerves, drove his fury.

He plowed through the unbroken snow to the cabin. He jammed his key into the lock, flung open the front door, and stomped inside. The wind seized the door and almost dragged it from his grasp. Snow billowed inside and drifted across the hardwood floor.

The cabin was chilly and dark. No heat. No power.

He blinked to adjust to the dim interior and grabbed his flashlight off his belt. An initial scan of the living room seemed like nothing was out of place.

Maybe she was still here, after all. Maybe everything was fine—

His gaze snagged on the books stacked the end table beside the leather sofa. Six books he'd never read, precisely spaced so that every side lined up exactly.

Not anymore. Three of the books were staggered, the top one balanced precariously, about to fall.

Pike went completely still, every sense heightened.

He pulled his gun and held it in the low ready position. A round was already chambered. He always kept a round chambered.

He moved cautiously from the living room into the kitchen. Drawers were yanked open haphazardly. Silverware and cups and pans lay scattered across the linoleum floor. The pantry doors hung open. A box of bran flakes was tipped on its side on the top shelf.

Outrage spiked through him. She'd done this. Ruined the sanctity of his home. She'd done it on purpose to aggravate him.

He would make the little slut pay. He'd break every bone in every finger of both hands. And he'd keep her conscious while he did it. Make her feel every agonizing *snap*.

He left the kitchen a mess, though he hated to do it, and moved to the hallway. He cleared the bedroom and the bathroom. She'd raided his closet, his drawers, and the bathroom cabinets.

He saw red. She'd touched his clothes. Rifled through his belongings. STOLEN from him.

Furious, he stomped back through the hall into the kitchen and threw open the basement door. He already knew what he would find but he went anyway, his anger mounting with each passing minute.

The basement was pitch black. And empty.

Back upstairs, he turned a slow circle in the kitchen. The mudroom door was open. Inside, he saw that she'd stolen the winter gear he stored for his hunting trips. And his skis.

He jerked open the back door. The silence was unnerving.

The dog. The damned guard dog. It was gone too.

His eyes tracked the footprints snaking around the yard, took in the chain laying useless and empty, the trampled snow and mud.

She'd let it go. She'd taken his damn dog.

Useless animal. If he saw it again, he'd shoot it in the gut and let it cower away to suffer and die alone.

He strode into the yard, studying the story outlined in the snow. She'd released the dog, then returned to the porch, put on the skis, and headed around the cabin toward the road.

It wasn't much of a road. An old, overgrown logging road hardly used anymore. She wouldn't find any passing cars to rescue her—not at Christmastime, not in this weather, and certainly not with ninety percent of the local transportation grounded until further notice.

She was miles from the closest town, locked deep inside thousands of acres of wilderness within the Manistee National Forest. There were hiking trails, snowmobile trails, and the occasional campsite or road, but this location was remote. Intentionally remote.

What was she doing? Where was she going? Did she even know?

He paused to withdraw the Zippo and cigarette pack from his pocket. He chose one and returned the pack to his pocket. He clicked the Zippo lid. Once, twice, three times. The receptiveness of the ritual was soothing. One of the few vices he allowed himself.

He hooded the end of the cigarette with his hand as he lit it. He breathed out a puff of smoke and watched it swirl in the frigid air.

He glanced at the sky again. It was late afternoon now. The clouds were dark and swollen. Snowflakes swirled in the gathering wind.

It would storm soon. Within the hour.

He wasn't worried. He was a skilled tracker. A stalker who'd honed his craft over months and years and dozens of victims.

The elements didn't bother him. He had the winter camping gear he'd salvaged from the back of his truck. His pistol. And the Winchester rifle.

The rage slowly settled into a low humming anger, into a familiar dark energy sizzling through his veins. The thrill of the chase. The electrifying elation as he drew closer and closer to his prey.

He dropped the cigarette only half-smoked and ground it into the dirty snow with his boot heel.

Gavin Pike was a hunter. It was time to hunt.

15

HANNAH
DAY TWO

Hannah awoke as the first light of dawn crept beneath the tarp flaps. She was shivering hard. Her throat and nostrils burned from breathing in the icy air.

The relentless cold was taking its toll. Her hands, cheeks, and feet felt frozen. She could barely feel them. That wasn't good.

She rolled over, her aching body protesting, and scooted forward. Squinting, she fumbled for her sunglasses, shoved them on, and crawled outside the makeshift tent, pushing aside the pine branches.

She grabbed the dirty boots she'd placed just at the shelter entrance and covered with pine boughs and shoved them on. She stood, her feet sinking into fresh powder well over eighteen inches deep.

The world was whiter and colder than yesterday. The temperature had to be hovering near zero, or maybe even below. Thick mounds of snow weighed down the branches of the birch, maple, oak, and pine trees surrounding her.

The storm was over, the wind a whisper, but snowflakes still swirled from the gray sky.

The fire had gone out sometime in the night. A thin film of white covered the charcoaled twigs and branches. She kicked it in frustration. Little chunks of snow, coal, and flakes of ash flew everywhere.

At least the snow would cover her tracks. That was the only good thing she could think of. Weariness pulled at her. She wanted to crawl back into her sleeping bag, close her eyes, and never wake up.

She needed to keep moving, needed to find some kind of manmade shelter by tonight. She might not make it another night. She thought she knew what she was doing, but she didn't. Not really.

Tears wet her eyes. She blinked them back. She was out of her element, exhausted, completely alone. She had no idea if she was going in the right direction, if she'd just missed a road or a house or a town and didn't even know it.

At least her canteen was full. Well, almost full. Allowing the water to slosh around would help keep it from freezing.

She'd weighed down her pack with an additional three Ziploc sandwich bags of water. To keep them from freezing overnight, she'd kept the canteen and the sandwich bags in the sleeping bag with her, along with her warmed rocks.

The water would last her maybe a day, but not much longer. She needed far more water to keep functioning. This wilderness couldn't last forever. She would find something. She had to.

She tried to push down the fear sucking at the edges of her mind. It didn't work. She forced herself to drink some water and eat a can of tuna, several fingers of peanut butter, and a few pieces of jerky.

She left one on the log for Ghost. The jerky strip she'd left out the night before was gone. Half-filled paw prints marred the snow around the log. Too large for coyotes.

She knew it was Ghost. She needed him to be here, just outside of sight, prowling the boundaries of the trees. Needed another living creature to know that she existed.

A sound came from the woods behind her and she whipped around, heart hammering. Saw nothing in the shadows, only trembling branches.

A squirrel scurried across the snow.

It took too long for her heart rate to slow. She tried to move faster.

Still shivering, her fingers stiff and numb—all of them, not just the damaged ones—she undid the tarp and brushed off the snow as best she could. She wound her sleeping bag and rolled the dry side of the tarp around it, then reattached both to her backpack.

Her movements were clumsy and awkward. Already weakened with a crippled hand, her big belly just got in the way of everything. Things took five times longer than they should have.

It meant she was slow. It meant something faster could catch her.

She relieved herself on the other side of the log for privacy—as if someone was going to come along the road—then shouldered her pack, groaning as she stood and rubbed her aching lower back.

She checked her compass to verify she was still heading south and slipped it back into her coat pocket. Using the log for balance, she managed to latch herself back into the skis, wrapped her remaining pole strap around her right hand, and started out.

Everything was ten times harder today. She was sore and tired. The snow was deep and soft, and instead of skimming the surface, her skis sank several inches and kept getting crossed or stuck. Every stroke was uneven and difficult and took more energy than she had to give.

"Come on," she whispered desperately. "Come on."

The hours passed incredibly slowly. The snow continued to fall, so she constantly had to brush it off her hood and wipe her sunglasses. She drank the water in her canteen and the sandwich bags and ate the last of her nuts and granola bars.

She had to pee several times, the pressure on her bladder irritating and constant. She grew more and more weary. Everything hurt. She fell several times. Uncomfortably swollen and off-balance, she felt trapped in an unfamiliar body.

It felt like she'd traveled miles and miles, but she wasn't that naïve. In this deep, unbroken snow, she might be traveling a mile to a mile and a half an hour, if she was lucky.

In the late afternoon, another snowstorm came barreling in, fierce and heavy and unexpected. She should've been watching the sky and set up her shelter long before it arrived.

She was so weary, she could barely lift her gaze from the ground. Another mistake.

There was no time to search for another fallen log. She unhooked her skis and stumbled off the road, struggling through knee-deep powder and avoiding the deeper snowdrifts.

Once she was out of sight of the road, she blinked hard against the snow and looked for a tree well, a swath of ground with far less snow beneath the canopy of an evergreen tree. The snow collected on the tree boughs rather than under the tree, creating a natural gap.

She found one beneath a huge spruce with thick, heavy boughs. She dug away the shallower snow and pushed it all to one side to create a small wall to block the wind.

Spruce boughs were a bad choice for insulation due to their prickly needles. A fir tree nearby provided softer boughs. She managed to chop several thin ones with her axe and dragged them to her shelter.

After setting up the tarp and sleeping bag, she burrowed in, too exhausted to think, to do or feel anything. She dreamed of monsters encased in ice and snow, frozen blue-eyed demons hissing white breath, their weapons icicles that pierced the heart and bled cold black water.

16

PIKE
DAY TWO

Pike had lost the girl's trail in the heavy snowfall the night before. Gradually, the snow filled the slip-sliding tracks her skis had left, leaving less and less of a trail to follow until there was nothing at all.

Pike wasn't worried. She was clinging to the road, to the promise of civilization. He was confident she wouldn't leave it. Not for a while anyway.

He trudged through the snow, black balaclava covering his face, the collar of his thick coat turned up, hood tied tight to keep out the freezing wind and biting snow.

He was no stranger to the cold. It invigorated him, energized him. Besides, if he was freezing, she was more so. It would hamper her, slow her down.

Hour by hour, minute by minute, he was closing the gap between them.

It was that thought that excited him more than anything.

He moved more slowly than he wanted, but it was paramount to find her. He wouldn't be overconfident. He wouldn't make a mistake.

He scanned his surroundings constantly—the dense forests of ash, elm, and pine, oak and hickory and birch; the underbrush burdened beneath mounds of wet snow, the small paths and dark spaces between the trunks; beneath the canopy of bare, snowy branches and needle-covered spruce and fir boughs.

The air was sharp and clean and smelled of pine and sap. He kept his breathing steady, his senses alert.

He'd slept well enough in his tent. A small propane Buddy heater and his winter sleeping bag kept him warm enough that he hadn't needed to bother with a fire. He still had plenty of food and water.

His thoughts turned to the power outage, to what it might mean. It was an anomaly. Something he hadn't planned for. He liked to plan for everything.

Pike knew human nature. Knew how people acted, thought, and believed better than they knew themselves. He based his every action and reaction on the soundness of this strategy.

He'd studied people long enough to learn their weaknesses, their mental defenses and justifications, their failures and temptations and self-deceptions, which allowed someone like him to move freely among them. A careful and cunning wolf among dumb, dull sheep.

The power would come back on. Life would return to normal.

But what if it didn't?

What if this was only the beginning?

He mulled that possibility over in his mind as he squatted beside a strange lump on the side of the road. He brushed and dug the snow away to reveal a sawed-off stump. It was nothing.

He rose and kept moving. No power for an extended period of time meant no heat, no food deliveries right on schedule, no water running through the pipes.

How long before chaos descended? A week? A month?

Chaos might be a good thing. As desperate people fought over food and dwindling supplies, the police would be distracted with trying to maintain order.

Pike didn't worry about food. He knew how to hunt. He knew how to take what he wanted.

But the ability to hunt his favorite prey without the concerns of law enforcement to take into consideration . . .

That was a tantalizing thought.

People would be dying of everything—disease, the elements, starvation, thirst—the victims of circumstance. So many dead and dying. Too many for the authorities to handle, to properly investigate.

Who would know if something—or someone—got to them first?

Less than ten miles from the cabin, he spotted something irregular off the right side of the road.

Several nearby evergreens had small lower branches cut off a few inches from the trunk. He jogged over to investigate. He felt one with his gloved fingers. A fresh cut.

He turned slowly, scanning the area. Behind a waist-high snowbank, several yards into the forest, a large pine tree had fallen. He glimpsed a spot bare of snow in the space beneath the log.

He bent and examined the scene. Three towering evergreens nearby blocked much of the falling snow from accumulating. The shallow snow beneath the log had been pushed and brushed to the sides, revealing the dirt and leaf litter beneath.

An unnatural configuration. Manipulated by human hands.

Pike's heartbeat quickened. "There you are."

A few feet from the log, he brushed aside a thin film of white powder and revealed half-burnt sticks and dead coals. She'd made a fire here.

He stood, brows furrowed, and took in the dozens of pine boughs littered about—some fresh with green needles, some dead and browned. She'd scattered them to look natural. But he could tell.

She'd built herself a small fire, made a soft bed of pine needles beneath the log, and burrowed in for the night. She had selected a good spot. One he might have chosen himself, had he been stuck in the elements overnight without a tent or camping gear.

Interesting. He hadn't known she had the skillset. He tucked that information into a corner of his mind and kept moving.

He continued to follow her. The fresh snowfall had covered much of the tracks, but he could still make out the shallow indentations of her skis.

She was definitely heading south.

This road would hook west in several miles, heading back toward Free Soil and Manistee to the northwest. What would she do then? Would she stay on the road, clinging to the idea that it would eventually lead to civilization, that civilization would save her?

Or was she heading south for a specific reason? Was she heading home?

The thought made him grin.

He licked his dry lips and wiped snowflakes from his sunglasses. He smiled at the snow and the trees and the gray darkening sky. He would take care of this particular problem.

And then he would be free. Freer than he'd ever been before.

The future looked bright indeed.

17

HANNAH
DAY THREE

Sometime around mid-afternoon on the third day, the snowfall finally relented.

Hannah's canteen was empty. She refilled one of the empty sandwich bags with snow and tucked it inside her coat and layers of clothing against her bare skin to melt it. It made her even colder, but she couldn't go without water.

She flinched at every noise. A swish and whoosh of wind through the trees, heavy snow thumping from branches.

Several times, she scrambled off the road, gripped in terror at a strange sound or the hint of movement out of the corner of her eye.

She hoped it was Ghost following her, but she couldn't be sure.

The sun hid itself behind a thick scrim of gray clouds, deepening the shadows beneath the trees. Hannah blinked through her sunglasses. Her eyes still ached and stung, but she didn't have to squint as much. Her eyesight was returning.

She crested a small hill, breathing hard. The snow-covered trees closed in on either side, so close she could almost touch the branches.

Welcoming the small break, she crouched, pushed off with her pole, and slid down the hill. It was steeper than she'd thought. She picked up speed, the sharp wind stinging her cheeks.

Her right ski dipped suddenly. The tip dug into the snow and struck something hard—maybe a rock. The ski stuck fast.

Momentum flung her body forward, her ankle wrenching painfully in the ski boot. The latch released, and she tumbled to the snow, arms flailing.

She half-turned as she fell, managing to land on her side rather than her stomach. She fell hard, knocked the air from her lungs. She tried to suck in oxygen, but it wouldn't come.

Her lungs burned. Her pulse thudded loud in her throat, her head. Stinging pain spiked up her right leg to her hip. Her ribs and shoulder hurt.

She opened her mouth, gasping, but still no air would enter her aching lungs.

She rolled onto her back and stared up through the branches, her gloved fingers clawing at her throat as if that would help. *Breathe! Please, just breathe!*

Finally, her lungs expanded, and she sucked in a huge mouthful of freezing air. Her throat and lungs felt seared. She coughed, trying to clear her airways.

Hannah lay there, stunned and hurting, for several minutes, just trying to breathe normally again. She needed to get off the ground. The snow pressed against her legs, butt, and back. Little drifts of it tumbled across her arms and sprinkled into her neck, down past her scarf to her bare skin.

She managed to sit up using her hands and arms, her stomach muscles useless. Her legs stuck out in front of her in the snow. She tried to move her right leg. A sharp pain speared through her ankle.

Careful not to jostle her injured ankle, she scooted back using her butt and her hands until she reached a thick maple tree at the edge of the road. She slumped against the trunk, defeated.

She didn't just have a deformed hand. Now she was crippled too. Pain and frustration and helplessness welled up inside her. A choking sob escaped her lips.

It was too much. All of it. She'd spent the last five years helpless and trapped. Her mind still couldn't grasp anything different. How stupid was she to think she could even try?

That she was any good at anything but being a beaten, broken, trapped bird in a cage.

A bird without wings. A bird who'd forgotten how to fly.

She should've stayed in the basement. She was dead anyway. About to freeze to death in the middle of nowhere. The next snow-storm would cover her body, and she wouldn't be found until spring. If she was ever found at all.

You know you'll be found, that voice whispered in her head.

Fear wrapped its hands around her throat and squeezed, squeezed until she couldn't breathe. Despair filled her.

Her fate was already determined, either way.

Either the killing cold would take her. Or *he* would.

"I can't do this," she murmured to no one. "I can't."

18

HANNAH
DAY THREE

Hannah was awakened by the sound of footsteps.

Minutes or hours, she didn't know how long she'd been asleep. Her limbs felt heavy, like her veins were filled with cement. The cold cut through her. Her head was foggy and thick with cotton.

For a minute, she didn't know where she was. Maybe she was dreaming. She'd rather be dreaming than awake in her prison, her trapped mind slowly going insane.

A twig cracked somewhere in front of her. In the woods past the road.

She turned her head to listen, shifting her body slightly. Rough bark snagged at her coat. Pain pulsed in her ankle. Not dreaming, then.

It all came back to her in a rush—the light going dark, the power off, the opened door, the mad dash to escape. The three agonizing days lost in the woods.

After tripping and twisting her ankle, she'd abandoned the skis, burying them as best she could in a snowdrift off the road, and hobbled into the woods to find a spot to rest. She'd curled up against the thick, wide trunk of an oak tree and fallen into a restless, exhausted sleep.

A crack in the forest. Closer now. A sharp rustle. She stared hard into the shadows. The forest stirred and whispered, alive.

Was it Ghost? Or something else?

Something large brushed past branches and underbrush. The rhythmic crunch of boots through soft snow. Getting louder.

Someone was coming. A person, not an animal.

Him.

Her heart bucked in her chest. She couldn't run. Not with her ankle. Not with her condition.

She shrugged down against the trunk of the oak and attempted to make herself as small as possible. She pulled her pack close to her side.

A man appeared through the woods.

A jolt of electric fear shot through her. She went absolutely still.

He came through the woods across the road, through a break in the trees. The man trudged closer, his head down, hands stuffed into his pockets, a navy scarf wrapped around his neck and the lower half of his face.

Not *him.* Someone else.

Relief didn't flood her veins. Other than her captor, he was the first human being that she'd laid eyes on in five years. He was still a man. And men were dangerous.

Especially strangers. Especially strangers on a lonely back road in the middle of nowhere, with no one else around to hear your screams for help.

She knew all too well how that scenario played out.

Panic clutched at her with steel talons. Fog filled her brain. She couldn't breathe. Could barely think straight.

He stopped fifteen feet away, startled, and stared—maybe as shocked to see her as she was to see him.

"Go away!" she mumbled, her voice still hoarse and raw.

He watched her for a moment without speaking. He was a big guy, maybe in his early thirties. Broad shoulders and muscular arms evident even beneath his thick, fur-lined parka.

He wore a gray beanie on his head. A faint chestnut stubble filmed his square jaw. His eyes were an arresting gray-blue.

He didn't look evil. But then, neither had the man who'd imprisoned her. She'd learned never to trust appearances.

"What the hell are you doing out here?" the man asked.

Instinctively, she shifted so her deformed hand was hidden, her arm shielding her belly. Hopefully with all the bulky clothing, he wouldn't be able to tell.

Her condition only made her appear weaker, more vulnerable.

She struggled to hide her fear. Predators preyed on fear, on weakness. But it was useless. Her terror took over, and she was helpless against it.

She felt faint. A rush of dizziness flushing through her, blackness hovering at the edges of her vision. Her mind threatening to go away.

"Just leave," she begged through chattering teeth. "Please."

His thick brows furrowed. "Lady, are you okay?"

He wore a large, bulging pack slung across his back. His hands were out of his pockets. He carried a gun. It was held low and down at his side, not pointed at her, but it didn't matter.

He could shoot her dead right here if he wanted. She had no defense other than a pathetic kitchen knife. Overwhelming helplessness washed over her.

What had she been thinking earlier, hoping for someone to come rescue her? As soon as she saw another person, she was reduced to a quivering mess.

"Are you lost?"

She could barely hear him over the blood rushing in her ears. She rocked back and forth, clutching her head with her hands. A low moan escaped her lips.

The darkness was coming.

She had to fight it, had to stay present. She focused on the ridges in the bark. Started a desperate count in her head. *One, two, three . . .*

"You got somewhere to go? Did you get stranded in the snowstorm? We're a long way from any trailhead."

Fear paralyzed her, froze her in place like a deer too entranced by a wash of headlights to save its own life. *Eleven, twelve, thirteen . . .*

"I'm not gonna hurt you," he said slowly, "if that's what you think."

She was weeping, shaking, her whole body shuddering with terror. *Twenty, twenty-one, twenty-two . . .*

Another long moment of strained silence passed. She could feel his eyes on her, studying her, analyzing her weaknesses. Figuring out how best to strike.

"Okay," he said. "Don't worry. I'm going now."

Footsteps marching away. The soft crunch of boots through snow. The swish of a body brushing against branches and underbrush.

Thirty-three, thirty-four, thirty-five . . .

She didn't dare move for a long time. It took even longer for her heart to stop bucking against her ribs like a frantic jackrabbit. *Seventy-six, seventy-seven, seventy-eight . . .*

Eventually, she reached one hundred. She closed her eyes, opened them. Forced herself to sit up, take a steadying breath, and look around.

The man had disappeared. Not by the road but through the woods. That's how he'd snuck up on her.

She saw the path through the trees now that she hadn't noticed before. A blue, rectangle-shaped blaze marked the trunk of a thick pine a few yards off the road. It was some sort of official trail.

He was gone.

It didn't mean he wouldn't circle back. Didn't mean he wasn't still a danger.

Her mouth tasted metallic. She'd bitten her tongue. She spat blood onto the snow.

She sagged against the oak's trunk, breathing hard, her body still trembling. She pulled her knees up to her belly as close as she could and tried to rest her arms on her knees, but she couldn't reach. Her stupid stomach was in the way.

A primal scream of frustration, fear, and anger shrieked inside her head, filled her chest with an immense, unrelenting pressure.

Furious with herself, she struck the ground with the palm of her damaged hand. It only hurt more.

Her ankle still hurt. She was still lost in the woods in the dead of winter, slowly freezing to death, out of water and nearly out of food. Her captor was hunting her.

And this man, this stranger, was a dangerous unknown.

When the tears came, she couldn't stop them.

19

HANNAH
DAY THREE

G host stood at the edge of the tree line across the road, not twenty feet away.

Hannah didn't know when he'd arrived. He might've been standing there for an hour while she sat in the snow and bawled like a baby.

She sniffled and wiped her face, her chest still hitching. "Hey. Hey, boy."

He tilted his head, watching her.

She strained her ears and listened. She heard no sounds other than her own breathing and Ghost's panting breaths. Maybe the stranger wouldn't come back. Maybe he'd leave her alone like he'd said.

She dug inside her pocket with stiff, fumbling fingers and pulled out the last piece of beef jerky. She still had one more package stashed away in her pack.

She tried to throw it to him, but her arm was so weak, it landed a yard from her feet. "Sorry, boy. Sorry, Ghost."

To her surprise, he trotted across the road, his oversized paws sinking into the snow. He didn't stop until he was a few feet away. He slurped up the jerky.

He didn't turn and run like she expected. He gave a soft whine. And he stayed.

Up close, he was huge. Taller than she was sitting down. His hot dog breath struck her face as he crept closer, his brown eyes never leaving her face.

He looked different. Stronger, healthier. Less haggard. Great Pyrenees were noble, brave, and incredibly smart. She saw all that and more as she watched him watching her.

She didn't move. Instinctively, she knew that any sudden movements might scare him off. She stared at the huge sharp teeth protruding from either side of his lolling tongue, imagined those powerful jaws sinking into tender flesh, shredding muscle and bone.

She should have been afraid of him, but she wasn't. This dog was the one thing in this wide terrifying world that she didn't fear.

She held out her unbroken hand, palm up. "That's it, Ghost. That's it."

He inched toward her fingers. Sniffed her gloves.

"You're okay. Come on."

Curiously, he nosed her left boot. He snuffled along her pant leg, to her belly.

She longed to pet him, but she wasn't sure if he would let her. He hadn't been touched in kindness in a long, long time.

He towered over her. He whined again, soft and almost sad.

Her gaze settled on his collar. The fringe of red staining his beautiful white fur. He'd worn the ugly, tight collar for so long that it'd rubbed his neck raw.

"I won't hurt you," she whispered, even though he was the one who could tear her face off. "I would never hurt you."

She reached out and groped for the buckle with her good hand. Ghost stood silent, watching her steadily. He didn't growl or snap at her. All good signs.

It took her a minute to unbuckle it with her stiff gloved fingers, but finally it dropped to the snow beside her thighs. She picked it out and hurled it into a snowdrift several yards away.

Ghost shook himself a few times and chuffed.

"How does that feel? Better, I'm sure."

He lowered his huge head and pressed it against her chest. Like he was grateful, like this was his *thank you*.

She released the breath she didn't remember holding.

Hesitantly, she reached out and touched the thick bristling fur ringing his neck, careful to avoid the raw ring where the collar had been. He pressed his head harder into her chest. She felt the warmth of him even through her coat.

She buried both hands into his fur. Felt the strength of bone and muscle beneath all that softness. "I hope that helps you."

He whined eagerly—happily—in response.

She lowered her chin and rested it on top of his head. She closed her eyes, inhaled the familiar, comforting scent of dog. His fur brushed against her numb cheeks. She could barely feel it. Could barely feel anything. "It's you and me. We're in this together, aren't we?"

Ghost flopped down next to her in the snow, his body radiating heat against her side. He placed his giant head on his oversized paws and gazed up at her. His bushy tail thumped the ground slowly, rhythmically.

Her lungs were ice. Breathing hurt. The bitter cold bit into her flesh, her body racked by shivering. Her teeth chattered.

She'd been so close to giving up, to lying there and surrendering to the unrelenting elements until the cold burrowed into her bones and froze her from the inside out.

But she hadn't. She was still here, still breathing.

She'd made her own shelters. Created fire. Lasted three days in the freezing wilderness.

And that counted for something. Every day she'd survived in that basement had counted for something.

She thought of Milo, of Noah, and home.

"I have to keep going, don't I?"

Ghost's ears pricked. His tail thumped in encouragement.

She had Ghost. She wasn't alone anymore.

And the dog was right. It wasn't in her to surrender. Not yet.

She closed her eyes and said a prayer for the first time in a long time. She'd believed her faith, like hope, had betrayed her. But maybe it hadn't.

Hope seemed like such a fragile thing, but it wasn't. It was still alive inside her. And maybe so was her faith.

Hannah gathered the last of her strength and pulled herself to her feet. She swung the pack over her shoulders, tightened her hat and hood, and rewound her scarf to cover the lower half of her face.

Her movements were slow and clumsy. Both hands felt useless, like they were already blocks of ice. The early signs of hypothermia.

But she already knew that. She was balanced on the knife-edge of survival.

She tested her right foot. Pain shot up her leg, but the ankle held her weight.

It wasn't broken. Probably not even sprained—just strained. It was swollen, and hurt like the devil, but the rest had helped.

She took a hesitant step. Sucked in a sharp breath. Took another step, her boots sinking deep into the snow. Every footfall difficult and strenuous and painful.

"I don't know how long I'm going to last out here, Ghost," she said between chattering teeth. "I really don't. But there's no point in freezing to death here when I can freeze to death somewhere else, somewhere closer to home, right? An hour. I can make it another hour. And then, maybe another hour after that."

As if satisfied with her decision, Ghost leaped to his feet. He shook the snow from his coat and bounded out onto the road ahead of her, leading the way.

20

LIAM
DAY THREE

Thirty-four-year-old Liam Coleman couldn't get the damn woman out of his mind.

He'd promised himself he wouldn't stop for anything or anyone. Not after what happened in Chicago. Not after everything he'd lost.

Liam had been flown to Chicago to visit his twin brother and sister-in-law for Christmas. They were in downtown Chicago when the EMP hit on Christmas Eve morning, three days ago.

He closed his eyes against the images of people running and screaming, the explosion, the dead bodies. The terrible memories intruded, threatening to unravel him.

He pushed out the horror and kept moving.

Moving was the only thing keeping him going, that kept the nightmares at bay.

He ducked his head against the falling snow and cutting wind as he trudged through knee-deep snow along the North Country Trail that bisected the Manistee National Forest.

Traversing the one-hundred-and-thirty-nine-mile portion of the

NCT through the national forest kept him far away from people, which was exactly what he wanted.

Once he'd entered the Manistee National Forest, he'd only passed a few cottages, campgrounds, and bait and tackle shops—all empty and abandoned.

He'd traversed miles and miles of endless stretches of savannahs and prairies. He'd traipsed along boardwalks over frozen marshland, occasional water plants poking through the snowdrifts, and crossed various creeks and rivers—Bear Creek, Cole Creek, Manistee River.

The NCT would take him north all the way to Mackinac Island and into the UP. The 4,600-mile National Scenic Trail stretched over eight states, from North Dakota to Vermont, but it was only the northern Michigan portion that concerned him.

Once the stolen 1979 Toyota Corolla had run out of gas—just south of White Cloud on 131—he'd purposefully avoided the high-ways. Before then, he'd hugged the coast through Saint Joseph, South Haven, and Holland and stayed west of Grand Rapids.

Very few gas stations remained open. Their pumps needed elec-tricity to function. Most of those with working generators or hand pumps were closed to the public, only providing fuel to first respon-ders, law enforcement, and the government.

Those still open were hotbeds of simmering violence as people desperate to get home to their loved ones argued and fought over ten gallons of gas. He'd already witnessed rioting and looting.

The chaos was beginning.

He'd read once that the nation was only nine meals from anarchy. In a bitter winter like this, with temperatures well below zero and the threat of freezing to death in your own home a real possibility, it was happening even faster.

Things would be different if only electricity was unavailable, and only regionally. People could pack their kids and family dog in the car and head upstate to Grandma's, or travel a hundred miles to stay at a hotel for a few days.

Residents of rural Michigan especially were no strangers to power outages lasting several days. They could handle the discomfort and hassle.

But millions of stalled cars? All the dead phones? People couldn't communicate with family members. They couldn't travel. They were stuck where they were. Trapped with what they already had on hand.

That sense of helplessness and isolation quickly bled into panic.

The emergency briefings he'd listened to on the car radio kept claiming this was a temporary issue and would be resolved soon. Liam didn't believe it. Pretty soon, no one else would either.

He hiked through towering forests of red pine. The huge rows of red pines had been planted by the Civilian Conservation Corps in the 1930s. Many now stood over seventy feet tall. He felt like an ant among giants.

He paused on a high ridge overlooking a scenic view of rolling hills forested in pine, spruce, and fir. The Little Manistee River snaked below him, frozen and glittering.

He took in the stunning scene, breathed in the crisp air. He found solace in nature. It had always calmed him, eased his stress and anxiety.

He loved it all. The brutal winter; the harsh, inhospitable landscape. Even the cold.

Nature was what it was. It wasn't cruel. It wasn't filled with malice, not like humanity. It was beautiful in its hardness.

But it didn't matter how spectacular his surroundings. Nothing could heal the hollow emptiness where his heart used to reside.

Liam took a minute to rehydrate and adjusted the straps of his go-bag across his shoulders. He took the pack with him everywhere, along with his everyday carry case.

His Gerber MK II tactical knife was sheathed at his belt along with his Glock 19.

He wished he had his AR-15 with him. He preferred a long gun to his pistol in these woods. He made a mental note to acquire one as soon as possible.

He rechecked his compass and the paper map of Michigan he always carried in his pack. It was about sixty miles to his homestead outside the tiny township of Mayfield, just south of Traverse City, and located outside of Traverse City State Forest.

His only goal was to make it back to his homestead. He didn't have much, but he had enough seasoned firewood to last the harshest winter. He had twelve months of supplies and woods chock full of deer, wild turkey, and rabbits to hunt.

His isolated, five-acre property had a well with a hand pump, a wood-burning stove, a generator, and a few solar panels. His house was filled with items he'd built himself—kitchen table and chairs, bookcases, a coffee table. He made his own soap and knitted his own blankets.

He was prepared. He had everything he needed.

He just had to get there.

Liam folded up his maps and tucked them back into his go-bag. It had taken him three days to travel almost two hundred and forty miles.

He could make it the rest of the way in four days of trudging through heavy snowfall—less if he could find a working snowmobile or UTV sans its owners.

Liam would never steal from anyone outright. He wasn't a thief. But he had no qualms about taking what he needed from the numerous empty houses along his route. He'd found the Corolla in the driveway of an abandoned home in the Chicago suburbs.

Millions of people were stranded far from home due to the holidays. Close to a third of Americans traveled over Christmas. If they couldn't use their stuff to survive, he could.

He'd felt a little guilty about the car; not so much about reloading his go-bag from the cupboards of a vacant rural home and taking shelter in their barn for the night.

He hadn't chosen the fastest or easiest path from Chicago back to his homestead. It *was* the safest and most secluded. The most isolated. And isolation was what he needed now.

He could survive the elements. His years as a Special Forces Operator had accustomed him to blistering heat and icy cold. He knew how to endure incredibly uncomfortable conditions to get the job done. He was used to hunger, thirst, and adapting to harsh environments.

Human beings were the unknown element. You never knew what they would do, what they were capable of. He kept his head down, remained alert, and tried to avoid contact with people.

The memory of that crazy woman flashed through his mind again. Her pale face. Her wild, fear-stricken eyes. He tried to push it away, but it only returned with a vengeance.

He dismissed her from his mind. He had no moral obligation to help anyone. That had been his sister-in-law, Jessa. The compassionate doctor, always trying to fix people. Not him.

His heart clenched like a fist. A sharp wave of grief welled up inside him. He pushed it down hard. He wouldn't think of the horror of the last few days, couldn't bear to remember the losses he'd suffered.

He had to focus on the task at hand to keep himself from falling apart. It was what he did best.

A white blaze on a red pine tree just ahead of him drew his attention.

Dusk was coming. The glimpse of sky he could see through the gnarled branches twisting above him had darkened to a deep, steely gray. It was an hour before sundown.

He unslung his pack and braced it against a tree so he could unzip one of the side pouches. He pulled out the Manistee National Forest visitor guide and trail maps he'd borrowed from a vacant ranger station he'd passed on the way up.

He studied the various dotted trails, trailheads, and campsites. A string of five or six cabins were marked about a mile and a half off the NCT at the Bear Track Campground.

He had no intention of spending the night out here in below zero temperatures. No reason to freeze to death in the middle of the wilderness with a perfectly good shelter nearby.

Liam turned onto the spur trail and picked up his pace. The slog through the snow was difficult and exhausting. His back hurt. He was more tired than he'd been for a long time.

She's going to freeze to death.

A voice in his head—a voice he recognized. He brushed it aside. He wasn't responsible for that strange woman. He wasn't a soldier anymore, wasn't bound by any code to offer aid and protection. She'd clearly refused any help, anyway.

She was terrified of you.

"So what?" he said aloud.

His words sounded harsh and loud in the stillness of the forest. Hollow and empty in his own ears.

Sounds were muted by the snow. In spring, summer, and fall, these woods were alive with birds singing, squirrels chirping, insects whirring, a wonderland for hikers and mountain bikers, campers, fishermen, and hunters.

In winter, it was a snowmobiler and cross-country skier's paradise. Not this winter. Not now.

She's scared and completely alone.

His only responsibility was to himself. Whatever responsibilities he'd held—and failed—to other people were gone now.

Responsibility, connection, love—it only brought more heartbreak. And his heart was already broken.

He glimpsed something through the trees forty yards to his left. A dark square shape that didn't fit with the slim vertical lines of trees clustered as far as the eye could see. A cabin.

He pushed Jessa's voice out of his mind as he plodded toward it.

Liam Coleman was meant to be alone. He survived alone.

21

LIAM
DAY THREE

The small cabin was no more than three hundred square feet. Maybe a hunting cabin or a lodge that belonged to the conservation officers. He paused inside the tree line and cautiously surveyed the area.

The building should be empty, but he always verified every assumption.

No smoke poured from the chimney. No vehicles parked beside it. No tracks anywhere in front or the sides of the cabin that he could see. It'd been snowing for a while now. That didn't necessarily mean no one was inside.

The cabin was built of wood plank with a steep shingled roof covered in a thick layer of snow. A chimney, which meant a fireplace. An outhouse a few dozen yards behind the cabin.

It wasn't built for year-round occupancy. But it would suffice for one night.

His heart rate increased a notch as he lifted his coat and drew his

Glock 19 from his holster. He had seventeen rounds in the upgraded magazine, an eighteenth round already chambered.

Staying within the tree line, his gun in the low ready position, he silently skirted the cabin. He saw no movement in the windows. Heard no sounds. No signs of life.

Before making a move, he studied the most concealed approach. Along the south side, the trees came within a few yards of the cabin. He circled around and closed in on the rear, using the trees for cover.

He darted to the back wall and ducked behind a chest-high stack of firewood. Keeping low, he edged up to a window to see what lay inside. He couldn't make out much—the window was scummy and frosted with snow. He glimpsed no movement.

He crept along the wall, edged around the corner, and approached the front door. Keeping most of his body concealed behind the wall for cover, he reached over and tried the handle. The door was locked.

A locked door posed no problem with his skill set. He quickly jimmied the lock, then immediately dropped prone. Any threat inside would likely shoot waist-high or above.

Sighting with the Glock, he "sliced the pie," searching carefully from 9-3 like on a watch. Seeing no one, he used the door frame to round the edge.

It was clear. The cabin was empty.

Inside was as he expected—a single room with plain plank floors and walls, wood cupboards and shelves for supplies along one wall, two single cots pushed against the opposite wall. Across the room, the wood-burning fireplace with a stack of dry logs ready to burn.

The cabin was chilly inside, but without the wind and snow, it felt almost balmy. It smelled stale and dusty and woodsy.

Once he got the fire going, it'd warm right up. He'd be able to cook a hot supper too.

His mouth watered—not because the MREs in his pack actually tasted good, but because he was so hungry. Thirsty, too. Hiking for miles through deep snow had taken a lot out of him.

He sat on the nearest cot for a moment to rest his weary legs. He set the gun down on the cot next to him, shucked off his go-bag, and pulled out his water bottle. It was nearly empty. He needed to melt more snow.

He emptied the water bottle and placed it back in the pack's side webbing. His go-bag contained forty-eight hours of emergency supplies—MREs, high-calorie protein bars, a Lifestraw water filter, water purification tablets, a first-aid kit, duct tape, a pair of goggles, two thermal survival blankets, extra wool socks and underwear, waterproof matches, a flint, and a Ziploc bag of Vaseline-coated cotton ball fire starters, sewing kit and multi-tool, a headlamp and flashlight, extra batteries, compass and paper maps, and three spare magazines for his Glock.

He was nearly out of hemostatic gauze and Celox blood-clotting granules. His tourniquet had also been used back in Chicago.

Instinctively, he thrust his hand into his pocket. Felt the soft scrap of lopsided, crooked knitting between his fingers. His only remaining connection to his past.

He felt everything he'd lost like an immense pressure crushing his chest. Bitter regret filled him. It tasted like ash on his tongue. It tasted like death.

He inhaled sharply, forced down the pain. Tried to think about something else, anything else. Focused on his plan, on surviving.

He tugged off his gloves and blew into his chilled hands. His ears were freezing beneath his gray knit cap. Snow melted in the fur of his parka hood and trickled down his neck.

She'll freeze to death out there—while you're warm and cozy in here.

That woman was crazy. Delirious, maybe. So small and pale, her eyes huge and frantic in her drawn face.

He didn't need anyone. Didn't want them.

He was done with that. Finished. That was the whole point.

Get to the homestead. Get to safety. Then he could shut out the chaos and cruelty of a world he wanted nothing to do with. He could live out the rest of his life alone and miserable and haunted.

Just like he wanted.

Just like he deserved.

You saw her, whispered the voice that wouldn't leave him. A female voice, low and warm and chiding. Jessa's voice. *You saw what she is.*

He had seen. The woman had tried to hide it. Pulled her coat over her middle and angled herself away from him, trying to shield herself.

But he'd seen it. The instant he saw her, he'd known.

The woman was pregnant.

22

HANNAH
DAY THREE

Hannah was freezing.

She bent her head against the driving wind. Forced her aching legs to push through the deepening snow. It rose higher than her knees, almost to her thighs. The trees closed in all around her, pressing closer and closer.

Her eyes burned. She was tired, so tired. Her right ankle pulsed dully. It hurt, but not as much as it had at first. Maybe that was because it was going numb.

She cupped her hands over her face and blew into her mittens to allow her own breath to warm her stinging cheeks. It didn't help. Her sunglasses had fogged in the extreme cold, and she'd put them in her pocket a while ago.

She didn't need them now anyway. Dusk had fallen. The whole world was a muddled shade of gray and growing darker by the minute. And colder.

She should've found shelter an hour ago. Or built herself a snow trench or an igloo, like the Inuit.

Every small, dragging step was a triumph. Her water was gone. She didn't have the strength to dig in her pack for the peanut butter, the only food she had left.

Her body was failing her. Her fumbling fingers were no longer cooperating. Her fine motor coordination had vanished.

Soon, her capacity to think rationally would freeze up as the blood left her brain and her extremities in order to warm and protect the vital organs of her core.

She'd survived two nights and three days out here. Could she make it a fourth?

Mother Nature was relentless and unforgiving. No matter how much she wanted it. No matter how strong her willpower.

The cold was a living thing, a savage and merciless predator. She'd loved the forest and winter as a child, but now it was hostile, actively aggressive.

Hunting her.

She realized abruptly that she didn't know where she was. The wide path of the road had disappeared. She was in deep woods. The road must have turned in another direction and she'd simply kept walking.

For how long? She'd been concentrating on the arduous task of putting one foot in front of the other and staying upright—she'd lost track, made a critical mistake.

Heart thudding loud in her ears, she twisted around, peered through the thick forest pooling with shadows. She couldn't see the road through the trees, the shadows, the blinding snow.

She needed to head back, to follow her quickly-filling tracks until she found it again. She had to stay on the road. It would lead to civilization eventually. It had to.

Despair bit at her. It had taken so much effort for each step, and now she had to backtrack, wasting even more precious energy. Energy she no longer had.

A rustling came from her right. Ghost darted through the trees and underbrush.

She blinked the snowflakes out of her eyes and searched blearily for the dog. He was nearly invisible in the gloaming.

"Ghost!" she called weakly. Her words were ripped away by the wind.

She took several plodding steps back in the direction she'd just come. Her boot caught on a hard chunk of snow, and she went down on her knees.

The scarf slipped off her face. She inhaled sharply. The freezing air went into her lungs and she felt them spasm.

She gasped. More cold air plunged down her throat and it was like her lungs were icing over and no longer functioned. It felt like drowning.

With awkward, cold-stiffened fingers, she struggled to pull the scarf back up over her mouth and nose. She exhaled several shallow, painful breaths. Between the scarf and her skin, the air warmed before she breathed it in.

Still, each inhalation burned her throat. Her lungs felt seared with cold.

Her thoughts came slow and sluggish. Fatigue tugged at her.

Maybe if she just sat down for a while. Maybe that was all she needed.

She was so tired. Just a rest. Just for a few minutes.

Falling asleep in the snow means death.

A deep *woof* sounded to her right. Ghost appeared, shooting across the narrow path and nearly barreling into her. His plumed tail slapped her shoulder and the back of her head.

She needed him. He knew it, somehow. He knew it and came to her aid.

Ghost circled her, almost dancing, paws lifting high in the snow. The fur around his black-lipped jowls were stained a faint red.

"You found a rabbit, boy?" she murmured. "Glad you found . . . food. You've got to . . . take care of your . . . self."

Her words were slurring. She was shivering violently; it was difficult to talk. She needed a rest. Just a few minutes more.

The dog nudged her face. He whined anxiously deep in his throat. His breath struck her cheeks, but she couldn't feel it.

Numbness wasn't good. She couldn't feel her feet either. Like they were two numb stumps. It was a bad sign. A sign of . . . but she couldn't think of the word anymore.

"I know, I know . . . I'll get up . . . soon."

She tried to climb to her feet. Ordered her numb and frozen muscles to move. She had to keep walking, to turn around and find the road again.

One more step. Wasn't that what she'd promised Ghost?

Instead, she lost her balance and toppled sideways in the snow. She rolled onto her back and gazed up at the bare branches whipping above her. The merciless wind moaning and howling. The endless swarms of snowflakes.

Tears froze in the corners of her eyes. Ice crusting in her eyebrows and eyelashes. She could feel the little hairs in her nose freezing.

Ghost flopped down beside her lengthwise. He pressed his long body against hers, like he was offering the warmth of his thick fur, like he knew exactly what to do.

With the last of her strength, she turned into him and buried her face in the soft scruff of his neck. She loved him in that moment. Loved this dog fiercely and completely like her own heart.

Movement deep in her belly. An elbow or a knee jabbing her ribs, her bladder, her lower back. She felt its weight, a swollen heaviness in her belly.

A parasite stealing her warmth, her energy, her very life.

Guilt pricked her, but it was too late to feel much of anything but exhaustion. And fear. She always felt the fear.

"I'm sorry," she whispered into Ghost's neck. "I'm so sorry . . ."

If she died, her captor would win.

She would never see her husband again, never wrap her arms around Milo or kiss his small rumpled head, inhale the sweet scent of him, laugh and sing classic rock lullabies with him.

A vision filled her, delicious and warm and beautiful. Milo giggling as he toddled toward her across the grass on his fat little legs, a Paw Patrol band-aid over one skinned knee. Hannah bending down, arms open wide as he crashed into her, wrapped his arms around her neck.

She stroked his black curls, kissed that soft, perfect olive-toned skin. *You came home, Mommy,* he said in his eager baby voice. *You came back to me.*

Tears froze in her eyelashes. She'd never get to tell him how much she longed to hold him again. She'd never get to tell him how she'd stayed alive for him all this time.

The darkness thickened all around her. She'd always thought of the color of cold as white, like snow, or maybe blue. But cold like this was black, the complete and utter absence of all light and color. Of life.

Ghost growled. The hackles along his back lifted beneath her gloved fingers. He leapt to his feet and darted in front of her.

Fear pierced the thick fog of her mind. She struggled to raise her head and search the shadows, the looming darkness.

What did Ghost see? A coyote? Another wolf? Or something much worse?

Something moved ahead of her. A dim shape took form—long legs, swinging arms, broad shoulders, a head covered in a gray beanie, furred hood pulled low.

The man. He'd come back.

Her throat seized. She couldn't scream or yell out. Couldn't make a sound.

"Lady, call off your damn dog!" the man shouted above the wind. He stopped five yards away, several birch and maple trees and a thicket of bushes between them. A flashlight in his hand. "I'm not here to hurt you."

Ghost remained in front of her, a great white bear, fierce and protective. He started up his savage booming bark that struck fear into the heart of anyone who heard it.

The man took a nervous step backward. He held up both hands, palms out. They were empty but for the flashlight. He wasn't holding a gun or a knife.

Didn't mean he didn't have one. Didn't mean this wasn't a trick.

Clumsily, she stroked the dog's back to calm him. "Shhh, boy."

He gave a disgruntled growl in response. But he obeyed.

The man glared at her for a long moment without saying anything. He looked angry and resentful, like he wanted to be out here even less than she did. "I found a cabin. Less than a mile north. With a fireplace and firewood."

She didn't believe him. Of course she didn't. The image of a warm, flickering fire danced in her imagination. What she wouldn't give for one right now . . .

"You'll die out here tonight," the man said. "With the wind chill, it's got to be negative thirty degrees."

It was hard to hear over Ghost's barking. Hard to think, to focus.

Sleep pulled at her, tugging her under. "Milo," she mumbled thickly. Her teeth chattering so hard she could barely speak. Her mind growing fuzzy. "I need . . . Milo . . ."

"Lady, believe me when I say that all I want to do is get you to that cabin, and then I'll be on my way. Will you just let me help you?"

Blackness sucked at the corners of her vision. The cold burying her, seeping into the marrow of her bones. Her body giving in to unconsciousness, no matter how hard she fought against it.

"Y-yes," she forced out between frozen lips.

Everything faded. The sound of his voice. Ghost's barking. The driving snow pelting her cheeks and forehead. The haunting howl of the wind.

Darkness prowled the periphery of her mind, growing larger and larger, circling her, drawing closer, tighter, until she felt herself slipping into icy black waters of nothingness.

23

LIAM
DAY THREE

With the dark, the freezing wind, the blowing snow, and the woman cradled in his arms, it took forever to return to the cabin.

Liam almost lost his way several times but managed to stick to his tracks and retrace his steps.

The dog followed closely at his heels, growling in fierce displeasure the entire time. It was disconcerting to have a creature with the strength and desire to rip your face off stalking you.

Liam didn't dislike dogs. He just wasn't a huge fan of dogs that wanted to murder him. If he'd known the woman had a giant killer of a dog with her, maybe he wouldn't have bothered after all.

But what was done was done.

At least the beast didn't make a move to attack him. Maybe the animal sensed somehow that Liam meant no harm. Still, he could've done without all the growling and teeth-baring.

Once inside, Liam lowered the woman onto one of the cots. The dog followed. He barked viciously, his hackles raised, lips curling back until Liam backed hastily away.

So much for that. Liam raised one hand in capitulation, palm out. "Okay, okay. I'm backing off, see? Calm down."

The dog's ears laid back against his skull.

Liam kept one hand on the hilt of his tactical knife. He moved slow and cautious, figuring that as long as he didn't act like a threat, the dog would leave him alone.

It seemed to work.

The dog lay on the floor in front of the cot, his enormous head resting on his paws, but his eyes alert and watching Liam's every movement.

First, he secured the cabin, locking the windows and the door. He kept a rubber doorstop in his go-bag for extra security when he traveled anywhere away from home. He used it now, wedging the doorstop beneath the cabin door so it couldn't be forced open.

He found a kerosene lamp on a shelf and lit it while he started the fire. He stacked the seasoned wood and reached into his go-bag for one of his two lighters. He also had waterproof matches and flint but typically went with the easiest option.

He opened a Ziploc bag filled with his favorite fire starters and took out a few large 100 percent cotton balls, each soaked in a grape-sized dollop of petroleum jelly. He pulled them apart to expose the dry fibers inside. They would burn strong for about four minutes.

Within a few minutes, he had a fire going. He stoked it with an iron poker until healthy flames crackled and popped.

Slowly, the cabin warmed. He pulled off his boots, socks, gloves, mittens, beanie, and scarf, and laid them along the mantle to dry.

He'd retrieved a camping pan from his pack and filled it with snow and a bit of water earlier. Now he placed a cooking grate over the flame and set the pan on it to melt drinking water.

He glanced at the woman. She was still unconscious. He needed to get her boots and socks off and dry her wet clothes, needed to pull the cot closer to the fire so she could get warm.

The dog was still between Liam and the woman. Glaring at him.

It was disconcerting to say the least.

How was he going to get close enough to the woman? The dog might attack him if he tried to touch her again.

"I'm not going to hurt her," he said softly, trying to sound comforting and unthreatening but probably failing completely. "There's no need to bite my face off."

The dog growled his disagreement.

Frustrated, Liam glared at the animal. He wanted to throw up his hands in surrender and stomp out of the cabin—good riddance to the dog and woman both—but he wouldn't last long out there in this storm either.

He strode barefoot to the window on his side of the cabin. He kept his body sideways so he could keep one eye on the dog, his right hand still resting on the hilt of his knife.

Outside, it was pitch black. The stars and moon hidden beneath the onslaught of snow. The wind shrieked and howled around the cabin.

A few hours out there could kill a grown man.

They were all stuck inside this cabin until dawn.

But that was it. The second the storm relented, he was out of here.

The dog tilted his head, studying Liam, sizing him up. Liam didn't need to wonder what the dog saw in him. He knew what he was—who he was.

He didn't care about the woman. Cared less about the damn dog. If he never saw another person for the rest of his life, it would be too soon.

He never should've gone back for her.

Almost against his will, he glanced back at the woman's pale, white face. Her eyes were closed. Her chest rose and fell softly. His gaze drifted across the rounded belly beneath her coat.

If she died, the baby died with her.

Damn it! He gritted his teeth. He longed to be at his homestead, where he was the one in control, where everything happened just as he expected, and nothing knocked him off his equilibrium.

Where he could grieve in peace.

Instead, he was stuck here—trapped in a tiny cabin with an injured woman and a monstrous dog.

He'd brought this down on himself. He was an idiot. A sentimental idiot.

Because he had to do something. As much as he resented her, himself, and this whole awful situation, he had no choice.

He was still a man of honor. That desire to protect and defend—it was still in him. It was who he was, whether he liked it or not.

Liam steeled himself, took a step toward the woman, the cot, the dog.

24

LIAM
DAY THREE

The dog watched him.

Liam took another step, hand still on his knife.

The dog lifted his head. Alert, suspicious.

"Not going to hurt her," Liam murmured. "Just trying to help."

The dog offered nothing. He was still undecided then.

Liam took two more steps until he was in front of the fire and a few feet from the dog. The opposite side of the woman's cot was pushed up against the wall.

The only way he was reaching her was through the dog.

The dog growled, bared his teeth.

Adrenaline spiked through Liam's veins. His primal brain screamed *run!* He didn't.

The dog leapt to his feet, hackles raised. Saliva glistening from his jaws. He was too thin and malnourished but still massive, his body thick with ropy muscles beneath that dense white coat.

"She's likely got frostbite," Liam said to the dog, like an explanation would make a difference. "Maybe hypothermia. I've got to warm her up."

He knew techniques to deal with a dog attack, even ones as large and fierce as this one. They all ended with a dead dog. He preferred not to use them.

This animal was defending his mistress. Liam respected that. Respected the dog.

He moved his hand away from the weapon at his side. He held out both hands again, palms up. The universal gesture of peace—if dogs understood that sort of thing. "I'm trying to help."

Everything in Liam told him this was a bad idea. But he forced himself to move forward anyway, his movements slow, measured, and unthreatening.

"I need to get her close to the fire."

With the dog on his feet facing Liam, Liam had just enough room to slide in beside him and reach the cot. Liam inched closer.

If the dog was going to attack, he'd attack.

There were worse ways to die.

The dog growled again, but it was softer this time. An *I'm not happy about this and I want you to know it* growl, not an *I'm gonna rip your throat out in two seconds* growl.

The dog took a step back, pressing his hindquarters against the cot, almost as if he were making room for Liam.

Liam would take it. "Thanks," he muttered. Carefully, he pulled the woman's cot closer to the fire so she got as much warmth as possible. "Now I'm taking off her wet outer clothing. That's all."

He bent over the cot and deftly unbuttoned the woman's damp coat. He lifted her head and upper shoulders and got it off her. Beneath her coat, the oversized hunter-green sweater and undershirts she wore were still dry. Liam left them on. She never woke up.

He moved to her oversized boots, unlaced and removed them,

and peeled off three pairs of damp wool socks. Her feet were white and freezing cold. Her heels and arches were wet and shriveled. On her toes, the skin was pale, hard, and waxy-looking.

The symptoms of trench foot and frostbite. Hopefully, mild.

She also had hypothermia. He wasn't sure how bad it was. She'd sounded foggy and delirious before losing consciousness.

He knew immersing only the torso in a warm bath was the best treatment. But there was no bathroom but the outhouse, no bathtub or running water. It was important not to rewarm her too rapidly, which could cause circulatory problems and lead to heart failure.

Not that he had the resources on hand to do so anyway.

He placed her socks and boots on the mantle beside his own to dry. He had an extra pair of wool socks that he hadn't used yet. He put them on her feet instead of his own. He could reuse his once they'd dried out by the fire.

He let the water over the fire get hot but not boiling and poured it into one of his water bottles. He placed it against her neck to help warm up her blood. He did the same with his second water bottle and without looking, placed it against her groin.

He shot a wary glance at the dog.

The dog stared back at him, black lips pulled back slightly, a constant, low rumble of disapproval in his throat. He watched Liam just as warily.

"Almost done." He tugged off her mittens, then her gloves.

The glove on her left hand stuck and refused to come off. Her fingers were stiff and bizarrely twisted. He had to carefully tug off each glove finger individually, but he finally removed it.

He drew in a sharp, startled breath. Her fingertips were red from frostnip. But that wasn't what drew his attention.

In the flickering firelight, her left hand was garish and misshapen.

Several of the fingers had been broken and never healed properly. Not just once. Multiple times.

Liam shuddered. He'd seen plenty of war wounds from his years in Iraq and Afghanistan. But nothing quite like this, and certainly not stateside.

What had happened to this woman? What would do something like that? Or who?

Just what the hell had he gotten himself into?

25

PIKE

DAY FOUR

Pike came across the remote cabin around midnight.

It was oppressively cold; he could barely feel his extremities. His winter clothing was top of the line, rated for arctic weather. It felt like the arctic now, with the snow swirling around him, the driving wind, the dense darkness.

He couldn't remember a colder winter.

But none of that mattered now. The adrenaline and excitement thrumming through his veins was warmth enough.

He'd found her.

With the light from his headlamp, he'd tracked the girl's path off the logging road into the woods—there the trail had gotten muddled. Mashed and trampled boot prints. Dog prints—*his* dog.

The damn dog was with her. She probably thought she'd saved him. Pike would cut out the animal's heart in front of her first. Then he'd take care of her.

He tamped down his fury and studied the tracks. She'd fallen several times. He could see where her knees and hands had sunk into the deep snow. She kept getting up.

She'd figured out her error and turned back to the road.

He smiled grimly as he followed the tracks. Human prey was infinitely more interesting than a dull animal. Animals were predictable. Humans could be surprising.

Rarely—but it was possible.

His smile faded when he noticed the second set of tracks. Large footprints. Deep indentations. Someone large and heavy. A man.

What the hell was this? Who was stupid enough to be out in the middle of nowhere during a snowstorm? Clearly, someone who deserved to die.

The intrusion of this second person checked him. Another dynamic to add to the mix.

A surprise.

He followed his quarry until the first set of tracks—Hannah's tracks—disappeared.

Only one pair of boots and one set of paw prints switched directions and crossed the opposite side of the road and continued into the woods heading north.

The second set of tracks were deeper now. Long, fast strides.

He went still. The pieces snapped together in his mind. The man had found her. He'd carried her.

Anger flared through him. She was *his* target. His prey. She belonged to him.

No one else was supposed to be a part of this game. The hunt was for her, and only her.

He forced himself to check his rage. He moved forward with more caution as he tracked her north through the woods.

He followed the smell of wood smoke to the cabin set in the

center of a small clearing. Smoke swirled from the brick chimney. A soft, yellow glow lit up the two windows.

He carefully circled the cabin, thinking, considering, careful to stay within the trees.

He circled the cabin again, furious but steady and focused. He prided himself on his ability to rein in his temper and control himself at all times—except for the rare, precious moments when he unleashed his full fury on his prey.

He longed to storm inside and eviscerate them both with his hunting knife. To feel her blood pulsing over his hands. To break her bones and watch the life bleed out of her.

To cut out the thing that belonged to him, the thing she'd stolen.

But he couldn't. Not yet. Not without knowing who else was inside the cabin. His skill set, his weapons, what type of challenge he presented.

Pike did nothing on a whim. His every action and reaction were carefully calibrated beforehand. He did not make mistakes.

And he would not make one here. The icy cold stung his face beneath the balaclava. It sapped his strength, his energy. His vitality.

The storm was so fierce now that visibility diminished by the second. He needed to seek his own shelter—set up his tent or build a snow trench to keep his body temperature up through the night.

He knew where they were. He would wait, watch, and strike when he was ready. Thirty perilous miles still stood between these two and the nearest real town.

Plenty of time for what he had planned for them.

26

HANNAH
DAY FOUR

Hannah woke with a start.

Her dreams were feverish nightmares, filled with blood and screams and demons with red, pulsing eyes chasing her down, their claws long as knives. She was running, running, always running but never able to escape, never able to run fast or far enough.

She sat up gasping, her heart jackhammering in her chest, her pulse a roar in her ears. Her head whipped around, eyes wide as she took in her unfamiliar surroundings.

She didn't remember where she was. She didn't remember any of this.

Instead of concrete, the walls and floor were wood. Instead of the single glaring lightbulb, flames cast a flickering glow over the small, single-room cabin.

She sat on an uncomfortable camping cot. Her coat was gone. So were her gloves. Her prickling, stinging feet were encased in a pair of blue wool socks she'd never seen before.

She wasn't alone.

The man was lying in a second cot across the room. His eyes were open. He was watching her with those steely gray-blue eyes. Intense and penetrating. Unnerving.

Instinct took over. Heart in her throat, she flung herself backward. She fell off the cot, landing on her butt and groping for the knife looped to her belt. It wasn't there.

She was defenseless. Utterly defenseless.

Terror coursed through her. She could barely see straight, couldn't think. The door—escape—she had to get out of here. Had to run before it was too late.

"Your knife is on the mantle," the man said evenly. "Didn't want you to accidentally cut yourself."

"Please, just let me go!"

He sat up slowly, never taking his eyes off her. "You aren't a prisoner. The door's right there."

She clambered awkwardly to her feet. Pain needled her toes and heels, her right ankle twinging, but she didn't care, barely even noticed.

She darted for the door, sure he would be after her in seconds.

She didn't take two steps before she tripped over Ghost, who lay on the wooden floor at the foot of the cot. She threw out her hands to break her fall. Her knees and palms stung from the impact.

Ghost jumped up, instantly alert, and pressed against her side. She buried her good hand in his fur, borrowing his strength, and struggled back to her feet again.

"Wouldn't do that if I were you," the man said.

She ignored him and stumbled for the door, Ghost still at her side. She tried to open it. It was locked. Blind panic flooded her veins.

"The doorstop," the man said calmly. "You have to move it."

Shaking, she bent down awkwardly, bending her knees, and

tugged the doorstop out of the way. Straightening, she flung the door open.

The frigid air struck her like a physical blow. The shock of it sucked her breath from her lungs. Snow blew into the cabin in swirling gusts.

The night was a cold, black thing crouched outside the cabin, waiting to devour her.

"You should shut the door."

Ghost whined in agreement.

She took an involuntary step backward, bracing herself against the cold. She stood in the doorway, swaying on her feet, fear gnawing at her insides, panic fluttering frantically at her brain.

The thought of being stuck in here against her will terrified her. She hated the claustrophobic feeling of being *trapped*. Hated it with every fiber of her being.

The man frightened her. What he might do. What he was capable of.

She couldn't go back out there. It was too dangerous. This was a choice between the terrifying unknown and certain death.

She refused to choose death.

She forced herself to shut the door. Apprehension churning in her gut, she leaned heavily against it, let the solid strength of the wood hold up her shaky legs.

There's no lock on the inside, she told herself. *You can leave any time you want to.*

She recounted the logs in the fireplace, the socks on the hearth, the planks of wood on the floor until her rapid pulse slowed and her shallow breathing evened.

"Okay," she whispered. "Okay."

"Good choice," the man said dryly. "Could you please put the doorstop back in place? It's just a precaution. It's what I always do."

Shakily, she obeyed. It wasn't hard to move if she needed. It wasn't like it was a lock. "How . . . how long was I out?"

"You've been out for nearly seven hours."

She shook her head. Seven hours? That was impossible. She licked her chapped lips, pressed her back against the door, her good hand still on the handle. "What—what time is it?"

"It's after two a.m."

"What day is it?"

He raised his eyebrows. "It's Saturday night."

"I mean . . . what's the date?"

"December twenty-seventh."

She sucked in a sharp breath. "And the year?"

His thick eyebrows raised further. "You don't know the year?"

"There's . . . a lot I don't know. Just tell me."

"Two thousand twenty-four. Almost two thousand twenty-five."

Darkness swept over her. Her legs buckled and she nearly collapsed. Ghost leaned against her thigh. He steadied her with his warmth, his solid strength.

She'd known. Of course she'd known. Over a thousand marks she'd scraped onto that concrete wall, day after day after day after endless day.

She knew she was well into the fifth year of captivity. But to hear someone say it, someone from the outside world, someone who'd been living and laughing and working and loving all this time . . . all that lost time . . .

It struck her like a punch to the gut.

She was taken on December 24th, 2019. Christmas Eve. That she remembered clear as day, even as other memories faded with time like those old Polaroid photos left too long in the sun.

He frowned at her. "Are you experiencing confusion? Memory loss is a symptom of hypothermia."

She shook her head. This had nothing to do with hypothermia. She felt unsettled, unmoored from herself, from reality. But she couldn't explain that to him. "I'm . . . sure it'll come back to me."

He stood abruptly, moved to the fire, and picked something up. He turned toward her and held out a white mug. "Here. Couldn't give you anything while you were out. You need to drink something hot and sweetened. With high calories. It's just honey and hot water. All we've got. But honey is a very good choice post-hypothermia."

He was right. Still, she stared at the mug warily, like it might transform into a snake and bite her.

"Look, lady. You can relax. If I wanted to hurt you, I would've done it already."

It wasn't the warmest welcome she'd ever had. Still, his awkward bluntness was faintly reassuring.

She took an unsteady step toward him, reached out, and snatched the mug. The ceramic was hot—almost too hot—in her hands.

Her stomach growled. Suddenly, she was desperately hungry.

She retreated to the relative safety of the cot and sat down, Ghost at her heels. She curled the fingers of her good hand around the mug and raised it to her lips. Steam heated her cheeks. She couldn't help herself—she sighed with pleasure as the warm sweetness slid down her throat.

She drank more of the sweetened drink. Inched closer to the crackling fire. Gradually felt warmth and energy seeping back into her body. Needles pricked her hands and feet as they slowly returned to life.

Still, Hannah didn't let her guard down for a second.

27

HANNAH
DAY FOUR

Ghost flopped back to the floor in front of the fireplace, stretched out his long body, and gave a satisfied yawn. Apparently, the tension was over for him.

Not for Hannah. She couldn't relax. Her muscles were tensed, her jaw tight. She had to remain vigilant, be ready to run at a moment's notice.

He saved you. Didn't matter. Just because this man acted nice didn't mean he was. She couldn't trust him.

Trusting the wrong person had cost her nearly everything before. She wouldn't make the same mistake twice.

The fire crackled. The cabin creaked. Outside, the wind howled mournfully. She studied the man out of the corner of her eye, still cautious.

He was tall, broad-shouldered, muscular. Chiseled features and those arresting gray-blue eyes. She'd been too terrified to notice before, but he was ruggedly handsome. Strong, his whole body radiated power and competence.

But there was something else. A tension in his shoulders, shadows behind his eyes, a grim wariness in his expression.

She glimpsed the gun holstered at his waist, the tactical knife on his belt. He was armed.

Nothing about this man suggested that he was harmless.

She needed to be careful. Very, very careful.

The man got up, added another log to the fire, pushed it around with the poker, and sat back down on the cot on his side of the cabin. He glanced at her. "How do you feel now?"

Hannah finished drinking and set the mug down on the floor. She crossed her arms and cradled her ribcage, hugging herself.

She felt drained and shaky. Still exhausted though she'd slept for hours. But the bone-chilling cold was gone. Her head was clear. She could think.

She touched her belly, felt movement, and quickly moved her hand away. "Better."

He studied her, his head cocked slightly. "What happened to you?"

"I—"

How could she tell him the truth? She couldn't. The words were locked in a vault somewhere down deep inside her. To speak them aloud would bring the evil here, would make it real and visceral, and she couldn't do that. "I don't know."

He frowned. "You don't know?"

"My car broke down," she lied. "I was walking, trying to find help, and I got lost."

He nodded, seeming to accept her word, and leaned back against the wall, his hands behind his head. "A lot of that happening lately."

They fell into a tense silence.

Ghost lifted his head, ears pricked, tail swishing on the plank floor. He was probably hungry and thirsty too.

She noticed the man had set out a bowl in the corner for Ghost. The water was still half-full. Drips of water splashed across the floor in a two-foot radius. This stranger, whoever he was, had at least been considerate enough to care for her dog.

"My name is Hannah," she said. "What's yours?"

The man hesitated. "Liam Coleman."

"Nice to meet you," she said, automatically polite. Old habits died hard, even after five years of disuse. "Thank you for saving me."

He shrugged, said nothing, seeming uncomfortable with the gratitude.

"Do you know where we are?"

"We're in the middle of the Manistee National Forest."

"On the northwestern side of the mitten?"

He nodded. "Above Muskegon."

She took it in. She'd been in Michigan all this time, just as she'd suspected. As a kid, she'd once camped along the Manistee River with her grandparents before they'd died.

"Do you have a phone? I need to—" Her throat tightened. She almost wept at the mere thought of Noah and Milo. That she might actually get to see her son again. To hold him. "My family. I—I need to let them know where I am, that I'm . . . alive."

He glanced at her, surprised. "You don't know?"

"Don't know what?"

"Phones aren't working."

"There's no service out here? I guess that makes sense."

"Not what I mean. Near as I can tell, phones aren't working anywhere. Not in Michigan, not in Chicago. The whole Eastern Seaboard and the Midwest are down; maybe the West Coast too."

Disquiet filled her. Foreboding prickled at the back of her neck. He wasn't making sense. "Down? What does that mean?"

"Power is out. Communications. Even cars. It wasn't just yours.

The computerized parts in almost every newer-model vehicle made in the last two decades got fried."

She shook her head, incredulous. Maybe he was insane. Or mocking her. Deceiving her with wild stories for his own entertainment. "That doesn't make sense."

"Believe what you want. It's not my job to convince you. But you won't be able to call home, not even when you get to a town."

She remembered the lightbulb flicking off in the basement. The fridge and generator silent. The security system down, the secure door unlocked.

Goosebumps pimpled her arms. For once, it wasn't because of the cold. She felt sick to her stomach. Could it possibly be true? Was this . . . whatever it was . . . the reason she was free right now?

"What could do something like that?"

"An electromagnetic pulse," Liam said. "An EMP."

28

HANNAH
DAY FOUR

"What's an EMP?" Hannah asked. Just the word sent shivers of dread up and down her spine. She hugged herself more tightly, inched closer to the fire.

"It fries electronics. Transformers. Anything with a computer chip, like phones, computers, and cars."

"What causes it?"

Liam sat up straighter and raked a hand through his dark brown hair. "A solar geomagnetic storm could fry transformers and take out the power grid. Or a high-altitude nuclear blast."

"A nuclear blast? Like with radiation?"

His expression darkened. "If it detonated in the atmosphere, say sixty miles up, it wouldn't cause a massive firebomb and mushroom cloud like with Hiroshima. The threat is in the high-frequency burst of electromagnetic energy."

He seemed deadly serious. She didn't want to believe him. She'd rather have it be some sick, twisted joke. But she could still feel the locked door opening beneath her hand, the lurch of hope in her chest.

She believed him.

It was too crazy not to be true. The irony of it didn't escape her. She'd fled her prison—only to find the world in far worse shape than she'd left it.

She tried to imagine life without smartphones or the internet. Tried to imagine entire states without electricity or heat in this brutal weather. Winter was only beginning.

She just hoped Noah and Milo were safe. That was all she cared about. Whatever crisis had just beset the United States, she would worry about it once she was home.

Right now, her complete focus was on staying alive.

She cleared her throat. "Is there any way to contact the police?"

"Why would you need to call the police?"

She licked her chapped lips. She didn't answer. Couldn't answer.

"I doubt anyone's out here looking for you, if that's what you mean. Law enforcement has their hands full already."

No one had been looking for her for a long, long time. If this EMP thing had really taken down the power grid, she was on her own.

But she'd always known that deep down, hadn't she? That getting home would never be as easy as breezing into the nearest police station and reporting her status as a missing person newly found.

It was up to her to get home. It always had been.

She pictured Noah and Milo as she'd last seen them five years ago. Noah tall and trim, with his wiry athleticism and easy, charming smile. He was dark-haired, like his Venezuelan mother. Easygoing until he was pushed too far, like his short-tempered, Irish-American father.

Whatever his faults, he'd never yelled at her, never hit her. Not once.

Milo was born with his grandmother's olive complexion, curly black hair, and huge dark eyes, nothing like Hannah's own chocolate-brown hair, forest-green eyes, and fair, freckled skin.

Milo was inquisitive and sensitive. Tender and affectionate, but also immensely stubborn, like she was.

Her throat tightened. Milo was three years old the last time she'd seen him. He'd be eight now.

How tall would he be? Would he still have that unruly mop of dark hair that always curled over his ears? Did he play soccer? Football? Did he still love Legos and singing Bob Marley's "Three Little Birds" at the top of his lungs?

Would she even recognize him?

She missed him so much; it hurt like a physical ache in her chest.

Hannah picked nervously at the frayed threads on the cuff of her sweater. "Do you know how far we are from Fall Creek? It's south of Grand Rapids. A small town just off the St. Joe River near Lake Michigan. That's my home. Not where I grew up, but where I lived—live now, I mean. With my husband. And my son. That's where I'm going."

A memory struck her, far in the blurry past of her *before*—shouting matches in the living room, tears and crying and arguments and ultimatums. A slammed door.

Hannah marching out into the cold, her cold breath puffing into swirling white steam, her self-righteous anger boiling through her veins. *It's over. I'm done with this, done with him. I'll take Milo and go back home to my parents. After tonight. After this one night for myself—*

But there was no after. No life after that night she stormed away in her car. She'd never returned. She'd vanished so completely it was like she'd slipped through a crack in the universe.

Her gut lurched. Her mind threatened to spiral away again.

"Never heard of Fall Creek," Liam said. "But I have a map. I can check."

Hannah clasped her hands in her lap, rubbed at her ruined hand to keep herself present. She was here now, not back in that concrete prison. Not trapped in a tragic past she'd wished she could change a million times. "Yes. That would be good. Thank you."

The man unzipped his pack, dug around, and pulled out a paper map. She longed to see it, but she was afraid to get any closer to him.

The door was ten feet from her cot. She felt like she could leave at any moment if she needed to. It was a false sense of security—she wasn't wearing her coat, and her boots were still drying by the fire—but she clung to it desperately anyway.

"Where are you headed?" she asked to distract herself.

He didn't answer for a minute. The silence lengthened, until she thought he might not respond at all. "Near Traverse City."

"What's in Traverse City?" she asked hesitantly. "Is that where your family is?"

Liam stiffened. He didn't look up. "I don't have a family."

"Oh. I'm . . . I'm sorry."

He didn't say anything, just spread out the map on the cot beside him. He traced a line with his finger. "Near as I can tell, you're close to two hundred miles from Fall Creek."

Her lungs constricted. "Two hundred miles?"

Without a car, it might as well have been a thousand. The journey seemed endless; the obstacles were insurmountable.

No, she told herself. They weren't. Nothing was, if it meant getting home to her family. If it meant freedom.

She'd adapted to every cruel and terrible thing the world had thrown at her so far. She'd adapted to her basement prison. She'd adapted to this harsh environment, managed to survive the woods and snow and killing cold on her own for days.

She would adapt to whatever came next.

The truth was, in some ways, she'd always been taking care of herself. Even back in the basement. Even then.

Ghost leapt to his feet. His hackles lifted. A low growl rumbled in his chest.

The hairs on the back of Hannah's neck stood on end. "Ghost? What do you smell?"

With a savage bark, Ghost ran to the door.

Something was outside.

29

LIAM

DAY FOUR

Liam peered out the window into the pitch blackness, Glock in hand. He couldn't see anything even if there was anything to see.

The night was thick and dark and foreboding.

Cold crawled in beneath the door and pressed through the thin windowpanes. Snow was falling so thickly, it appeared solid. The cabin creaked beneath the howling onslaught of the wind.

Ghost barked several times in warning—deep, cacophonous booms that hurt Liam's ears in such close quarters.

The hairs rose on the back of his neck. He checked the window again. Threat assessment was ingrained in every fiber of his being.

"It could be an animal," he said. "Maybe a fox or coyote."

"Maybe," Hannah said in a small, quivering voice.

He turned away from the window and glanced back at her. She was hunched on the cot, her legs pulled as close to her chest as she could with her big belly, her eyes huge in her pale, drawn face. Her whole body trembled. She looked terrified.

"What do you smell?" he asked the dog.

Ghost shot him a disgusted look, like it was obvious. He stopped barking but gave a low, terrible growl.

It made Liam uneasy. He wished he could see better. Wished he could go out there.

It was negative fifteen degrees outside at least, not including the vicious wind chill. Even animals were smart enough to take cover in weather this lethal.

After several minutes, Ghost stopped growling and retreated to the warm hearth by Hannah's side. He flopped onto his stomach with a dejected chuff.

Liam circled the inside of the cabin for another twenty minutes, checking the windows, on high alert for any noise or movement. There was nothing but the wind, the snow, the darkness.

Finally, he holstered the Glock, went back to the fire, and poked around in the wood bin until he found a piece the right size. He carved one end into a knife edge, then jammed the shim between the top and bottom window so it couldn't be jimmied open. Just in case.

The woman watched him, wide-eyed and still suspicious of his every movement.

He stoked the flames with the poker, then poured the water from the snow he'd melted earlier into his water bottle and took a long swallow. He glanced at her. "You want some?"

She nodded, dug a canteen out of her backpack, and passed it to him with her right hand, her left hand curled uselessly against her stomach.

What had happened to her? Why was she really out here?

He didn't ask. It was none of his business.

He'd done his good deed. He'd saved her life, brought her to shelter. That was all that could be expected of him. He couldn't handle anything else.

They would part ways at dawn—or as soon as this storm relented.

He returned to the cot, opened his pack, and removed most of his supplies. He spread them out on the cot to reorganize and recheck what he had.

He liked things to be organized and easily accessible.

He left the roll of five hundred bucks in twenties and fifties at the bottom of his pack. He hadn't eaten into his funds yet, too wary of interaction to approach a store or gas station.

His Gerber MK II tactical knife and Glock 19 were securely attached to his belt.

His small everyday carry case was still in his coat pocket. It contained his multi-tool, stainless steel tactical pen, small LED flashlight, two lighters, small folding knife, and a handkerchief wound with more paracord.

She eyed the cot. "You have a lot of stuff."

"I like to be prepared."

He'd had a chaotic childhood, to say the least. A father more interested in using his fists to control rather than love his sons. Liam had always hated feeling at the mercy of others, of being beholden to adults who should've had his best interests at heart, but didn't.

He believed in being ready for anything. Nothing would take him by surprise. Nothing would ever leave him feeling helpless or defenseless again.

"Me too," she said so softly that he almost didn't hear her.

He repacked his go-bag carefully, organizing it so he could get to what he needed quickly and efficiently. He'd need to get more medical supplies as soon as possible. And he could use a long gun.

"Are you a soldier?" She watched him, nibbling her bottom lip nervously. "You look like you've served in the military."

He had, but it wasn't something he liked to talk about.

The military had been his salvation. A way to escape his

depressing home life. He'd joined up the day he'd turned eighteen, eventually earning the distinction of serving as an elite Delta Operator.

After eight years of seeing too much and doing worse, he'd been medically discharged for a back injury. Five crushed discs jumping from choppers and airplanes with Special Forces.

He worked out regularly to remain fit, but he couldn't run and jump like he used to. He hated it, but he'd learned to live with it. Along with the bad memories. The nightmares of combat, of fear and pain and death.

He'd learned to live with a lot of things.

"Something like that," he muttered, staring down at his hands.

A beat of awkward silence.

"What do you do?" he asked, because it seemed rude not to after her barrage of questions.

"I'm a—" she hesitated. "I used to be a singer. I was going to school for music education. But I . . . I don't sing anymore."

He didn't say anything. The wind moaned. Tiny bits of ice ticked against the windows.

"You said you don't have a family. None at all? No parents? No brothers or sisters?"

Emotions rose in Liam's chest unbidden—remorse, guilt, loss.

His father had been a low-life drunk who'd barely kept food on the table and seldom kept his fists off their mother, a depressed woman who'd never been much of a mother.

They were both dead now. Had been for years.

His only other family was his twin brother, Lincoln, and his sister-in-law, Jessa.

Gregarious, outgoing Lincoln with his infectious laughter, his constant optimism, his extravagant love of life. The complete opposite of Liam, who was shy and withdrawn and lonely, even as a child.

His twin's absence carved a hollowness in his chest, an empty space where his heart should be but wasn't.

And Jessa. Compassionate, calm, and steady. Her long black braids framing the regal structure of her face, her warm smile and radiant, light brown skin. The most beautiful woman he'd ever known.

Liam had one other living family member. He couldn't think about that. It would undo him.

Grief surged through him. Regret like acid burning the back of his throat.

He blinked. Forced out the terrible memories. The whiff of jasmine perfume. The screams and the blood and the stench of burning jet fuel.

"You need rest," he said more sharply than he intended.

She flinched.

Guilt stabbed him. He hadn't meant to hurt her. Softer, he said, "And you should eat something."

"I'm out of everything but peanut butter." She spoke the words cautiously, carefully, like if she said the wrong thing, he'd snap at her again. Or worse.

The guilt worsened. He looked away. "I have some chili stew. I'll heat it up for both of us."

Anything to distract him from his own shame. From the memories that haunted his every step, invaded his dreams.

After he heated the chili over the fire, they ate in tense silence. The flames roared and crackled as another log caught fire.

He didn't feel like talking. Neither did she.

She sat hunched and cowering in her corner and didn't ask any more questions. She poured half her chili into her own camping pot and set it on the floor for Ghost, who wolfed it up in a couple of bites and licked the bowl clean.

When he finished, Ghost nosed at the door, needing to relieve himself.

The woman moved the doorstop, let him out, and slammed the door shut as a gust of snow blew into the cabin. The cold hit them like a slap. Wind moaned through the trees. The branches groaned and creaked and scraped the roof.

A minute later, Ghost returned, alerting them with a deep booming bark. He shook his coat, spraying snow everywhere, and curled up before the fire with a smug, satisfied expression.

She glanced at Liam warily, her mouth pressed into a thin line.

"What is it?"

"What do we do?" She waved her hand, embarrassed. "When we have to go?"

"The outhouse is ten yards behind the cabin."

She blanched.

"It's that, or pee into a pot in here."

She glanced at the door, at him, at the door again. Wrinkled her nose. "Outside it is."

"Maybe don't go to the outhouse," he said, reconsidering. She was likely to get disoriented in the storm, and then he'd have to freeze his butt off to find her. "Just go right outside the cabin and come back."

They shrugged on their coats, boots, and all their winter gear, and took turns doing their business. Liam had never missed a functioning toilet inside a warm building more than he did right now.

Once they were back inside, he put the door stop back in place and added more logs to the fire. "As soon as this storm stops, I'll be on my way. You can stay here as long as you need to."

She looked a little taken aback. She bit her chapped lower lip and nodded.

He cleared his throat. "I wish you luck on your journey."

"Thank you." She glanced at him with those big, doleful green eyes before dropping her gaze to her clasped hands. Those eyes were disconcerting. Green as moss, as the deepest forest.

"Get some sleep," he said brusquely.

She lay on the cot, facing him, her eyes open and staring. He'd noticed when she retrieved her kitchen knife from the mantle but pretended not to.

She was scared of him. He hated that. It made him angry. Not at her, but at whoever could do that to another human being.

He tried not to think about the pregnant woman out there tomorrow, on her own. So small and wan and afraid of everything.

She wasn't his responsibility. Wasn't his problem, he told himself again and again. The words rang hollow in his own ears. He slept fitfully that night. Not from fear, but something else. The sorrow creeping up on him. The what-ifs, the should-haves circling in his mind, relentless. The regret and self-loathing like a block of ice in his belly.

The storm raged all that night and into the next day.

They spent most of the fourth day eating, heating more melted snow to wash themselves down, and lying on their cots, drifting in and out of sleep to the sounds of the crackling, hissing fire and the cabin creaking and settling, the snow pelting the windows, the wind moaning.

He and the woman were both mentally and physically exhausted. Their bodies craved the extra rest. Eventually, they both succumbed to it.

Sometime during the middle of the second night, the howling wind abated. He raised his arm and looked at his mechanical watch. Only 3:23 a.m.

He laid back on the cot, adjusted the go-bag beneath his head, and closed his eyes. He needed as much sleep as he could.

His own journey wasn't over yet. Not by a long shot.

30

LIAM
DAY FIVE

Liam was up just as the first fringe of dawn brightened the cabin windows.

The snow had stopped falling and the wind had died down, though the relentless killing cold snuck through the cracks in the window frame with bitter, seeking fingers.

The storm was over.

Time to leave.

The woman still slept in her cot, curled into a fetal position beneath her sleeping bag, her knees tucked beneath her stomach, her long hair a tangled mess around her face. She looked so young, so vulnerable.

You shouldn't abandon her. Jessa's voice in his head again.

He could almost feel her presence beside him. An ache washed through him, a painful pressure ballooning in his chest. The grief a visceral, physical thing.

Grief did that to you. Scooped you hollow from the inside out. So did regret.

She wasn't real. The voice wasn't real. Wasn't *her*.

He blocked it out and kept moving. He retrieved his dried socks, boots, coat, and scarf, and put them all on. It felt good to be dry again. It wouldn't last long.

He added more logs to the fire and stoked it, making sure it would burn for several more hours. He ate a can of peaches, a handful of nuts, and half a protein bar.

On the mantle above the fireplace, he left her a meatballs in marinara sauce MRE, a can of peaches, and a can of black beans, both opened in case she didn't have a can opener, and the other half of the protein bar.

He had a few days' rations left. Food wasn't a problem. Water he could melt with a pan and a fire. He'd be good and hungry when he returned to the homestead, but he'd get there.

He could go days without food if he needed to. Hydration and maintaining his body temperature were critical.

He put on his gloves and knit hat, wrapped his scarf around the lower half of his face, and shrugged on his pack. He did a quick weapons check, then headed for the door.

Ghost lifted his head and watched him without a sound.

He considered saying something like goodbye but didn't see the need for it. The woman needed her sleep more than any pointless remarks from him.

He'd already told her he was leaving in the morning. There was nothing more to be said.

Liam opened the door and stepped outside, closing the door quietly behind him. Thin orange and red clouds drifted across the lightening sky. The sun might actually show itself today.

He pulled out his compass and the map of Michigan and took a moment to orient himself.

If he headed northwest, he'd pick up a spur trail that led back to the North Country Trail, which he'd take another sixty miles or so until just before Traverse City. From there, he'd find an eastern route to Mayfield.

Three or four more days, and he'd be—

Liam stopped abruptly.

Directly ahead of him, less than thirty feet away: a fresh set of footprints.

They weren't his.

His adrenaline spiked. He lifted his coat and drew his pistol. He turned in a slow circle, scanning the shadows, the gnarled underbrush and pine, oak, and hickory trees.

No sounds. No movement.

He retraced his steps from the day before yesterday from the cabin to the woods. He'd circled the cabin once himself to clear the area.

His old tracks just inside the tree line were nearly buried. The new tracks were half-filled with fresh snow, but they were clear.

A second set of footprints traced his own. Not once, but several times, as if the person had paced around the cabin again and again, like a mountain lion circling its prey.

The hairs on his arms stood up. Ghost had heard something. Someone had been out here in the middle of the night, in the storm. Watching them.

What the hell?

He brought the pistol up and re-scanned the woods, tense and alert and ready for anything. Once again, he missed his long gun. He was only effective out to fifteen yards with the handgun. He needed the punch—and the range.

He followed the tracks, his stomach sinking, anger growing with each step.

This was all wrong. What was he missing? He'd been on his own, minding his business, just trying to get home. He'd stumbled across a woman in the woods and decided against his own self-interest to help her.

Was the woman bait, meant to lure him into a trap? What was going on?

Liam stopped in his tracks. Not ten yards from the left side of the cabin, something lay in the snow. The carcass of an animal.

A coyote. He recognized the gray-white tufts of fur, the pointed ears and narrow muzzle. The animal had been flayed.

It lay on its back, its skin opened in two bloody flaps on either side of it. The internal organs were laid out like the courses of a feast —heart, lungs, stomach, the intestines draped grotesquely around the creature's neck.

Liam's gorge rose in his throat and he fought down the sour-sick acid burning the back of his throat. This was no roadkill. No half-eaten prey. There was nothing natural about this at all.

It was a warning.

A threat.

31

LIAM
DAY FIVE

"No!" The cry shattered the stillness.

Liam's head snapped up.

The woman stood in her socks in the doorway, her expression stricken. She wore her coat, though it wasn't zipped. Her rounded basketball belly protruded underneath her sweatshirt.

Her face had more color, but her eyes were still too big for her face, huge and green and terrified.

"It's him," she whispered.

"Who's him?"

She shook her head. She took a stumbling step backward and sank to her knees in the opened doorway. A low moan escaped her lips.

Liam strode toward the cabin, trying but failing to rein in his building frustration. "Who the hell is *him*? You know who this is?"

She shrank away from him, trembling. Rocked back and forth. Covered her face with her hands.

Ghost bounded protectively in front of her. He didn't growl, but his lips curled back from his impressive canines. He stared Liam down.

Liam knew better than to take another step. He stopped and kept his hands at his sides. His grip tightened on the Glock. "You know something. Tell me."

Another long minute passed. She rocked and moaned, oblivious to anything but her own fear.

Liam gritted his teeth. "Fine. Have it your way." He turned on his heels and started to walk away.

"Wait."

Her hoarse voice was so soft and pathetic, he almost didn't hear her.

He stopped. He couldn't help himself.

"He—he's after me. He wants me back."

Liam turned around and faced her. "Who?"

She dropped her hands from her face. Her eyes were glassy with terror, her pupils huge. Strands of her wild dark brown hair stuck to her wet cheeks. She was still shaking, but she'd stopped rocking back and forth. She lifted her chin. "The man who took me."

"You said your car stopped working."

"It did. It didn't break down five days ago. It broke down five years ago."

He heard what she said. The words were too incredible to take in. He gaped at her. "What?"

"I was stuck on the side of the road at night. My stupid phone died. And then this guy stopped to help me. I thought—it doesn't matter what I thought. The man—he stole me. He stole me from my family, from my home. He kept me locked up in his basement, in a hunting cabin somewhere in these woods. Five days ago, on the day of that EMP thing, the power went out. I don't know how it affected his security system, but the door opened."

She sucked in a ragged, hitching breath. She clutched her deformed hand to her chest and rubbed the broken, twisted fingers absently, like she didn't even realize she was doing it. "I took what I could and I ran. I ran before he could come back and find me. But I knew . . . I should have known . . . that he'd keep looking for me, that he wouldn't just let me go."

"You knew?" Liam sputtered, anger warring with his shock and dismay. "You knew, and you didn't say anything?"

"I didn't ask for your help," she said, the barest hint of accusation in her voice. She had him there.

"You didn't think to mention the psycho stalking you?"

The tears dried on her cheeks. Her eyes flashed with something behind the fear. A hint of will, of defiance. "I—I didn't trust you."

He spread his arms, gesturing at the mutilated carcass behind him. "And now?"

She visibly deflated. "I didn't think he'd find me so quickly . . . I didn't think . . . I'm so sorry."

It was difficult to maintain his own anger. She was clearly petrified. Her shattered fingers told Liam everything he needed to know. Anyone who would torture another human being by repeatedly and painfully breaking their bones was a sadistic psychopath.

And now he was on their trail.

Her trail. Not theirs. Not Liam's.

He owed nothing to her. Nothing at all.

What are you going to do?

He gazed at the woman, every cell in his body screaming at him to walk away, to turn his back, to leave this drama—this burden—far behind.

He was a man haunted. Unmoored and untethered. Meant to be alone.

He couldn't stop staring at her deformed hand. At her rounded belly. The vulnerable child inside her.

Memories flooded through him. His blood rushed in his ears. That instinct to protect and defend still somewhere deep inside him.

Almost against his will, he thrust his free hand into his coat pocket. It was still there. The incredibly soft, tiny little slip of knitting. His fingers closed over it.

He squeezed the fabric a single time, let it go. Felt his broken heart shatter all over again.

The woman pulled herself to her feet, bracing herself against the door frame, her bad hand resting on her swollen belly beneath her opened coat. She watched him, wary and silent, waiting.

Waiting on him to decide the next move. To determine their fate.

The big white dog stood at her side, pressing himself protectively against her legs, his old-soul eyes locked on Liam. Like he, too, was asking Liam what he was going to do.

Don't walk away, Jessa's voice said in his head. *Please don't walk away.*

Liam didn't.

32

HANNAH
DAY FIVE

Hannah and Ghost weren't alone.

She wasn't sure how she felt about it yet.

Liam Coleman trudged ahead of her, breaking through the thick snow, creating a trail for her to follow. He kept his strides shallow so she could easily step inside his footprints.

He carried his pistol in both hands, constantly scanning for any threat. He kept a close eye on Ghost, too, in case he smelled anything.

She hadn't asked for Liam's help. She'd been terrified to accept it.

But she couldn't do this on her own, and Liam knew it.

"I'll take you home," he'd declared that morning after he'd secured the area and made sure Pike wasn't lurking nearby.

"You don't have to," she'd said. Ghost had bounded from the cabin and pressed himself against her side. She buried her good hand in his fur, letting his strength seep into her. "You're not obligated."

Liam glowered at her. "You have a psychopath stalking you. You're pregnant and exhausted. How were you planning to protect yourself?"

She opened her mouth, closed it. Everything in her wanted to push him away, to deny his help, to claim she didn't need it. She didn't trust him.

Sensing Hannah's anxiety, Ghost growled, rumbling deep in his throat. She tightened her grip on his fur. "It's okay, boy. We're just talking."

Ghost settled down but didn't take his gaze off Liam. He didn't totally trust the man either.

She didn't want to rely on anyone but herself. Depending on someone else felt like walking over thin black ice, already cracking beneath her feet, just waiting to give way.

Her captor had hunted her down. He'd left the dead animal he'd tortured and flayed as a threat—as a promise—to her.

Likely the only reason he hadn't killed her last night was because of Liam's presence. That and he liked to play games. She knew that.

Liam had already saved her life once. This made twice.

It wasn't simply that Liam Coleman was a man, and therefore a fit protector. This particular man was a soldier. A warrior. Strength and power radiated off him.

It was in the way he held his pistol low and ready, the wicked-looking knife at his belt, how he moved with precision, confidence, and control. How he was always watching, always assessing, always alert.

He was a man who knew what he was doing.

She felt a flutter in her belly. A slow, turning slide. An elbow against her ribs. A head or a butt pressing against her bladder. Always her bladder.

She thought of her family. Of getting home to Milo.

She wasn't making decisions only for herself.

In the end, it wasn't even a choice.

"Okay," she'd said.

He'd looked simultaneously relieved and discomfited. "I'm gone the second I get you home. Understand? I'll take on no obligation beyond that."

They stared hard at each other for several long seconds. Him scowling, her trying not to flinch, Ghost intently watching them both.

Maybe Liam really wanted to help her after all. Though "want" was too strong a word. He acted like being with her was the last thing he wanted.

And yet, here he was.

"Thank you," she finally said. "Truly."

Ghost tilted his head at her and chuffed doubtfully, as if saying, *Are we really doing this?*

"Yes," she answered him. "We are."

Liam turned away from her. "Get your things."

She collected her stuff, Ghost right beside her, nosing into everything. It didn't take long.

It took longer to dress in her multiple wool socks, her sweaters, her coat, scarf, gloves, and finally to sit awkwardly on the cot and yank her boots on, her belly constantly in the way.

"How long until we're out of this forest?" she asked once she'd shouldered her pack and joined Liam in the clearing.

She carefully avoided looking at the flayed coyote carcass a few yards away. Ghost investigated it before shaking his head and sneezing in disgust.

He'd studied the map while she was getting ready. He traced a tiny dotted red line with his gloved finger. "I passed by the town of White Cloud not far off the NCT on my way up. It's about forty, forty-five miles south. We stay on the NCT until then. Three or four days." He looked at her and frowned. "Maybe five."

She blanched. "Five days?"

"We're breaking trail in two feet of snow in freezing temperatures. And you're pregnant." He eyed her. "You can't do it?"

He was looking at her with pity. She despised that look. Hated how weak and pathetic it made her feel. She drew herself to her full height. "I can do it."

"Good." Still, he glanced down at the map again. "Branch is closer to twenty miles, but it's southwest and a bit out of the way. We'll see how it goes."

"And after that? Will we walk the entire one hundred and fifty miles?"

"Not if I can help it. We'll stock up on supplies and find an older snowmobile, a UTV, something. Maybe even a car, if we're lucky."

She didn't ask how they would find this magical transportation, like they'd just stumble over it in the snow, keys in the ignition and the tank full of gas.

They stayed off the road. Liam used his map and compass to find the North Country Trail. It hardly looked like a trail with all the heavy snowfall—only a break in the trees. Everywhere she looked, trees and snow and more trees.

It was easy to get confused, to get lost.

But Liam trekked on with confidence. Clearly, he knew his way around the woods, knew how to survive anywhere. Of course he did. Why was she not surprised?

For the next several hours, she trudged after him, step by weary step. She took two pee breaks. Liam hated stopping for anything, and so did she, but it couldn't be helped.

As the day warmed into the teens, they were careful to discard layers to keep themselves from sweating. Evaporation would lower their core body temperatures and heighten their risk for hypothermia.

Hannah had no desire to go through that again. She'd gotten lucky once.

Ghost brushed against her legs, thrust his head beneath her hand, then darted off through the trees after some invisible quarry. Sometimes he trotted on her right, then her left, then he busied himself checking out some bush or tree or squirrel behind them.

A second later, he'd bound ahead of them, black nose sniffing the air, plumed tail pointed straight back.

He looked healthier already, his coat shinier, his ribs filling out. She wished she had more beef jerky to offer him. It was a good thing he could find his own sustenance. They didn't have any to spare.

What would Ghost do if he came face-to-face with his former master? Would he return to him obediently? Or would the dog remember that her captor had enslaved them both?

Hannah hoped to never find out.

Around noon, they took a break for lunch: more cold food out of cans.

The sun shone bright in the clear blue sky. The pristine snow sparkled. The air was sharp and crisp in her lungs and smelled like pine needles.

Surrounded by such wild beauty, she could almost forget the evil that hunted her.

Almost.

Still, she was tense and edgy. She kept looking anxiously over her shoulder, searching the shadows, jumping at every rustle, crackle, and swish.

She *felt* him. In the ache of her broken fingers. In the icy pit of her belly.

He was coming for her, for what she carried inside her. Because of that, he'd never stop. Not until he found her and got what he wanted. Then he'd gut her like the poor creature he'd left for her in the snow.

She was traveling with a strange man she distrusted, a killer hot on her heels. In the middle of a crisis the likes of which this country had never seen.

Fear dogged her every step. Hannah quickened her pace, as if she could ever outrun her own terror.

33

LIAM
DAY SIX

Liam paused at the crest of a hill and pointed. "There's a house up ahead."

It was late in the afternoon, only a few hours before sundown. They'd need to find shelter soon. They'd been hiking south for two days, and by Liam's count, had traveled about twenty miles.

Using Hannah's axe last night, he'd built a sturdy shelter with chopped branches which he covered with his reflective-side-down emergency blanket and an insulating layer of snow. Inside the shelter, he layered thick pine boughs, and used his pack and more pine branches to block the entrance.

It was barely large enough for the two of them, but their own body heat warmed the small space and made it bearable, even comfortable.

Ghost dug himself a den in the snow right outside. Liam remained alert, Glock in hand, all night.

He was tired, but he was used to going long periods of time on only three to four hours of sleep. In training, he'd lasted months.

He kept a stash of caffeine pills in his go-bag for situations just like this.

Now, he studied the house below him. They were still within Manistee National Forest, but they were getting closer to the outskirts, to roads and homesteads and tiny blink-and-you'd-miss-it towns.

He'd been on the lookout for empty houses. This was the first one they'd come across, only he didn't think it was empty.

The woman—Hannah—came up beside him. She was short, the top of her head just below his shoulder. Everything about her was small and fragile and vulnerable.

His heart beat a little harder. He couldn't help himself. She stirred that protective instinct in him, the one he'd been sure was dead.

No matter the pain that haunted him, she deserved protecting.

"Where?" she asked, her voice muffled beneath her scarf.

"Across the meadow through the trees. There, at your nine o'clock. See the clearing?"

She nodded. "I smell smoke."

So did he. It was faint, drifting invisibly on the cold, crisp air. "Means it's probably occupied."

"Good. Then we can ask for help. And maybe some food."

"They won't want to help us," he warned her.

"How do you know?"

"Experience."

Her eyes flashed. "I guess we'll find out."

He tucked his gun into his coat pocket, unslung his pack, and dug through it for his binoculars. He peered through the trees, trying to make out the shape of the house. A row of thick spruce still partially blocked his view.

He needed to get closer.

"You have your knife on you?"

She nodded.

"Keep it ready. I'm going to get a better look."

She lifted her coat, unknotted her big, unwieldy kitchen knife, and gripped the handle in her right hand. It took her too long to reach it. In an emergency, it wouldn't help her.

The blade looked like it was about to fall out of that awful knot job at any moment. She needed something better. A better knife, to start with.

One more thing to add to the list.

Ghost pushed up between them. He wasn't just huge, he was incredibly heavy—one hundred and forty pounds, maybe more—and nearly knocked Liam off balance.

It was almost like he was elbowing Liam out of the way. He clearly didn't want Liam anywhere near Hannah.

"Deal with it," he said to the dog.

Ghost glared at him.

"What?" Hannah asked.

"Nothing." Liam shook his head and turned back to Hannah. The dog was a good thing. He'd protect Hannah while Liam did what he needed to do. "I mean it. Stay here. And keep the dog with you."

Light snow had begun to fall. Thick wet snowflakes twirled slowly from the gray sky and landed on his head, his shoulders, his nose, and eyelashes. They needed another heavy snowfall to fill in their tracks and slow down their pursuer.

He could be right behind them, but Liam didn't think so. The psychopath had left the dead animal two days ago, and then he'd retreated, like a coward. Maybe he liked the waiting, the watching, the hunting.

He'd show up again, but he'd likely attack on his own terms.

Glock in hand, Liam circled the house, keeping a few rows of trees between himself and the clearing. The two-story clapboard house's white paint was peeling, the snow-covered porch sagging. Smoke spiraled from the chimney.

The garage door was closed. A small shed and a larger barn or storage building were set back thirty yards behind the house. Tracks zigzagged back and forth between the barn, the shed, and the house. It was definitely occupied.

He preferred to break into empty houses, but they didn't have a lot of options. With two people eating through his supplies, he only had some nuts and two MREs left.

They needed high-quality calories to keep their body temperatures and energy up to slog through all this snow. And Hannah needed even more for the baby.

A direct approach was best. He hated to do it, but he'd need to holster his pistol beneath his coat. Knocking on a stranger's door while armed didn't send the friendliest message. The homeowners might decide to greet them with a hail of buckshot before they had a chance to introduce themselves.

He backtracked to where Hannah waited obediently, Ghost standing guard beside her. At least she could follow directions. As could the dog.

"I'm going to the door. You stay here."

She shook her head. "I'm going with you."

"No."

Her chin lifted slightly. "They're more likely to open the door to a woman."

He saw it again—that flash of something. Stubbornness, a hint of defiance. A glimpse of who she might have been before the psychopath got his claws into her.

She didn't like to be told no.

And she was right anyway. What lay behind the door was less dangerous than what waited out there. "Fine. We both go. I do the talking. You don't speak. The dog stays."

"The dog comes."

He holstered his pistol and glowered at her in frustration. "I said—"

The hairs on his neck lifted. He sensed something out there. Something watching.

Liam went for his gun.

The crunch of snow behind them.

Ghost whirled around, abruptly on full alert. He let out a resounding bark, hackles rising.

The distinct racking of a shotgun echoed in the crisp air. "Don't either of you move a muscle!"

34

LIAM

DAY SIX

"Raise your hands! Now!" a raspy voice demanded behind them.

Liam raised his hands, cursing himself for putting away his Glock a moment too soon.

"Turn around now. Nice and slow."

Adrenaline surging, Liam turned around. Beside him, Hannah did the same. She still held the butcher knife.

Ghost shouldered in front of Hannah, keeping himself between her and the new threat. His hackles raised, he barked a savage warning.

Ten yards away, tucked between two towering pine trees, an old Hispanic woman stood in the snow, feet planted wide, a Remington Model 31 pump-action shotgun gripped in her hands.

"I ain't got much patience for trespassers," she snarled. "The last ones are in a pile behind the barn, matter of fact. Waitin' to be burned, since the ground's too frozen for buryin'."

She had to be nearing eighty years old and wore saggy long-johns and shin-high boots beneath a flowered housedress and an unzipped camouflage coat. Her bronze face was heavily wrinkled, surrounded by wisps of white hair sticking out beneath a furred-earflap hunting cap.

The shotgun aimed at Liam's chest wavered in her shaky hands.

"These hands are shakin' from arthritis, not fear," she growled, as if reading his thoughts. "And this close, you and I both know this beauty won't miss."

"We didn't mean to trespass," Hannah said. "We're lost."

Liam was surprised at the steadiness of her voice. He'd expected her to dissolve into a lump of useless terror, the way she had on their first meeting. But she didn't.

"That's what the last pair said. Invited 'em in for tea, and next thing I knew, they were up to robbin' me blind. Thought they didn't need to bother tyin' me up, seeing as I was so old." She cackled. "Showed them wrong, didn't I?"

Neither Hannah nor Liam said anything. What was there to say to that?

"It's colder than a witch's tit in a brass bra out here. And I ain't even wearin' a bra." She gestured at them with the shotgun. "Drop your weapons."

Hannah dropped her knife in the snow.

The old woman turned to Liam. "Now you."

He didn't move.

The woman spat into the snow. "Didn't you hear what happened to the last two? I wasn't born yesterday. I put this down, and you'll have two rounds in me from that nine-mil pistol beneath your coat. Don't think I didn't see you holding it for the last ten minutes."

The hairs rose on the back of Liam's neck. She'd been watching him case her house. She must have already been in the woods before they arrived.

Strange that he hadn't heard her or seen her. She must have snuck up downwind to hide her scent from the dog.

As if she'd read his thoughts, she said, "I was out collectin' kindling and heard your dog. Good luck for me. Bad luck for you."

He didn't believe in bad luck. Only mistakes. He was losing his edge. He was tired, weary, sick of the constant snow and trees and more snow.

It was a poor excuse. He had to do better. Once they got out of here alive.

"I ain't askin' again."

Liam gritted his teeth, reached beneath his coat, and unholstered his Glock, careful not to lift the coat and reveal the knife sheath on his left side.

"Remove the magazine. Toss 'em far apart."

He obeyed.

"Now the rest."

"I don't have—"

"Lie to me, and I promise you'll be beggin' to meet your maker before this is through. Drop your knife, boy."

With a sigh, he removed the Gerber and tossed it to the ground. It landed blade-first in the snow a couple of yards away.

His hands hung loose at his sides, his muscles tense. If she got close enough, he could disarm her. He just needed to wait for the opportunity to present itself.

She would make a mistake, and he'd be ready to move when she did.

"Turn around. Go. March yourselves to the back of the shed. You'll see where to go."

"You don't have to do this," Hannah tried again. "We meant you no harm."

"Oh yeah?" The old woman angled her chin at Hannah. "Then what in tarnation were you plannin' with that knife, girlie?"

"Protection," Hannah said. "There are lots of bad people in the world."

"Lots of liars too," the woman said. "All the crazies are comin' out of the woodwork now."

Liam couldn't agree more, but he knew better than to say so. He didn't take his eyes off the woman or the gun. Her finger was a hair's breadth from the trigger. It trembled as badly as her hands.

She might shoot them whether she meant to or not.

Ghost kept barking. He didn't leave Hannah's side, but it was clear he wanted to. His whole body was quivering with barely restrained fury. The dog didn't like the gun pointed at them any more than Liam did.

"Quiet your dog," the woman said. "Or I will."

Hannah dropped her left hand to Ghost's ruff. "Hush, boy."

Ghost quieted but for the rumble deep in his chest—a warning that he was ready to act the second Hannah gave her consent.

The woman glanced at Ghost. "You got him trained well."

"He's not trained," Hannah said. "This is just who he is."

The woman grunted—whether in approval or disgust, Liam couldn't tell. It was hard to read anything beyond the scowl contorting the network of wrinkles spanning her face.

"We're leaving now," Liam said. "Put your gun down, and we'll walk away."

"I let you go, you'll just come back tonight and kill me in my sleep."

"We wouldn't do that," Hannah said.

"You want what I have. Everyone does now."

Liam felt Hannah's eyes on him again. "The power going out. It happened to you too."

The woman snorted. "Where've you been? On vacation to la-la land?"

Hannah stiffened. "Something like that."

"Uh-huh," the woman said suspiciously. "Don't play dumb with me. It'll just make me wanna kill you more slowly. Or maybe I'll kill your dog first, and let you watch."

"No!" Hannah cried. "Please. He didn't do anything wrong."

The woman shuffled closer—now fifteen feet away. Her gun trained on Liam.

Liam tensed. His hands curled into fists. He willed her just a few steps nearer. He could reach her before she got a shot off.

His reflexes were faster. And the one who moved first always had the advantage. The fraction of a second that it took her to react would be enough.

Hannah was trembling, but her words were clear and steady. "Let him go. Do what you want to us, but leave him alone."

"Hey, now," Liam protested, keeping his voice neutral and unthreatening.

"I kill you, I'll have to kill the dog first. He'll have my throat before he lets anyone lay a hand on you, girl. That's plain as the nose on your face." Her hands shook and she adjusted her grip on the shotgun. "And it'd be a cryin' shame to kill such a beautiful animal."

Adrenaline surged through him. His muscles tightened, coiled, prepared to lunge for her and to take her out. It wouldn't take much to break her frail neck.

He planted his back heel in the snow, readied himself.

Hannah took a small step forward. Ghost moved with her.

Hannah was getting between him and the woman. Weaving

around her would shave a fraction of a second off the crucial time he needed. What the hell was she doing?

He wanted to reach out and grab her, but sudden movement would draw the old lady's attention. Ghost's growls reverberated in Liam's chest. He grimaced.

"You like dogs," Hannah said. "I can see that."

The shotgun wavered. "Don't got much use for people, but dogs I've always had a soft spot for. Maybe the only soft spot I got left."

"Dogs are loyal. Treat them right, and they'll be your best friends forever," Hannah said.

The old woman lowered the muzzle slightly but kept her finger balanced on the trigger. She glanced at the dog again. "I know Pyrs. They're the closest to canine royalty as exists, I reckon."

"They are."

The woman worked her jaw like she was considering something. "Not just anyone can command the respect of a dog like that. I may be old, but my eyes are still good. So's my mind. Doesn't take a blind man to see that dog loves you, girl. And you right back."

"I do," Hannah said quietly. "I really do."

She took another step. "I don't know what I did to deserve a dog like Ghost, but I love him for it. He's brave and loyal."

"I had one like that." The shotgun muzzle lowered a few inches more. "A German Shepherd named Snickers. Smartest animal you've ever seen. Big, beautiful, with jaws that could crush bone in a second flat. Trained her myself." The woman's face creased into a network of wrinkles. Her thin lips twitched into something resembling a grin. "She was mine for fifteen years. Never let me down a single time. Ran off intruders more than once too."

Liam's mouth opened. He just stared at the woman. His brain couldn't process how quickly everything had just been flipped on its head.

A half-second ago, he'd been prepared to snap the old lady's neck. She'd threatened to kill them. Now she was smiling like she'd just won a pie-making contest.

The crazy old woman dropped the shotgun into the crook of her arm and stuck out her hand. "Name's CiCi Delacruz. It's a pleasure to meet you."

35

HANNAH

DAY SIX

Thirty minutes later, Hannah sat in the old woman's warm kitchen, a hot cup of lemon eucalyptus tea in her hands, delicious steam heating her frozen face and fingers.

CiCi Delacruz bustled around, pulling freshly homemade bread, peanut butter, and homemade jam and applesauce from her cupboards and spreading them across the table.

In a heartbeat, she'd transformed from heartless killer bent on their destruction to nurturing grandmother. It was bizarre, but not at all unwelcome.

She'd allowed them to retrieve their weapons. Hannah's kitchen knife lay on the kitchen counter. Liam held his pistol, his tactical knife sheathed at his belt.

CiCi's own shotgun was leaning against the cupboard below the wide basin of the farm sink. Once she'd decided to trust them, she'd gone all-in.

Ghost lay on the scarred wooden floor next to Hannah's chair.

His tail thumped appreciatively when CiCi brought him a bowl of dog food.

"Still had an unopened bag," she said as she poured him a huge bowl. "I've treats where that came from too."

"What do you know about what happened?" Liam asked around a thick slice of bread spread with homemade strawberry jam. He balanced his plate on the edge of the counter, eating with his left hand as he stood guard beside the back door.

"I wouldn't have known anythin' had happened at all if I hadn't been listenin' to my late husband Ricardo's ham radio. People are plain goin' nuts. Folks reportin' empty grocery stores from New York to Los Angeles. Lootin' and break-ins and bodies piling up everywhere."

Liam leaned forward, his gaze sharpening. "It hit the entire continental US then. What about Hawaii? Other countries?"

CiCi peered at him beneath a crown of wispy white curls. "My antennae isn't strong enough to reach that far. But I've talked with folks who can. Hawaii has power. Parts of Alaska. But no one's heard a thing from anyone in the rest of the States who does. One guy in Texas says he chatted with friends in the UK. They're fine. Well, they've got power. But their financial system is in crisis. What happens in the US affects everyone. You believe it's an EMP like some of 'em are sayin'? Or some ginormous solar flare?"

"A nuclear EMP, not a solar flare," Liam said. "A solar flare wouldn't just affect the US but much of the planet. An EMP from a high-altitude nuke would be more localized. Probably more than one nuclear blast if it's affecting most of the United States. Maybe a coordinated attack from a rogue nation. What's the government reporting?"

She wrinkled her nose. "They just keep replayin' the same emergency broadcasts: 'Stay calm, keep warm, and remain indoors; this is a temporary phenomenon, power and services'll be restored shortly. Aid is forthcomin'. 'Forthcomin' my saggy britches."

"They're trying to prevent a panic," Hannah said. "Offering reassurance."

"Not sure what good reassurances do the poor families freezin' to death in their own homes," CiCi said grimly.

Hannah chewed her sandwich in somber silence. What was happening in Fall Creek? Were Noah and Milo okay? Their old house had a fireplace, if they still lived there. Did they have enough wood to keep it burning twenty-four-seven? Did Milo still have enough to eat?

When she'd lived there, she always made sure they had four weeks' worth of food and supplies stored in the garage. It had been the source of many fights between her and Noah when money was tight. And money was always tight.

Where she'd grown up in the UP, you couldn't rely on stores always being fully stocked. Snowstorms could knock power out for days. You had to be ready, just in case.

Was Noah ready for this? Was he protecting their son? Apprehension tangled in her gut. She longed to be home so badly, it hurt like a physical ache in her chest.

"Do you think small towns will last longer?" she asked.

"Longer than cities, anyway. Maybe they'll have a chance if they band together, or if someone remembers the old ways of doin' things."

As late afternoon drifted into twilight, CiCi lit two beeswax candles on the kitchen counter and sat down opposite Liam and Hannah. The scent of lemon and honey filled the small, homey kitchen.

"Out here, I got to rely on a generator anyway. Save it for the important stuff, though—hot showers and the washin' machine. Candles and oil lamps work just fine for light. Got a well with a hand pump, septic system, and the woodburning stove. Don't go into town more than once a month, so I make sure I got enough to last me a while."

"Your generator is still working?" Hannah asked, thinking how everything had gone silent in the basement, even the generator's low rumble.

"It's old as sin and not connected to anythin' computerized and electronic, so yep. Heard on the radio that some folks' generators went out too. They make everything with computerized bits these days. It'll be a hard, hard winter. I know that."

Liam peered outside into the gathering darkness. "And the trespassers who came to your house?"

"They probably came up from the closest town once the stores were emptied out— Branch to the southwest, or the bigger town of Baldwin further southeast. There'll be more. My Ricardo and I lived out here on our own for forty years. We weren't born yesterday."

She glanced at her shotgun leaning against the cabinet. "I know just how to handle 'em."

CiCi kept talking, but Hannah barely heard her. Exhaustion tugged at her eyelids. Her muscles ached from days of hard travel. Her lower back hurt.

With her stomach full and her body thawed, she felt like she could sleep for a week.

A pressure on her bladder tugged her back into wakefulness. She shifted uncomfortably in her seat. "May I use the bathroom?"

"Let me show you," CiCi said.

Hannah followed CiCi up the narrow, creaking stairs to the second floor. Ghost leapt to his feet, lumbered to the base of the stairs, and whined anxiously.

"Stay with Liam," Hannah said. "Help him guard the house, okay?"

Ghost cocked his head and gave her a dejected look, but he stayed downstairs.

Upstairs, the walls were papered with a faded print of yellow roses and winding green vines. Photos in dusty frames hung on the wall—Cici and her husband in youth, in middle age, and older, both of them smiling, happy.

In the bathroom, she relieved herself, thankful beyond words for an actual toilet. She swore never to take the bathroom for granted again.

As she washed her hands with a yellow bottle of hand sanitizer, her gaze fell on the small shelf below the mirror. It was crowded with prescription pill bottles. They had long, complicated names she didn't recognize.

When she opened the door, CiCi was waiting for her on the other side. "Bad heart."

"What?"

"It's what I've got." The woman angled her chin toward the bathroom shelf behind Hannah. "You seem like the curious sort. Reckon you saw the pills."

Hannah hesitated. She hadn't thought about the millions of people dependent on medications. If the delivery trucks stopped, they wouldn't be delivering life-saving medicine to pharmacies or doctors' offices either. Or hospitals.

How many hundreds of thousands of people were going to sicken and die over the next weeks and months as their meds ran out?

Too many.

"What are you going to do when you can't get refills?" Hannah asked.

CiCi shrugged in resignation. "What everyone else is gonna do. Go 'bout my business and stay upright for as long as I can. What else is there?"

"I don't know."

"No one knows when their time is gonna come. I've had myself a full life. I'll go when I go, and I'll go in peace."

CiCi's words made sense in a way that not much else had for a long time. "Aren't you afraid out here all alone?"

CiCi frowned. Wrinkles fanned out from the corners of her dark brown eyes. "Alone is a state of mind, nothin' else. You remember that. So is fear."

"There are bad people out there. Bad people who would hurt you in a heartbeat."

She licked her lips, wanting to tell the woman about *him*, to warn her. The words clogged in her throat. Saying them out loud—it was impossible.

CiCi's eyes narrowed. "Child, we're all running from somethin'. I learned long ago not to live in fear of the next boogeyman. Let them come, I say. I have plenty of ammo."

Hannah nodded, relieved. The tightness in her chest eased. "Thank you again for your hospitality. You didn't have to show us such kindness."

"Kindness!" CiCi grunted. "I was dead-set on shootin' you."

"Well, thank you for not shooting us."

CiCi grinned. She shuffled for the stairs, then stopped abruptly. She turned back and stared hard at Hannah, her wrinkled jaw working, her sharp gaze never leaving Hannah's face.

Hannah waited patiently for the woman to say what she wanted to say. If she'd learned anything worthwhile during her years of captivity, it was patience.

Finally, CiCi nodded to herself. "I've got somethin' for you, girl."

36

HANNAH
DAY SIX

Hannah entered CiCi's bedroom. It was a bright, airy room with a quilted lavender bedspread and lacy curtains.

"I'm not lonely here, but I'd be lyin' if I said I don't miss someone to talk to. When my Ricardo was alive—" CiCi's eyes grew distant for a moment. "Well, that's neither here nor there, now is it? No use gettin' all misty-eyed for the things dead and gone. It's the living that matter now."

CiCi cleared her throat, turned, and went straight to her closet. "You can't keep on wearin' those baggy men's clothes. I got some warm gear that'll fit you well enough."

Hannah's chest went warm. "Thank you."

"You're welcome to stay the night."

"That's very kind. I'll talk to Liam."

"I've even got an extra nightgown, if you want."

Hannah went stiff, her jaw rigid. She shook her head. She would sleep in her clothes and boots. Easier to get up and run. A nightgown made you vulnerable.

Cici saw her face and nodded. "Fair enough." She opened the closet and pulled down an old box from the top shelf. She removed the lid and pulled out a gun. "A Ruger American .45. The compact version. Seven round magazine."

Hannah stared at it, eyes wide.

"It's mine, but I use the Remington now. Old age bests us all in the end. I can't shoot like I used to, not with these damn arthritic hands. A shotgun still gets the job done. I've got no need for this one anymore. Seems like you might."

Hannah shook her head, took a step back. "I can't take this."

"Sure, you can. You just hold out your hands. Easy as pumpkin pie. The 'thank you' is optional. It's yours, either way."

"I don't know how to use it."

CiCi winked at her. "Lucky for you, you've got a good-lookin' companion who does."

Trepidation flushed through her. She wasn't even sure why. "I can't repay you."

"You hear me ask for anythin'? I'm old enough to do what I damn well want to."

CiCi grabbed Hannah's good hand and thrust the gun into it.

Hannah's fingers closed over the cool gray metal. It was lighter than she'd thought it'd be. She stared down at it. Such a small thing to contain so much power. Capable of killing a man. Maybe even a monster. "Thank you."

"You got somethin' to protect, don't you?"

It took a moment for Hannah to realize the old woman meant the life growing inside her. Dread and doubt twisted her insides. "I guess I do," she managed lamely.

"How far along are you?"

"I'm not sure."

The woman's gnarled eyebrows shot up to her hairline. "Surely, you got an idea. I know I wouldn't forget the fun of a good roll in the hay."

Hannah blinked back a rush of bitter tears.

Instinctively, she touched her stomach with her deformed hand. Usually, she tried not to.

Her swelling stomach was a constant reminder of him, of what he'd done to her, of the evil he'd put inside her. It hurt too much to try to explain.

CiCi seemed to sense her resistance and took pity on her. "I thought six months when I first saw you, but up close, I see you just carry small. You're much too thin. All skinny arms and legs and belly. But you're carrying low. The babe's already head down, I'd guess. You're close, aren't you?"

CiCi had just confirmed her fears. Worry gnawed at the back of Hannah's mind. She was running out of time.

What would she do when it came? She had no idea. She'd done her best to push it out of her mind, to not think of it.

She couldn't think about what happened last time. What he'd done.

The darkness came calling, whispering in her mind. Her chest went cold. A wave of dizziness washed over her. She leaned on the nearby dresser, her legs weak and shaky.

"You all right?" CiCi asked, sounding almost far away.

The blood. The pain. The thin, ragged cry.

Terror moved through her, mounting like waves upon a roiling sea, black wave after black wave. Desperately she scanned the room, searching for something to count, for a way to anchor herself.

The faded gold stripes in the ancient wallpaper. *One, two three* . . . She counted them again and then a second time. *Thirty-five, thirty-six, thirty-seven* . . .

"What's wrong, honey?"

Hannah blinked. The warm, cozy room came slowly back into focus. The old woman with her flowery housedress, long johns, and compassionate eyes in her wizened face.

She sucked in her breath, forced herself back to the present. She was safe. He wasn't here, wasn't hurting her.

But he was still somewhere out there, prowling the hundreds of miles of national forest. Maybe making his way closer, ever closer.

"I . . . I'm sorry." Hannah wiped cold sweat from her forehead. Guilt pricked her. She was being hunted. She needed to warn CiCi that the evil that tracked her might come here too, to this warm and cozy home. "I need to tell you something. You might not want us to stay. There's—there's someone after me. A bad man. He wants to hurt me. He could come here."

CiCi snorted. "Honey, I know how to take care of myself."

"But if he—"

"I'm plenty familiar with bad men and what they do. That's what my Remington is for."

Hannah nodded politely. "But—"

"Weren't you listenin' before? I live alone way out here, and that's my choice. I'm goin' to live and die on my terms and I'm grateful for each day, come what may." She clucked her tongue. "Don't you worry none 'bout me."

"Okay," Hannah said. At least she'd tried. "Okay."

"It's none of my damn business, but I'm gonna say it anyway." CiCi took hold of her arm just above the elbow and squeezed. "I see fear in you."

Instinctively, Hannah shied away, but CiCi wouldn't let go. The old woman's eyes bored straight into her, like she could see all the way into the dark pit of her soul.

"That's what I mean," CiCi said. "There's two kinds of fear. Healthy fear keeps you alive. It's that gut instinct we women tend to ignore. You listen to that, you keep breathin'. Fear warns you to pay attention. To get out. To stand your ground and fight. Fear's the body's warnin' system. Without it, we're the deer trapped in the middle of the road stunned by oncomin' headlights. Roadkill every time."

"And the other kind of fear?" Hannah asked hoarsely.

"That second kinda fear takes hold of you and don't let go. It sinks its claws in and turns you into somethin' you're not. That fear destroys you from the inside out."

Hannah swallowed. She didn't say anything. She wasn't sure she could. But she knew exactly what CiCi meant. She lived it every second of every day.

CiCi released her arm. "You got that fear in you, but you don't have to keep it, girl. You're the only one who can choose. It don't matter what's out there." She tapped her own chest. "It's what's in here that counts."

"How—how do you get rid of it?"

CiCi rolled her eyes. "If I could tell you, it'd be too easy, wouldn't it?" She tilted her chin at the weapon clutched in Hannah's hand. "Start with that. You'll figure it out from there."

37

PIKE
DAY SEVEN

Pike watched the shabby white clapboard house through the scope of his rifle. The smell of wood smoke filled his nostrils. He needed a cigarette, and badly.

Smoke billowed from the chimney. The curtains were open. He caught brief glimpses of movement through the kitchen windows. A hunched old Hispanic woman.

Three pairs of boot tracks and one dog clearly led to the front door and inside. The old lady, the girl, and the man with her.

He'd tracked them here easily enough, always staying downwind. All he needed was the damn dog alerting them.

First chance he got, he was shooting the mutt in the head.

Big fat snowflakes tumbled down from the gray evening sky. It would be dark soon. It had been snowing for a while and wouldn't let up anytime soon.

No matter. Their tracks were deep and easy to follow.

Pike slung the rifle across his chest, readjusted his pack, and rose from his prone position beneath a large fir tree. He brushed snow and brown pine needles from his coat and pants.

He pulled out a cigarette and put it to his lips. He fished out his Zippo and stood turning it in his fingers, the old familiar weight of it, before at last clicking it open and flicking the flint wheel once and raising the flame to his face.

He tasted the smoke in his lungs, felt the nicotine speeding to his brain. He smoked the cigarette down, dropped it to the snow, and crushed it under his boot toe.

Now he was ready. Keeping inside the tree line, he made a slow circle around the house, searching for where the tracks picked up again.

It hadn't taken him long to realize the woman was alone in the house. They'd already left by the time he reached the house.

They'd been here. That was what mattered.

Scowling, he circled again. The snow was falling harder, obscuring his vision further than a few dozen yards. That shouldn't matter. Human tracks in two feet of snow were clear as day. A child could follow them.

He still didn't find them. Where were they?

He slogged through the snow, retracing his steps to the edge of the clearing. Footprints crisscrossed the yard, leading to and from the woods in several directions.

Carefully, he scanned the property again until he found two sets of prints and the dog's. The dog's paw prints were spread wide and far apart, like it was bounding ahead of the man and the girl.

They'd exited the house, crossed the clearing, and entered the woods in a southwestern direction. The prints weren't from boots. They were wide and shallow. Snowshoes.

Once inside the woods, he lost the tracks within a few hundred yards. The snow was windswept, peppered with fallen pinecones and small branches and littered with animal tracks. Regular, brush-like indentations were barely visible beneath the newly fallen snow.

He cursed under his breath. They'd attempted to cover their tracks by brushing pine boughs behind them.

Even without the pitiful attempt to deceive him, the shallow tracks would fill quickly. He would lose them in less than an hour at this rate.

After the woods, they could hit any one of a half-dozen small towns, depending on where they exited the Manistee National Forest.

He turned and glared back at the house, rage filling him, searing through his veins, boiling his insides. His fingers tightened on the rifle.

The occupant of that house had done this. The lone decrepit old woman. She'd harbored them.

Maybe she knew where they were headed next. She would tell him, and he could intercept his prey with a surprise ambush.

Even if she couldn't tell him anything useful, it didn't matter.

He would make her suffer for helping them. She would pay, bone by bone.

Dusk had fallen. The shadows deepened over the snow, the moon completely hidden. Using the cover of dusk, he crept across the clearing to the side of the house. He peered inside the window into the kitchen.

An oil lantern glowed on the counter. The woman wasn't in the kitchen.

Through the hallway leading out of the kitchen, he glimpsed a small living room and a set of wooden stairs leading up to the bedrooms.

He moved silently to the second window. This one offered a good view of the living room through the thin lacy curtains.

The old woman was slumped in an oversized La-Z-Boy brown chair. Her stockinged feet were up on an ottoman, a glass of water on the end table beside the chair. A shotgun leaned against the chair next to her legs.

A book lay open on her chest, which rose and fell gently. Her eyes were closed. She was dozing—or maybe already asleep.

Pike's lips curved in a slow smile.

Excitement built inside him. His pulse quickened. This would be child's play. An appetizer before the main meal. Something to hold him over.

The frigid air scalded his throat, burned his nostrils. It didn't bother him. He barely noticed the snow blanketing his head and shoulders. He was focused, alert, completely dialed in.

He inhaled the wood smoke, the clean white snow, the sharp pine, and damp and loamy earth beneath it all—every sense alive and thrumming with power.

Still crouching, he moved silently to the rear door into the kitchen. He slipped off his hiking backpack and the rifle and set them both on the back steps beneath the porch overhang.

He only needed his knife and his bare hands for this.

From one of the pockets of his pack, he pulled out a slim lock pick case. Lock picking was a skill that had served him well dozens of times. Today, it worked again.

He inserted the pick into the keyhole of the old lock, felt for the tumblers, and listened carefully. He heard the satisfying click.

He slid the door open, degree by degree, anticipating a creak or squeak, but it opened smoothly and silently. He closed it quietly behind him.

He stood for a moment in front of the door. He let his eyes adjust, his ears straining for any sound, any movement, but he heard nothing.

His boots were wet from the melting snow. He considered taking them off to move with utter silence. It wasn't needed. She was a weak old woman. Even if he didn't surprise her, what could she possibly do to him?

He reconsidered. She did have the shotgun.

Caution had gotten him this far. Smarts and cunning. Preparing for every contingency, no matter how simple or easy the task appeared.

He bent and unlaced his boots, removing them with great care. He moved without a sound in his wool socks, prowling with the ease and grace of a panther through the kitchen into the living room.

The brown leather La-Z-Boy faced away from him, toward the fireplace. The fire snapped and crackled. The flickering firelight cast heavy shadows.

The room smelled of cinnamon, charcoal, and the faint medicinal smell that always seemed to emanate from old people. He hated it.

Pike drew his tactical knife from the sheath at his belt. The razor edge gleamed, the edge honed so sharp it would split a human hair with ease. Or a human throat.

Pike snuck up behind the woman. Killing her quickly would be as simple as gutting a deer or slicing the throat of a hare caught in a snare.

But he wanted her alive long enough to give him the information he needed. What happened after that depended completely on his mood.

He raised the knife.

The old woman swayed to her feet, the shotgun gripped in her arthritic hands, trembling finger on the trigger.

38

PIKE
DAY SEVEN

His fury surging, Pike lunged in and smacked the weapon out of the old woman's hands.

The shotgun went off with a thunderous boom. His ears rang from the blast. He faltered for a second, dazed.

The shot missed, the muzzle aimed toward the window instead of at him. The blast shattered the glass and peppered the bookshelf on the wall to his right with buckshot.

The shotgun clattered to the floor.

The old woman bent to retrieve it.

Pike came to his senses and kicked it out of the way. It went skittering across the floor and struck the brick lintel of the fireplace.

He whirled on the woman and punched her in the face with his left fist.

She collapsed into the chair, blood gushing from her broken nose. She let out a low moan and a string of unintelligible curses.

He shifted his knife to his left hand and seized her shriveled upper arm with his right. Without a word, he hauled her up and dragged her stumbling and lurching into the kitchen.

He hurled her into a chair. She landed with a soft thud.

He punched her twice in the stomach. She gasped, choking. The fight went out of her. She crumpled in on herself, shriveling before his eyes like a dried-up old raisin.

She should've been put down like a dog years ago.

"Where are they?" he snarled.

"Who?" she forced out between ragged breaths.

"This can go two ways for you. Easy or hard. The choice is yours."

She gazed up at him, hatred blazing in her eyes. "Go to hell."

He waved the knife at her. "Where did they go? I know they were here. I know you let them in this house, in this very kitchen. I can smell wet dog everywhere." He angled his knife at a bowl of half-eaten dog food and drool-laced water next to the fridge. "See?"

"That's—that's from my dog."

"Oh yeah? Where is it?"

She glared up at him silently.

He sheathed his knife and seized her wrinkled left hand. She tried to pull away, but she was much too weak to fight him. "One finger per answer. You give me the correct answer, I won't break a finger. You lie to me? Well, you can guess the consequence."

"You." Her rheumy eyes widened. "You're the monster. The one that put that fear in her."

Recognition was far too underrated. It was the one negative to what he did, what he was. He never received the accolades or the glory.

"I'm not afraid of you," she said.

"You should be." He smiled. "Shall we begin? I know she was

here. All you have to do is tell me where she's going. Just a word or two. That's all."

She groaned and hunched over, her skin ashen. A withered old hag. She mumbled something, her voice so hoarse and scratchy, he couldn't hear her.

"What did you say? You ready to talk now?"

She rasped an unintelligible response.

He squatted in front of her, still holding her hand. "Tell me. That's all you have to do. This will all be over soon. You tell me and it all ends. The pain goes away. I go away. I walk out that door and you never have to see me again."

Of course, he was planning on walking out the door, but not before he'd finished what he'd started. It would be intensely pleasurable to snap her bony neck, to watch the light fade from those defiant eyes.

To know that he was the one with absolute power, absolute control, absolute authority. He ruled death itself.

The old woman whispered her answer.

Still smiling, he leaned in close.

She raised her chin and spat in his face. Globules of bloody spittle splattered his cheeks, nose, and eyes.

Pike flinched and reared back, nearly falling.

He wiped the disgusting slobber from his face with the back of his arm. Anger flared through him. It took every ounce of his self-control not to seize his knife and end her right then and there.

That wasn't enough. Not nearly enough.

"I'll never tell you a thing!" she shouted.

He tightened his grip on her hand, feeling her fragile bones creaking and grinding beneath the pressure of his thumb. Anticipation quickened his heartbeat.

"Everyone does, in the end," Pike said. "Everyone."

39

LIAM
DAY SEVEN

L iam pushed across the snow in his snowshoes, Hannah right behind him, the dog ambling through the trees beside them. The day was windless, snowflakes falling fast and silent, muting all sound.

The snowshoes spread out their weight and kept them from slogging through deep snow with every step. They'd both used snowshoes before, though Hannah's were too big for her, and she struggled to find a smooth, steady rhythm. Her condition made it even harder.

Before they'd left, CiCi had given them two pairs of snowshoes—hers and her late husband's. "I'm not goin' on any arduous treks with this old body," she'd said with a dismissive wave. "Not these days. Ricardo would be pleased knowin' his things were put to good use."

She had also insisted they spend the night, since dusk was already falling by the time they'd eaten and warmed up. Hannah needed a warm, safe place to sleep, so despite Liam's misgivings, they'd stayed.

They'd showered, scrubbed their itchy scalps and grimy bodies, and washed their clothing. CiCi had cooked them a delicious meal of the last of her pot roast, mashed potatoes, and green beans.

As enjoyable as it was, he hadn't allowed himself to relax. Not for one second.

He blinked the exhaustion from his eyes. The sharp sting of the cold kept him alert. He hadn't slept last night, not really.

In the military, he'd learned to extend his ability to stay awake by going into a sort of meditative state. A "cat nap" of sorts, where he slipped into a very light sleep, shutting down anything extraneous beyond awareness. The caffeine pills he'd popped didn't hurt either.

Liam had guarded the house until dawn, watching for the psychopath.

He wouldn't get the better of them again. Liam wouldn't allow it.

Ghost had taken it upon himself to patrol the house too. He moved constantly from the kitchen to the dining room to the living room and back again, sniffing at the doors and windows and throwing Liam occasional disdainful looks, like he didn't trust Liam to get the job done.

After an uneventful night, they'd eaten a hearty breakfast and left CiCi's that morning. The woman had insisted on packing their backpacks with another fresh loaf of bread, two boxes of Ritz crackers, two cans of tuna fish, and a small jar of peanut butter. Their canteens and water bottles were filled with fresh water.

"It's no feast, but it'll get you to the next town," she'd said, shooing them away when they tried to thank her.

When they'd left, they used large pine boughs to brush across their tracks for the first several hundred yards into the woods, and then changed direction to throw off their pursuer.

The thick fat flakes tumbling from the sky would cover their tracks soon. Hopefully, it would be enough.

Liam held the Glock in both hands, constantly scanning the trees around them and behind them, checking their six and searching for shadows or movement that didn't belong.

He saw nothing but snow and trees and more snow, heard nothing but their own ragged breaths, their snowshoes swishing, the occasional puff of clumps of snow falling from branches or a squirrel scurrying through the underbrush.

Despite their exertion, Hannah's teeth wouldn't stop chattering. She looked miserable but did her best to keep up with him. She never once complained.

She just kept going, jaw clenched, a line between her brows, her eyes almost glassy with the intensity of her focus.

She wouldn't tell him she needed to stop. He'd have to do the stopping for them, or she'd collapse on the trail.

He felt a pang of pity for her—and a growing, if grudging, respect.

"Here," Liam said, pointing several yards off the trail. The trail was straight in both directions, so he had a clear line of sight. A large, flat boulder about five feet in diameter lay to their right. "Time for lunch."

She nodded gratefully and sank onto the rock. She hunched forward, her hands cupped in front of her face, and breathed on her chilled fingers. Her face was ghost-pale and windblown, her eyes and nose reddened.

A fire would warm her up, but it would take too long and was too risky. They needed to get more distance between them and the psycho.

He'd decided they should stop in the tiny village of Branch to shore up their supplies, find shelter for the night, and look for transportation. As much as she might argue otherwise, Hannah couldn't hike for miles day after day. Not in her condition.

By his calculations, they were less than five miles from Branch.

They had four hours until dusk. Once they reached the town, they could find an abandoned house, barn, or maybe even a hotel still open if they were really lucky.

Liam had the cash if they needed it.

They ate the tuna fish and Ritz crackers from CiCi. Ghost drank his fill from the water Hannah poured into her camping pan.

The dog trotted in circles around them, his plumed tail waving like a flag as he kicked up snow with his paws and let out self-satisfied *woofs*. At least someone was enjoying the snow.

Hannah shoved an entire cracker into her mouth and chewed hungrily. Big wet snowflakes settled on her hood, her shoulders, her eyelashes. "What do you think this town will be like?"

"No idea," Liam mumbled.

"What were the other places like? On your way here?"

"Bad and getting worse."

"What about Chicago?"

Liam stiffened. He saw the planes overhead again, heard the explosive crash. The terror, the running, the blood. Jessa's desperate, beseeching eyes, gazing up at him. *Please, Liam. Please.*

He blinked the terrible images out of his head. "Chicago was Hell."

She didn't say anything for a few minutes. Just chewed and swallowed and drank more water. She wiped her runny nose. "I miss people."

"I don't."

"You don't?"

"It's better to be alone."

She was quiet for a moment. "Alone is terrible. Alone is the worst feeling in the world."

Shame pierced him to his core. He chose to be alone. Because his past hounded him relentlessly. Because he was a man haunted.

The things he'd lived through in Afghanistan and Iraq, in war-torn countries all over the world . . . they stalked his dreams, tormented him. He'd seen the worst humanity could do to each other. And it had scarred him.

To him, solitude was a comfort.

And a copout, Jessa whispered in his ear. He saw Jessa's face in his mind's eye, the disappointment in her eyes.

Hannah hadn't been given a choice. It had been taken from her.

He watched the snowflakes drifting in swirling, lacy curtains all around them. Snowflakes landed and quickly melted on his cheeks, his nose. Cold and feather-soft.

"People do awful things to each other," he muttered guiltily. "People are dangerous. Especially now."

A shadow passed across her face. An intense pain behind her eyes. Terrible things had happened to her. She knew the things humans did to each other—she didn't need him to tell her that. "Not everyone."

He was surprised she had any faith in humanity left. He didn't. "We've just been plunged into chaos, with finite and fast-dwindling resources. Put food, shelter, and survival on the line, and people will stab you for a loaf of bread."

"I don't believe that," she said softly—so softly, he almost didn't hear her. She finished eating, slowly wrapped up the crackers, and stuffed them back in her pack. "I—I can't believe that."

She gazed up at him then, snowflakes clinging to the damp strands of hair poking out from beneath her hat and furred hood. Her eyes were as green as the fir and spruce trees surrounding them.

They pinned him, steady and unblinking. Disquieting. "Some people are bad. There is evil in the world. I know that. But there are also good people. People like CiCi."

People like Lincoln and Jessa. The two people he'd loved most in the world. He looked away. "They're anomalies."

An ache swelled in his chest, acute loneliness and regret threatening to consume him. Conflicting emotions running too close to the surface. It hurt too much.

He pushed it out and focused on what he needed to do next instead. He unslung his pack, rested it on the rock, and pulled out the map and compass with his left hand, his Glock still in his right. "We need to go."

Without a word, Hannah stood and shouldered her own pack. They adjusted their scarves over their faces and set off.

Two damaged people just trying to survive this damn cold.

Hours passed as they struggled on in silence. The snow crunched beneath his snowshoes like glass, fell in thickening sheets. His chest burned as the frozen air was dragged deep inside his lungs. Dusk was fast descending.

The snow hadn't let up all day and didn't look like it would soon. Two-and-a-half feet of snow would deepen to three feet or more before morning.

The woods thinned out. Occasional houses peeked through the trees. They came across a few campsites and paved roads. A farm or two.

They were closing in on civilization. He could feel it, cold dread building inside him, as steady and relentless as the falling snow.

Liam stopped. "I estimate we have an hour to go to reach Branch. It's almost dark. I have a headlamp and you've got a flashlight. We can make camp, or we can keep going."

It was the first time he'd given her an option. Maybe he was getting soft, but he didn't want her to push herself further than she was capable of.

She blew out a crystalized cloud, her bad hand pressed against her lower back, a pained expression on her face. "We keep going."

"You sure?"

She nodded, resolute. "Yes."

Trepidation roiled through him. A town meant people. And people were a threat. Whatever lay behind them, he feared what lay ahead would be worse.

40

PIKE
DAY SEVEN

Gavin Pike hunched his shoulders and ducked his head through the driving snow. The wind blew harsh and cold, but most of his face was covered and goggles protected his eyes.

He'd stolen the old woman's purple snowmobile from her garage. The 1999 Polaris Trail Touring took a few tries to get started, but once it did, it ran like a well-oiled machine.

He drove south on North Hamilton Road, eating up the miles, only swerving occasionally to avoid a stalled car or truck mounded with snow. It was a rural road in the best of times. Now, it was absolutely empty.

He was done with the forest. Done with struggling through deep snowdrifts to track his prey on foot. He'd leveled up with the Polaris. He had to take a longer route, but it didn't matter.

The old woman had lasted far longer than he'd expected. Longer than anyone he'd previously dealt with.

No doubt she believed she was acting courageously, heroically. But heroics meant nothing. She'd broken in the end.

That was the beauty of it. The exquisite, scintillating perfection of humanity: they were all so frail, so weak. Nothing but a bag of meat and bone and flesh, just like any other creature.

It didn't matter if you were special forces or a CIA spy or a terrorist. Apply enough pressure in the right place, and *snap!*

The distal, middle, and proximal bones of the phalanges. The five flimsy metacarpals. The scaphoid and trapezoid capitate of the carpels. The ulna. The radius. They all broke.

Everyone broke. Getting them to that point—watching the hope drain out of them, the despair take hold, the terrible realization in their eyes—you held absolute power, you were absolute death, and they were utterly helpless before your wrath.

He smiled beneath his balaclava, his lips chapped and cracking from the cold, but he barely felt it. Barely felt the snow or the wind or the darkness closing in, the shadows lengthening.

He knew where they were going. He would get there first.

He'd have plenty of time to set up an ambush.

Let the games begin.

41

HANNAH
DAY SEVEN

"There it is," Hannah said.

Liam snapped off his headlamp. Hannah turned off her flashlight and stuck it in her pocket. Cold nipped at her exposed skin as her eyes adjusted to the darkness.

She could just make out the dim shapes of trees and bushes all around them. They'd exited the forest on a hill, the small village of Branch, Michigan spread out before them.

The place was blink-and-you'd-miss-it small—a main street lined with a handful of hunched one- and two-story buildings and a few clustered neighborhoods, everything smothered in white.

Smoke rose from the chimneys of several dozen houses. Dozens more had candles or battery-operated lanterns glowing from their windows. She saw a few bonfires burning in backyards, dark shadows huddled close to the fire for warmth.

More than half the homes were dark and silent. Either their owners were away on holiday, or the owners had left in search of a hotel or family and friends to stay with.

Or maybe the owners were still inside the dark cold houses, families hunched beneath every blanket and sheet and towel in the house, children and parents dressed in as many layers of clothing as they could wear, shivering and desperate.

Hannah shivered herself, her teeth chattering. She felt her body heat leaching out of her, degree by painful degree. Her legs were sore. Her whole body felt like she'd just run a marathon through the Arctic Tundra.

CiCi had given her a pair of thermal underwear and fleece-lined pants still held up by the makeshift paracord as it was more comfortable against her belly than a belt. A fleece undershirt and hat with built-in earmuffs.

Her clothes were better fitting and warmer now, but it was still freezing out.

What she wouldn't give for a warm bed, a soft mattress, a pile of thick, cozy blankets. What she wouldn't give to be back in CiCi's warm, cozy lamp-lit kitchen.

Right now, just getting out of the snow and wind would be enough.

She started forward, but Liam put his hand out, halting her. "Wait. We have to be careful."

Hannah wrapped her arms around her chest and hugged herself. She wished Ghost was here, but thirty minutes ago, he'd flushed a hare from some bushes, given chase, and disappeared.

She always felt better with him near her, steadier, more centered. Safer.

"We should avoid Main Street," Liam said. "Look for an empty house off by itself. And be discreet. It's best if no one knows we're here."

She nodded without speaking.

"If we get separated, meet back at that hill. See those three spruce trees at the crown, with the tree stump right in the center? Hide in there, and I'll find you. That's our rally point."

She didn't want to think about being separated and completely on her own again. For all the suspicion and distrust she'd felt toward him, he'd done nothing to harm her.

She was alive because of him. She'd come to rely on his quiet, steady presence.

"Follow me. Stay right behind me. Do whatever I say. If I say run, you turn and run. Don't stop. Don't look back."

She nodded soberly. Liam started forward and she followed closely behind.

They crept down the snowy hill, trying not to slip or make a sound to betray their presence. Hannah almost stumbled over her own snowshoes twice, but Liam caught her arm.

They skirted the first street. Then the next.

A row of small houses with narrow backyards separated them from the mom-and-pop businesses on Main Street: a small general store, gas station, bank, a Dollar General, a couple of restaurants.

They crept through one backyard, then another. They avoided the houses with lights or smoke. Most of the homes were quiet and dark.

It was eerily silent. The snow absorbed all sound. It felt like creeping through a frozen ghost town.

Hannah's heart rate quickened. Blood roared in her ears.

She stared hard at each house as they passed. The blank black windows stared back at them like eyes. She imagined people inside, watching them.

Liam stopped abruptly. She nearly ran into him.

He twisted around, seized her forearm, and pulled her against the side of a brick house. He pressed his back against the wall next to her. He gripped his pistol in both hands.

"What is it?"

"Listen."

At first, she didn't hear anything. Then she did. The low rumble of engines. Several of them. They were drawing swiftly closer.

Voices echoed sharp and crisp in the night air. Thumping sounds. A dull heavy thud and the crash of glass breaking. Someone screamed.

"Wait here." Liam darted into the darkness. She waited, terrified, her heart jackhammering so loud she could barely hear a thing.

Less than a minute later, he returned. "A bunch of people just drove into town. Looks like they're taking what they want by force."

"It's only been a week," she said, incredulous. Even after everything Liam and CiCi had told her, it all had still seemed unreal. Until now.

"Long enough."

"How many?" she whispered.

"Counting by the flashlights, at least three different groups of five to seven people moving through the town. They're looting what's left of the stores. And some of the houses."

"W-who are they?"

"These aren't desperate people stealing from their own to live. They're from somewhere else. They're looking for food. Gas, if they can find it. Going to rob the town and bleed it dry. Looks like they're starting on the south side of town and working their way north."

Fear clamped down on her. "What do we do?"

"We have to get out of here," Liam said. "Before we're trapped."

42

HANNAH
DAY SEVEN

S houts rose into the night. Someone screamed. A gunshot went off.

Hannah flinched. Her heart slammed in her chest.

"Should we go back to the w-woods?" she asked through chattering teeth.

Liam glanced down at her. In the darkness and with his hood over his face, she couldn't make out his features. He was studying her, examining her. Assessing her strength.

She tried to stand taller. The freezing wind tugged at her scarf, pulling the flap covering her mouth and nose free. Her nostrils were dry and irritated. Every icy breath raked her throat.

She pushed the scarf back into place with stiffening fingers. "How close is the n-next town?"

"Walkerville is twenty-two miles."

She couldn't make it that far, no matter how determined she was, no matter how much she wanted it. She knew it. Liam knew it.

"They're right on top of us," Liam whispered. "We need to keep moving. Stay behind me. Go when I signal you."

He crept along the side of the house, peered around the corner, then darted across the yard between the houses to the cover of the next one.

He checked to make sure the next house was clear, then gestured for her to follow him.

Several houses down and across the street, a woman screamed. More shouts and yelling. Banging, crashing sounds.

"You can't take everything we have!" a female voice cried. "How am I supposed to feed my children?"

"We've got to feed our own children," another female voice responded—lower, harder, angrier. "Now stay back, or I swear I'll shoot you."

Fear rooted Hannah in place. She couldn't move, couldn't breathe.

She knew what human beings were capable of. Their greed and cruelty. Out here, with no one to stop them or tell them no . . .

Across the quiet expanse of yard, Liam gestured to her again, increasingly agitated.

She needed to move. She couldn't. She shrank back against the wall, shivering and cowering. Dizziness washed through her.

Darkness wavered at the corners of her vision, her mind threatening to go blank on her. She fought it, searched for something to count, to anchor her. She couldn't go away, not now, not here.

"Try the one with the red door!" a man shouted. He sounded close. Less than a hundred feet away. Maybe closer.

A flashlight swept across the snow. The beam washed the house in light.

She froze, waited breathlessly for a shout of alarm. The rush of voices and bodies and guns coming to discover them.

The flashlight beam wavered.

"You see something?" a deep voice asked.

"See what? It's just a dog or a coyote or somethin'. Scared of your own shadow, man? I told you, there ain't no cops out here. We got this place to ourselves."

"Yeah, yeah. I'm sure you're right."

"Get a move on, Thacker. I'm freezing my balls off out here."

"Thought your balls were too small to freeze."

"Screw you, moron."

Harsh laughter. Footsteps trudged away in the snow.

Her pulse thudded in her throat, her skull. She pressed against the wall, her pack grinding against her spine.

A soft crunch and a thud. Footsteps again. The flashlight beam sweeping across the fronts of the houses, sliding between the twenty feet of snowy side yard separating Hannah from Liam.

Only one man had left. The first had remained behind, still suspicious, not quite sold on the coyote theory.

Hannah glanced frantically around her, desperately searching for an escape, for somewhere to hide.

The house's backyard was barren. A snowy expanse of nothing. A few sparse trees thirty yards away. Past that, a large field and the hill, the forest beyond it. Way too far to reach without being seen.

She remembered the gun in her coat pocket. The Ruger .45 CiCi had so kindly given her.

But she had no idea how to use it. Couldn't even hold it with both hands, given her deformed fingers. And she'd left the kitchen knife behind at CiCi's house.

She hated her own helplessness.

The footsteps crunched closer. Between the two houses. Heading straight toward her.

43

HANNAH
DAY SEVEN

Hannah turned her head and met Liam's gaze, her eyes frantic. He crouched behind the corner. His gun was gone. He held something else in his hands. Something long and sharp, gleaming darkly against the white snow: a knife.

A shadow appeared between the houses. A tall, broad man dressed in a parka with a black ski mask pulled over his face. He held a flashlight and a baseball bat studded with ugly-looking nails.

Liam exploded into motion.

"What the—"

The man only got out two words before Liam punched him in the throat. The guy made a gurgling, gasping sound as he staggered back, trying desperately to suck air back into his windpipe.

Liam didn't give him a second to react. He came at him again.

The thug flung up his bat to deflect the blow, attempting both to defend himself and attack at the same time.

Liam ducked easily beneath the weapon, spun around him, and

gripped the man in a headlock from behind. He dragged the choking man behind the house out of sight.

He crouched over the man, and the knife flashed in his hand. Black blood spewed from the man's neck. It all happened so quickly. The man hardly made a sound.

Hannah stared, stunned, her mind still trying to process what had just happened.

Liam wiped the blade on the back of the dead man's parka. He sheathed the knife beneath his coat, rolled him up against the house, and kicked fresh snow over the blood spatter.

He drew his pistol again. Keeping it low and ready, Liam turned back to Hannah, who remained frozen against the wall of the first house. He motioned for her to hurry.

This time, her legs worked. She moved. She didn't look at the body as she passed only feet away, careful to avoid the concealed blood.

Liam said nothing. She said nothing to him. She was too cold to talk, too cold to think.

They crept from house to house, building to building. They passed a fast food joint, a mechanics shop, a Dollar Store, and a darkened gas station with a half-dozen people struggling to siphon gas from the non-functioning pumps.

She glimpsed the beams of flashlights cutting through the falling snow. Hunched figures darting through the darkness.

The ruckus on main street grew louder. Men were shouting. A woman screamed. Several gunshots went off as people whooped and hollered.

The thugs spread out, ransacking houses and breaking into businesses, hauling out supplies stuffed into big black garbage bags. Most of them carried baseball bats, crowbars, and rifles.

"Don't think you can just steal from us!" an older man yelled, fear and anger in his voice.

A man laughed. "Ain't nobody here to stop us, old man."

A crash sounded, and the old man cried out. Several dull wet thuds swiftly followed. The old man let out an anguished moan.

They were beating him—to death it sounded like.

She paused, horrified, torn between fleeing and doing something to help. Liam turned, grabbed her arm, and hauled her along.

At the south end of main street, a half-dozen trucks were parked in the middle of the road in front of the local grocery store. Several still had their headlights blazing, snow twirling in the hazy cones of light. Six snowmobiles and a few winterized ATVs outfitted with snow chains sat next to the trucks.

The looters were everywhere. More people were being dragged from their homes and beaten mercilessly. Their attackers shrieking and hooting in crazed bloodlust.

Hannah and Liam needed to find cover, and fast. They needed to find someplace no one would want to loot. A place without value.

There. Through the swirling snow. She touched Liam's arm and pointed ahead to a modest brick building just past the bank they were hidden behind.

Two of the windows were shattered, fresh graffiti scrawled across the exterior walls. A stray flashlight beam lit up the interior through the jagged windows—shelves and shelves of books.

A library. No food or drink allowed. No reason for anyone to want to break in.

Liam dashed ahead of her, made sure the area was clear, then motioned for her to follow him. The library was near the south end of Main Street, a few hundred yards from the waiting trucks, snowmobiles, and ATVs.

Only a few men stood guard. She and Liam would be quiet. No one would even know they were there.

The rear door was ajar. A roof overhang kept the snow drifting against the door from being too high to jam the door open enough for Hannah and Liam to slip inside.

They were inside, but far from safe.

44

HANNAH
DAY SEVEN

Liam paused inside the darkened hallway and put his finger to his lips. He crouched and unhooked his snowshoes, then Hannah's. He instructed her to wait in place while he crept ahead and cleared the building.

She waited, shivering hard, straining to hear the violence echoing outside.

Without a headlamp or flashlight, the hallway was awash in shadows so deep it was difficult to see past her own hand.

In a few minutes, he returned as silently as he'd left. She never heard him make a sound. He beckoned her deeper inside.

The large main room was high ceilinged with the check-out desk in the front, surrounded by an open area with a dozen study tables. Located to the left was a children's section: waist-high shelves filled with picture books, a colored rug, and bean bag chairs. To the right were two sets of glass entrance doors and a line of large windows—three of them broken.

Dim light flooded through the windows, highlighting the maze of long, tall shelves crammed with books.

"Stay down and away from the windows," Liam said. "Find a spot in that corner. Take the snowshoes with you. I'll be there in a minute."

She bent awkwardly—her belly in the way—and picked up the snowshoes. She shuffled past the check-out counter and the tables through a long row of shelves to the rear corner.

She unslung her pack and leaned the snowshoes against one of the shelves just as Liam returned, lugging three bean bags. She could just make out a yellow one, green one, and a third either navy blue or black.

Liam spread them out in the corner. "You sleep. I'll take watch."

"What about y-you?"

He grunted. "What about me?"

"Don't you n-need to sleep?"

"Not with them out there."

She sank into the yellow bean bag and rubbed her hands together. She pressed her good hand to her mouth and blew into her cupped fingers, letting her own hot air warm her numbed cheeks.

It was still frigid inside the library, but at least she was free of the snow and freezing wind. She longed for a fire to thaw her icy insides, but smoke would be a dead giveaway.

Liam took off his gloves, unzipped his pack, and pulled out the crackers and peanut butter. He dipped a cracker in the peanut butter and handed it to her. "Eat first. And drink something."

She nodded wearily. He was right. She was starving. She ate the cracker in a few bites. Liam handed her several more. She swallowed them all down, the peanut butter thick and smooth on her tongue.

A memory flared through her mind. Little Milo giggling, his mouth and cheeks and fingers smeared with Jif. He'd gotten into the pantry while she was cleaning the bathroom, eaten half a jar before she'd found him.

Peanut butter had been his all-time favorite food. If they slathered veggies in the stuff, he'd even eat broccoli and Brussel sprouts.

Her throat tightened. Did he still love peanut butter? Would she ever get home to find out?

She would. She had to. They would make it through this night. She and Liam together. And Ghost, wherever he was out in the woods. He would wait for them. She believed it.

Hannah tried to sit up and reach for her pack for her canteen, but her body rebelled. She was too tired to move.

Liam went to her pack, tugged out her canteen, and handed it to her.

She drank deeply, the cold water soothing her burning throat. "Thank you."

She handed it back to him empty. They would need more water soon.

Hopefully, the thugs would move on soon, leaving this poor town to its own misery. Then they could start a fire and melt more snow or search for water in the staff break room, behind the reception desk, or there might be water left in the library pipes.

She tried not to listen to the distant shrieking and shouting, but she flinched with each crack of a gunshot.

She removed her hood, took off her knit cap, and dusted off the melting snow. She retied her messy bun with shaky, numb fingers, pushed the damp strands behind her ears, and put her hat back on. Steadied her breathing.

She glanced warily at Liam. "You killed that man."

He shoved a hunk of peanut butter sandwiched between two

crackers into his mouth and barely chewed before swallowing noisily. "Had to be done."

She turned that thought around in her head for a moment. Should she feel horrified? Outraged? Guilty? Should she hate this man? Fear him? Run away from him?

She didn't trust him. She didn't trust anyone, not even herself. But she didn't fear him anymore.

That didn't mean he wasn't frightening. The way he'd killed that man, his movements so agile and quick, like a great jungle cat—a panther or a tiger, a creature whose very nature was to kill.

A shiver ran through her. The man Liam had killed wasn't a good one. They were robbing and beating townspeople out there. They were stealing from people who had little left to care for themselves, taking what would essentially seal these family's fates.

The thug would've warned the others and put her and Liam in further danger.

Could Liam have knocked the guy out instead? Maybe. But she was already learning how Liam's mind worked.

Leaving the thug alive left him a threat to their lives. Ending him ended the threat.

"Okay," she mumbled, as if he cared.

He hadn't asked for her permission or her judgment, and he didn't ask her opinion now. He didn't seem to care what anyone else thought about him, least of all her.

She was too tired to argue with him anyway.

Liam finished the sleeve of crackers and capped the peanut butter. He placed the jar back in his pack and zipped it. He took a small length of cord from a side pocket and tied his snowshoes to the back of the backpack.

He slung the straps over his shoulders. "Get a few hours' rest. As soon as the hostiles clear out, we keep going."

She curled up across two of the bean bags, her weary body sinking into the comfortable softness. She was incredibly grateful that she wasn't lying on the cold ground or a dirty mattress in a locked basement.

Anything was better than that.

Liam picked up the third bean bag and draped it over her thighs and torso for added warmth.

"You should take it," she argued feebly. "You need one too."

"I'm fine."

Liam positioned himself at the end of the row so that he could see both the entrance doors and the windows. He sat down and leaned against the shelf but kept his pack on his back and the gun in his lap.

She could just make out the whites of his eyes and the gleam of the pistol in the dim light. He would remain awake and alert so she could rest. Always the soldier, watching over her.

Gratitude filled her, but before she could say anything, sheer exhaustion took over. Her eyelids drifted closed. In only a few moments, she was asleep.

Her dreams were dark and disjointed and laced with terror. She was screaming, running across black ice, a leering demon with a red slash of a mouth chasing after her, the ice breaking open like jaws, splitting beneath her with a terrible *crack, crack, crack* . . .

She awoke abruptly to a tense hand on her shoulder and fear snarled in her belly.

A blurred figure hunched over her. "Shhh. Don't make a sound."

45

PIKE
DAY SEVEN

As he'd planned, Pike beat his quarry into town. They were on foot; he had the snowmobile.

He hadn't planned on the thirty thugs rampaging through the tiny town, looting every store, pharmacy, gas station, and home they could find.

The occasional gunshot echoed in the frigid air, mingling with screams, shouts, and raucous laughter.

Most townspeople gave in quickly, cowed by the unexpected violence. Some were left alone. Others were dragged from their homes and beaten in the streets.

He'd taken up a position north of town and cased the area with binoculars until he'd gotten a good overview of what was going down.

These weren't hardened criminals or trained soldiers. They were low-level thugs who thought themselves bigger and badder than they really were. Likely, one was the brains of the operation and had worked the others into a frenzy of greed, fear, and violence.

It wasn't a bad plan. Take first before others take from you.

Attack the smaller towns with few defenses and zero police presence. Strike at night in one fell swoop, and steal everything you can carry.

He might have done the same himself if he didn't have a more pressing agenda. Gavin Pike was an expert at utilizing every situation to his own advantage. This was no exception.

He trudged through snow back to where he'd parked the ancient purple snowmobile behind some trees.

He adjusted the rifle across his back, then removed his balaclava and stuffed it in his pocket. The cold stung his face like a slap, but he ignored it. He didn't want to look dangerous, not yet. His innocuous, placid features were one of his greater assets.

Pike affixed his goggles and started the motor. He checked the gas. Still half a tank's worth. He'd need to find gas soon.

He drove the snowmobile into the center of town, right through Main Street. A few dozen abandoned cars collected snow along the curb on either side of the street, but nothing blocked or hampered his way.

Nine or ten men dressed in thick winter gear were gathered around the gas station, all working on siphoning gas from the pumps. They turned toward him as he roared up.

Several grabbed hunting rifles they'd set down nearby. A few semi-automatics. Others brandished baseball bats and crowbars, or aimed the beams of their flashlights in his face.

He squinted, irritated, but kept his expression calm and placid. He slowed and maneuvered to the edge of the parking lot, then cut the engine and sat for several moments, waiting.

It was an age-old ploy, and an effective one. Make them wait, let them get nervous and edgy, wondering what you wanted, who you were. Get them to come to you.

One of the men stepped forward. A tall, skinny Caucasian man.

It was hard to tell any distinguishing details beneath the thick gray coat, hood, and scarf shielding the lower half of his face.

He held a rifle with both hands, though it was loosely aimed at the ground. For now.

"You best be moving on," the man said gruffly. He spoke with confidence, without any hesitation or doubt. Likely, he was the leader.

"Without that Polaris, though," said an African-American woman next to the leader. "We're going to need that."

"I'm sure we can work something out," Pike said agreeably. He had no desire to get himself shot by some idiot. He was more than capable of holding his own, but he didn't see a reason to resort to violence yet.

An idea was sprouting in his head, a way to use these fools to his own advantage.

The black woman was shorter than the man, and much heavier. She gestured at Pike with her shotgun. "Get off. Now. We'll take your pack off your hands too. And that rifle."

"Wilcox will escort you through town to make sure you find your way," the man said. "This place isn't somewhere most folks would choose to be tonight, if you know what I mean."

Another scream ripped through the night.

The thugs watched him, waiting to see him flinch. He didn't. Instead, he pulled out his badge and flashed it at them.

The woman took an instinctive step backward. Several of the men gathered behind them muttered low curses.

"Officer Gavin Pike." Pike left out the part about only being a reserve volunteer. What they didn't know only strengthened his position. "I'm afraid you folks are breaking the law on at least a dozen counts. Probably more."

The thugs exchanged wary glances, unsure what to do.

It'd only been a week since the blackout began. They were just getting used to the idea that the police might not control things anymore.

"My daughter has no food," the woman said defensively. "We're just doing what we have to."

"Where's the government?" whined a short, skinny guy behind the woman. "Where's FEMA? They've abandoned us. Just left us behind. They're forcing us to do this."

"I'm not going to arrest you," Pike said quickly to assuage their concerns.

It was best not to give them time to think anything through for themselves. Eventually, they'd realize they could kill a cop—real or fake—as easily as anyone else. Luckily, they hadn't come to that conclusion yet.

A few of them looked relieved. The others—including the woman and the leader—still stared at him suspiciously, their fingers near their triggers.

He kept his posture easy, his shoulders loose. He loosened his hood to make sure they could see his bland face, his charismatic smile.

"Look," he said in his friendliest voice, keeping the badge front and center. "We're all just trying to survive these next few weeks or months, right? We've got families to feed. And where's the government? Where's FEMA? I don't see any aid drops, do you?"

The thugs watched him, most grim-faced. A few nodded. He was speaking their language. "I've got no beef with you. This isn't my jurisdiction. Isn't my problem. Thing is, I've got a murder a few miles back that I've got to take care of. A nice little old lady killed in her own home."

The woman stiffened. "We ain't got nothin' to do with that."

"I already know who did it," Pike said easily. "Just got to catch the bad guys, that's all. That's what I could use your help with, actually. I know nothing comes for free, especially now. I've got two thousand dollars in cash. A thousand now, a thousand after, if you happen to find the man and woman I'm looking for."

It was a gamble to admit he had something they wanted, but he was still banking on their instinctive apprehension of the law. It worked.

"Cash?" one of the men asked.

"That's what I said. All the banks are closed, no paychecks getting issued right now, and credit cards are just squares of plastic, but cash is always king. I'm sure you know of a few stores still open, demanding greenbacks in exchange for goods."

A few nods. Several stares were less hostile, more greedy.

"You see the girl, you bring her to me."

"What do they look like?" the woman asked.

"He's tall, in his thirties, brown hair cut short, military bearing. He'll be with the girl. Dark hair, Caucasian, skinny but pregnant. They might have a big white dog with them. Hard to miss, those two. They've both got packs crammed with ammo and two M16s." That last bit was completely made up, but Pike knew how to read an audience. "I've got no use for the weapons and gear. They're yours."

Several of them exchanged looks. Semi-automatic weapons were useful in their new line of work.

"You want the man alive too?" the woman asked.

Pike shrugged. "Let's just say the man isn't my concern."

Pike never even got off the snowmobile. The leader came to him, puffing out his chest like a cocky rooster.

"And your rifle too," he said loudly so the others could hear. "That's part of the deal."

Without a word, Pike unclipped the strap and handed the

Winchester to the punk. He wasn't worried. He would take it back shortly, and then some.

Men like these needed to feel they wielded power over others in order to let their guards down. That was what Pike needed.

He gave the man the thousand dollars with a smile on his face. It was a cheap price to pay.

Now he would watch and wait. This time, Pike would be ready for them.

This desolate, snow-laden town would be the end of the line for all of them—the girl, Soldier Boy, the mangy dog.

The only one leaving this place alive was him.

46

HANNAH
DAY EIGHT

Hannah flailed, striking out desperately with weak fists, blinded by the darkness and sheer terror.

It was *him*. Looming over her, ready to hurt her, to torture her, to kill her, to break every bone in her body, shattering her from within, from the inside out . . .

"Shhhh!" a voice whispered. "It's me."

She swam up through the depths of the nightmare, struggling toward reality. She wasn't in the basement. She wasn't dying. Her bones weren't splintering.

Liam. Liam Coleman crouched beside her, eyes wide and white in the darkness, his features barely visible. His finger pressed against her lips.

She didn't know how long she'd been asleep. It felt like minutes but could have been hours.

Everything came back in a rush of dread and fear and bone-chilling cold. The frigid night. The town. The screaming and shouting. She and Liam running for their lives.

They were in the library, hiding from the deranged hoodlums looting the town.

Fear shot through her. She scrambled up to a sitting position, the bean bags rustling and crackling beneath her weight. The noise loud as explosions in the tense silence.

She eased off the bean bags onto her hands and knees beside Liam.

Sounds were coming from the front entrance. The tinkling of broken glass. A thud and damp footfalls on a tile floor. A muffled curse.

The looters were inside the library. Why? For what? There wasn't anything of value here. No gas, no food, no water, no money, and no people, as far as they knew. Unless someone had seen her or Liam.

Liam met her eyes and pointed at her, then the carpet in front of her. He pointed to himself and motioned down the aisle of books. He wanted her to stay put. He was going after the bad guys.

She nodded numbly, too scared to speak or make a sound lest she give their position away.

Still crouching, Liam moved silently between the rows of books and disappeared into the darkness.

Heart hammering, mouth bone-dry with panic, she scooched on her butt into the corner. She reached for the nearest bean bag with her bad hand but couldn't close her fingers to pinch the fabric.

Angry tears sprang to her eyes. She couldn't even pick up a stupid bean bag.

And she was alone.

47

LIAM
DAY EIGHT

L iam stalked his targets.

It was well after midnight. His body was exhausted, but he didn't feel it. That would come later.

He crept from shelf to shelf, always keeping a row between himself and his quarry, using the narrow space between the tops of the books and the shelf to get a bead on them.

Three men. Two with pistols. One with a rifle. The two with pistols held flashlights. They huddled in the entrance foyer, speaking quietly with each other, deciding what to do.

Whatever Liam did, he needed to do it quietly. It would only take a second for one of them to sound the alarm and draw reinforcements.

He could escape, slip out soundlessly and effortlessly without the hostiles knowing any different. But Hannah couldn't. He could run for miles without stopping, could execute anyone who dared to pursue him with ease, but she couldn't.

She was the weak link. She changed everything.

Liam needed to be very, very careful. He waited, assessing the situation.

Maybe they were looking for a break from the wind and snow. Maybe they didn't realize a library wouldn't have food. They'd simply walk out, and he wouldn't have to do a thing.

"This sucks," one of them grumbled.

"Why are we even doing this? Nobody's here."

"The guy said. They've got an M16. A backpack full of ammo. You know what we could do with that?"

"Can't keep warm with it, now can we?"

"Stop your whining and get moving."

Liam only had one kind of luck. It wasn't the good kind.

They weren't leaving. Even worse, they were searching for someone specific and wouldn't be easily dissuaded.

Adrenaline thrummed through him. His muscles tensed. Memories of his years in combat seared through his mind—bullets zinging past his head, grenades exploding, the dying screams of his fellow soldiers.

In war, every second was a life-or-death decision. Every move might be the last one you'd ever make. There was no time for indecision or second-guessing. Only action.

The library wasn't large. Three men searching meant they'd find Hannah within a few minutes at most. If they spread out, he could eliminate them one at a time. Use his knife or snap their necks. He needed to move quickly.

The hostiles strode deeper into the library. The first one shifted left and swept the children's area with a flashlight. The second headed straight toward the check-out counter.

The third one strode to the closed door next to the children's area and nudged the door open with the muzzle of his pistol.

Liam had already checked it—a craft room with kid-sized tables and colorful chairs and cabinets filled with construction paper, glue, and sequins.

He slipped the gun into his coat pocket and drew his tactical knife again. The Gerber or his hands—both were quiet. The noisy Glock was a weapon of last resort.

Liam skirted the aisles in complete silence. He kept one bookshelf between himself and the two broken windows in case they had a lookout posted outside.

He reached the far wall and the half-opened craft room door. He slipped inside, a shadow among shadows.

Thug number three faced away from him, checking the space between the cabinets and the far corner, which was blocked by an oversized trash can.

Liam's focus narrowed to a razor point. He lunged, fast and lethal. Four swift steps and he placed the point of the blade in the indent at the base of Three's skull, where the bone was thin, and slammed upward at a 45-degree angle.

The knife slid in soundlessly, scrambling the hostile's medulla oblongata and cutting off his motor senses immediately.

Liam released the hilt, the blade still inside Three's brain. He seized the man's shoulders before he crashed to the floor and lowered him slowly, gently, snaking his ankle around the leg of the chair next to him, and moving it a few inches back as he laid his target down on his side.

He slid out the knife, wiped it off on the back of Three's pant leg, and pocketed the man's pistol. He barely glanced at the body. Three had been dead before he hit the floor.

Every sense alert, his muscles tensed, Liam moved to the left of the half-open craft room door. He hesitated.

No sounds immediately in the vicinity. A thud and a curse

through the wall to his right. Thug One was still in the children's area.

Liam moved quickly but cautiously from the craft room and scanned the area, knife held low and at the ready.

Movement to his left. A shadow out of the corner of his eye. Thug Two was headed down the third row closest to the wall of broken windows. Still five rows from Hannah's location.

He didn't want One still active at his back. He made a quick calculation—he had the time.

Liam turned around the corner and strolled into the children's area. He kept his shoulders and arms loose, his posture unthreatening.

One barely looked up. He expected one of his friends to return. He wouldn't see Liam coming until it was too late.

The thug leaned over a row of desks set up with ancient desktop computers, pistol in one hand. He'd set the flashlight on one of the desks, and the beam threw deep, quivering shadows.

Liam glimpsed dark skin, a full beard, and a thick tattooed neck beneath the unzipped collar of the man's coat. "I really don't think they're here, man. I mean—"

One finally glanced at Liam. His eyes widened in surprise.

Less than three feet away, Liam reached him before he could even open his mouth or reach for his weapon. He lashed out with the knife, stuck him in the side of his thick neck right in the carotid.

One gurgled and flailed. Blood sprayed in a dark arc.

Before Liam could grab him, One's right arm bounced off the nearest computer monitors with a *thunk*. The monitor shuddered but didn't fall.

Liam laid the man on the carpet. He pulled out the blade and slid it across the man's jugular. One didn't make a sound louder than a gurgle.

227

Blood had spattered Liam's face and coat. He barely noticed. He pocketed the pistol, covered the dying man's mouth with his hand, and went still, listening hard.

"You say something?" Two called from the stacks. "Ray? Mason?"

Instantly Liam was up and headed for the main room. He adjusted his grip on the knife, wet and slick with blood. His pulse quickened in concern.

By the sound of Two's voice, he was only an aisle or two from Hannah.

48

LIAM
DAY EIGHT

Liam sprinted past the check-out counter and maneuvered between the round study tables, everything just dim shapes in the darkness.

Heart racing, he reached the stacks and quickly cleared each one, gun up. He moved to the second-to-last aisle. It was empty.

He stopped and listened, every sense on high alert.

No sounds. No movements. Even the chaos outside had fallen into a tense, muffled quiet.

Two would've made a noise if he'd found her. Hannah would've yelled or screamed a warning.

Liam couldn't see her, but he felt her, small and terrified and shaking like a leaf. Helpless and depending on him.

A footfall to his left. A boot scraped on carpet.

Liam crouched and peered through the space between the tops of the books and the next shelf to the next aisle. A flicker of movement. A darting shadow.

More footsteps, faster now. Two was running. Not toward Hannah or back to the entrance, but toward the wall of windows.

Somehow, Two had figured out that he was both alone and not alone.

He was making a break for it.

If Two reached the rest of his group, he'd bring back twenty of his goons, maybe more. Too many even for Liam to fight off.

Liam dashed down the row and rounded the endcap, nearly knocking several thick tomes off a shelf. He caught sight of Two fleeing across the library just as he reached the windows.

The thug vaulted over the waist-high shelves and hurled himself through the broken window, his rifle slung across his back. Jagged shards snagged at his coat and jeans, but he went through.

The man pitched forward and rolled with a pained grunt. He scrambled to his feet and shot off across the library parking lot toward Main Street, shouting the alarm, flashlight beam bobbing like a beacon for Liam to follow.

Liam followed but angled himself to miss the glass shards raking at his boots. He hit the snow awkwardly, the jarring landing sending pain streaking up and down his spine, irritating old war wounds.

The bracing cold struck him like a slap in the face. The wind howled mournfully. Great gusts swept the snow into drifts several feet deep.

His eyes adjusted to the night. Everything was gray snow and dim black shapes, no moon or ambient light to aid his vision. But Two and the other thugs had the same disadvantage.

Heavy flakes swirled into his eyes, stuck in his eyelashes. He blinked them away, ignored the pain, and forced himself to straighten. Two was a wavering shadow barely visible ahead of him. He had a fifty-foot head start.

Liam was sorely tempted to use his Glock, but he didn't have a clear shot. He needed to get closer. He had to chase Two down.

He sank well past his knees with every slogging step. Liam had his go-bag with his extra ammo. His snowshoes still attached to the back with a knot of paracord.

Fresh adrenaline dumped through his system as he pumped his burning thighs, pushing himself harder and harder. He should've taken the time to put on his snowshoes. Too late now.

Two was faster than he was. No one was running in this snow. It was like a nightmare chase through thick Jell-O or deep water.

And Liam was slower than he used to be. Once upon a time, no one could outrun or outmaneuver him. The crushed disc injury he'd sustained in Afghanistan had slowed him a step. Maybe more.

No matter. What he'd lost in speed, he would make up for in persistence, stamina, and sheer determination.

Two made it to Main Street. He floundered down the center of the road, raising his knees high, nearly jumping from step to step. Snow mounds as high as his head crowded either side of the street.

Less than a hundred yards away, four dark shapes separated from beneath the gas station overhang. Four hostiles. All armed. He could make out the sharp outlines of baseball bats and rifles. Four wavering flashlight beams pierced the darkness.

Adrenaline surging, Liam lunged behind a parked vehicle and sheathed his knife. He'd clean it later. He drew his Glock.

With a round already chambered and the magazine full, he had eighteen rounds, counting the one in the chamber. Three preloaded, seventeen round magazines in an easy-to-reach pouch of his go-bag. Plus, the two confiscated pistols and whatever rounds they had left.

Noise didn't matter now. He'd already been spotted.

Two reached the others and gesticulated wildly, jabbing back toward the library, his voice an indistinct shout above the wind. More shouting.

The others turned in Liam's direction and brandished their weapons.

Five hostiles slogged fearlessly down the center of the street. They didn't separate. No one dropped back to cover the others.

They weren't trained soldiers, weren't enemy combatants or insurgents. Just punks and low-life hooligans.

That didn't mean they weren't dangerous. Or wouldn't get lucky. He'd learned that the hard way.

Liam snuck nearer in the darkness, moving from vehicle to vehicle as cover.

Soon, he was thirty yards closer, and they'd lost sight of him in the dark and snow.

"Where the hell did he go?" a burly Hispanic man shouted.

"He was right here!" another one cried, this one female. "I just saw him a second ago."

"I'll kill him!" Two said, enraged. "I'll pluck out his damn eyeballs! He killed Mason and Pete! I know it!"

"How did he get a jump on you?" said the third guy, who was so young, his voice still cracked.

"It was dark in there!" Two whined. "He murdered Mason! What was I supposed to do?"

"Pay attention!" The fourth man was short and fat, carrying a shotgun pressed against his shoulder, slowly scanning the surrounding buildings through his sights with each step. "He could be anywhere."

Liam snuck behind a Honda Accord and reached an older-model minivan. The snow drifted as high as the family stickers attached to the rear window—a stick mom, two stick kids in soccer uniforms, a little stick dog.

He was fifteen yards away now.

He crouched behind the engine block, rose onto his haunches, and braced his hands against the hood. He peered through the falling snow and sighted the head of the first hostile—the burly Hispanic, an orange beanie yanked over his ears, no hood.

Liam squeezed the trigger twice.

49

HANNAH
DAY EIGHT

Hannah huddled in the corner. Her knees were drawn up against her swollen belly, her spine pressed against the bookcase, knobby hardcovers poking her lower back through her coat.

She shivered as she listened to the sounds outside. The cold burrowed into her skin beneath her clothes, even with the bean bags pushed up on either side of her.

Several minutes passed. She didn't know how long it had been. She was afraid. She missed Ghost. She hoped he was safe, hoped Liam was okay.

A noise gradually filtered into her consciousness.

The soft thuds of boots on carpet.

She lifted her head, blinking in the darkness.

A grunt. The thud of a chair knocking over.

Had Liam returned? She opened her mouth, but no sound came out. Some primal instinct kept her quiet. She wouldn't give herself away, not until she knew for sure.

The footsteps drew closer.

Her pulse sounded loud in her ears. She held her breath, straining to hear.

Screaming and shouting in the distance. They seemed louder now, more intense, angrier.

The footsteps stopped.

Click.

Hannah stilled.

Click, click, click.

Her heart went cold as a block of ice.

Him.

He was here. In the library. With her.

50

HANNAH
DAY EIGHT

The sickly-sweet scent of clove cigarettes overwhelmed her senses.

Hannah had to move. She had to move right freaking now.

Terror glued her in place. He would find her, he would hurt her, he would do worse than he'd ever done. His worst was unimaginable; his worst was an evil she knew better than anyone.

Her deformed fingers pulsed with familiar agony, like he was breaking them all over again, pressing down harder and harder, watching her with that dangerous smile. *Snap, snap, snap.*

No! *Wake up! Hannah, get up!*

She was on her hands and knees. She didn't know how, didn't remember doing it, but she was up and moving, crawling desperately away from him, from that devastating *click, click, click.*

The lighter lid flicking open and closed and open again as he studied her, contemplated what harm he would inflict upon her next. He'd liked the sound of it. It excited him.

She crawled along the far wall, perpendicular to the stacks, toward the windows. The darkness was alive, darting and shifting and scuttling into the corners.

She didn't want to believe it, but she knew—knew it was him with every fiber of her being.

"Hannah," said the familiar mocking, sing-song voice.

Her bones vibrated beneath her skin. Her heart shuddered inside her chest.

Blackness hovered over her eyes, the dark sucking black hole of nothingness threatening to take her under, to bring her somewhere else, somewhere numb and empty.

But she always came back. She always came back, and when she did, he would still be here. Would still be coming for her.

She fought to remain present, to keep her brain clear even as terror crashed through her in great cresting waves.

She desperately wanted to curl into a ball and cover her head with her hands like a child shrouding her face with a blanket—if she couldn't see the monster, then he wasn't really here. He didn't exist. He wouldn't really tear her to pieces with his claws, his fangs.

He would.

This monster was real: not a figment of her imagination, not a nightmare, not even a memory. He was here.

She had to hide, to get away.

The books. She could count them as she moved. It was too dark to read their spines, but she knew their reassuring shape, loved the dusty familiar smell of them.

They centered her, brought her back.

One, two, three . . . Eighteen, nineteen, twenty . . . Forty-two, forty-three, forty-four . . .

The panicked fog in her mind receded just the tiniest amount. It was enough.

She crawled past one aisle, then another, the dark tunnel of each row harboring a monster about to leap out at her. *Where was he?*

"Hannah . . ."

Her head snapped up. She strained to discern the direction of his voice. Somewhere behind her and to the left. The shadows hovered and quivered all around her.

She placed each hand and knee as quickly and quietly as she could, careful not to bang the metal shelves with her boots. Her heart thudding loud as a drum, her breaths torn from her lungs in rapid shallow pants she was sure he could hear across the library.

She risked a glance behind her. Her backpack leaned against the yellow bean bag, two pairs of damp snowshoes stacked on the other side. She bit back a moan of dismay.

If he'd only suspected her presence before, as soon as he found her things, he would know for sure. He would find her. And then . . .

Her mind shied from that thought, threatened to go away.

She fought her way back. Counted the books.

Ninety-six, ninety-seven, ninety-eight . . .

She crossed the fourth aisle. The fifth.

His footsteps behind her, drawing inexorably closer.

Click, click, click.

Maybe she could swing around behind him and escape through the front entrance. Or make it to the broken windows. The wall of windows was thirty feet straight ahead.

"Are you here, Hannah?"

It sounded like he was right on top of her, like he was going to round the corner of the aisle behind her at any second. He'd see the backpack. Then he'd see her.

She had to get out of his future line of sight. She turned left at the next bookshelf and headed down the aisle.

Thick, blocky nonfiction books lined the shelves. She nearly bumped one sticking out too far in her haste. It wobbled.

She twisted around, managed to snatch it before it fell.

With trembling hands, she eased it back into place, using the palm of her left hand rather than her useless fingers.

The stacks consisted of fifteen rows of shelves, interspersed with three perpendicular walkways so patrons could move easily between the maze of shelves. She paused ten feet deep, halfway between the outside wall and the first walkway.

Slow and careful, she pushed herself from her hands and knees to her feet and crouched as low as she could so he wouldn't see her through the narrow spaces above the tops of the books. Heart thudding, she prepared to run.

Not like she could run far like this, pregnant and exhausted.

The footsteps had stopped.

When? Just now? Or a few seconds ago?

She listened hard, struggling to place him in her mind's eye. Had he reached her original hiding spot yet? Was he behind her still, or . . . ?

"Hannah, Hannah, Hannah . . . " His voice was eerily disembodied, seeming to echo off the books and shelves and carpet and brick walls, like it was coming from nowhere and everywhere at once. "You left your things behind, Hannah. You want to come and get them back?"

She closed her eyes. Bit her chapped lower lip. Tried to remember how to breathe.

He clucked his tongue. "I know where you've been, Hannah. The question is, where are you going?"

Indecision gripped her. Head for the door. Or the window.

Which one? Which was a mistake? Which one led to escape?

"You thought I wouldn't find you? You thought you were smarter than me?"

Footsteps, heading toward the bank of windows. Toward her.

No more time to think. She scurried down the aisle, still half-crouched, belly low and aching, her good hand touching the metal shelf for balance.

Click, click, click.

The sound faster, harsher. He was getting agitated. Losing patience.

She rounded the corner of the next row and jammed her back against the endcap. White plaques at eye-height listed numbers and letters too dark too read. Her frantic brain couldn't have unscrambled their meaning even if she'd tried.

"Did you think I'd let you just leave? You have something of mine. I want it back. I'll cut it out of you, and then you can watch it die while I break every bone in your miserable body."

She bit back a moan. Her legs were trembling and weak, her bowels watery with fear.

"Are you listening to me, Hannah? HANNAH!"

51

HANNAH
DAY EIGHT

Every hair on Hannah's body lifted. Chills raced up and down her spine.

He moved closer, ever closer. "You know you belong to me. You and everything you have is mine. You won't get away with what you did. Not this time. I've been incredibly patient with you, Hannah. Gracious, even. But I'm done with that. After what you did? Causing me all this trouble? I never should have let you live."

Click, click, click.

Hannah clamped her good hand over her mouth, her chest hitching, tears of panic gathering in the corners of her eyes, blurring her vision.

She pushed herself off the endcap and shuffled to the next aisle. Only three rows from the windows.

"You should already be dead, Hannah. You will be, very soon. I would have made it pleasant for you. Or at least, not nearly as unpleasant as it will be now. You won't like what's coming next. I can promise you that. But you know what's coming next, don't you?

"You know what you deserve. Why don't you come out, little mouse? Stop these useless games. It doesn't matter. It doesn't make a difference. None of this does. You are mine. That thing growing inside you is mine. You will not take it from me. Do you hear me, Hannah?"

His voice wormed inside her, writhed into her skull, her brain. She couldn't get it out. She couldn't get away.

Darkness in her head. Darkness flapping in her chest with frantic, desperate wings.

She was dying. She was breaking all over again. Shattering into a million pieces.

"You know what? I'm a generous man, Hannah. I think you know that. I think you know how kind I've been to you. Too kind. Too merciful. You come out now, you show yourself to me, and we'll start over. Maybe I can be merciful again. Maybe we can take this last week all back and pretend it never happened. What do you think about that?"

Her whole body shaking, she faced the books, blinked rapidly, tried to focus, tried to count. *One hundred and seven . . . one hundred and eight . . .*

"Hannah, Hannah, Hannah."

Her pulse racing, her breath coming in loud, ragged pants. Too loud.

"This isn't you, Hannah. You've always been so obedient. So . . . pliable. That's what I liked about you. That's what made this whole thing work. Don't you get it? You're ruining it all, Hannah. What I do now won't even be my fault. You're making me do this, little mouse. Making this happen. I know you don't want that. I know you don't.

"Come on out. I already know you're here. We both do. What's the point of prolonging the inevitable? It's cold. I'm cold. You're cold.

Let's just go home. Come on, Hannah. All this? I can make it go away."

Click, click, click.

She was afraid to move. Not sure which direction to go.

"Hannah!" His furious voice bounced off the shelves, the ceiling, the floor, muffling it, sending it in all directions. He might be across the room. Or he might be whispering in her ear, right behind her.

In the distance, a flurry of shouts and gunshots.

She flinched. Was that Liam? Liam being shot, or Liam doing the shooting? Maybe he was dying right now in the snow, bleeding out because of her.

She pushed that thought down, shoved down the despair bubbling up. Had to focus on getting out, no matter what.

She mouthed a desperate prayer. If God was out there, if He was watching, she needed help.

"Hannah! ENOUGH! Come here!" he shouted.

She almost went. Heaven help her, her treacherous body nearly obeyed instinctively. She gripped the ridge of the metal shelf to hold herself in place, clamping down so hard her nails bent.

Click, click, click.

There. He was in front of her now. In the next aisle or the one after that, between her and the windows.

How he'd gotten ahead of her, she had no idea.

A scream pushed out from deep inside her, but she clamped it down behind her teeth, mashed her lips closed, biting her tongue. Warm tangy blood leaked into her mouth.

Slowly, soundlessly, she began to edge down toward the end of the second aisle, toward the large open area with the study tables, the check-out counter, the entrance beckoning to her.

Once she reached the end of the stacks, she would run.

A sound from outside.

She hesitated, her brain struggling to place it. Was that—

A shadow separated from the other, inanimate shadows. This one deeper, darker. Alive.

She screamed. A cry of desperation, of primal terror.

It lunged at her. Something hard struck her stomach.

She doubled over, gasping for breath, sucking in oxygen that wouldn't come. A low, pulsing pain radiated from her belly, spreading to her hips, her ribs, her thighs.

The shadow struck her again, backhanding her across the face and knocking her to the floor. She gasped and clutched her stomach, wincing, eyes stinging from the pain, the fear.

The shadow transformed into the heft and substance of a man. Sinister, malevolent, no less of a monster.

He smiled. His red slash of a mouth was barely visible, but she didn't need to see it. It was seared into her memory. She'd never forget it, not for a second, not until her dying breath.

She scrambled backward on her hands and feet, scrabbling like a spider until her back hit the bookshelf and she was stuck, trapped, nowhere left to run.

She screamed again, louder this time. The sound echoing and bouncing off the ceiling, the floor, and against the walls, as if the library itself were screaming, as if the scream emanated from the books themselves.

"You think someone is coming for you, little mouse?" He loomed over her as she cowered before him. "I promise you, no one is coming. That idiot you were with? The moron you manipulated into helping you? He's taken care of. He won't be bothering us anymore."

He had killed Liam. Liam was dead. She was completely and utterly alone.

She hadn't thought her fear could intensify, could worsen. But it could.

Things could always get worse.

52

LIAM
DAY EIGHT

Liam fired.

The burly man's head whipped back in a fine red mist. He collapsed sideways.

The woman screamed.

Two whirled around, stunned, flailing for the rifle still slung across his back.

Liam aimed and fired again. A double-tap. The first round hit his target's right shoulder. The man spun. The second round slammed into the side of his head above his ear. Two crumpled to the snow.

The fat one didn't hesitate. He ran for the nearest snowed-under car across the street, stumbling and righting himself and falling again as he dove for cover.

Two more hostiles came running out of the grocery store across the street waving pistols. Another three appeared in front of the bank up the street and headed his way.

The windshield above his head exploded, followed by the sharp report of a rifle. Gummy glass fell into his hair. A barrage of rounds shredded the air, slamming into the buildings on either side of him.

There were too many of them. Eight or nine now, taking cover behind cars and buildings, all aiming their firepower in his direction.

Liam felt every second passing like a bomb ticking inside his head. They had too much time. Time for the hostiles to consolidate their forces, for a few of them to circle around and flank him.

He was just one man. No one had his six.

And there was still Hannah.

Muzzle flashes in the darkness. Bullets whined and thunked into the stone façade of the building behind him. He risked a glance back.

It was a bakery named The Mix-Up. The blaze-orange awning sagged beneath the onslaught of snow. Shards of glass glittered across the sidewalk. Every window and the front door were shattered, the place ransacked.

He raised himself and laid down cover fire, squeezing off five rapid-fire shots. In the brief reprieve as the hostiles scrambled for cover, Liam backed across the sidewalk and ducked into the darkness of The Mix-Up Bakery.

The interior was long and narrow, a glass display counter to the left, a half-dozen yellow booths to the right. Directly ahead stretched a hallway to the bathrooms, staff room, and exit.

A week after the grid went down, the place was still infused with the sweet and yeasty scents of cinnamon rolls and freshly baked bread.

He headed for the exit, his boots squeaking on the tile. As he hurried down the dark hallway, he reached behind him and retrieved the first extra magazine from a side pouch of his go-bag.

He did a tactical reload, quickly switching out the pistol's magazine for the fresh one and stuffing the used mag in his pocket.

He thought of Hannah. Thought of how he'd failed everyone in his life. His twin brother, Lincoln. Jessa. The baby.

The terrible images flashed through his head—the wreckage, the dead bodies, blood everywhere. Lincoln on the ground, staring dully. Jessa's desperate, fierce eyes locked onto his.

Liam was a warrior. A protector. He'd dedicated his entire life to war, to battle, to defending the defenseless. But when it counted most, he hadn't been able to save them.

He was weary and battle-broken. He'd lost everything he cared about. And yet.

He was still here. Still fighting. He wasn't even sure why. It just wasn't in him to give up or turn his back. He thought he could run away from himself, but he couldn't.

Liam refused to fail anyone else.

He would kill every man here with his bare hands before he did that.

Sounds from outside the bakery. Crunching boots. A hissed curse. They were coming after him.

Anger seared through him: anger at the world. At himself. Disgust and self-loathing fueled him, drove him. His muscles tensed, adrenaline icing his veins.

Let them come.

53

HANNAH
DAY EIGHT

Hannah let out a low moan of despair. She tried to shield her face with her arms, but he batted them away with the toe of his boot.

"Oh no," he said almost gleefully. "You get to see this. All of this. Every excruciating, exquisite second. I owe it to you, don't you think?"

"Please," she mumbled. "Please . . ."

"I gave you a chance. Didn't I? You didn't listen. You chose to disobey me. You've left me with no choice. I wish I could say it pains me to do this, Hannah, but the truth is, I've been relishing this moment for a long time."

He squatted on his heels. Though it was dark, she could still make out the maniacal gleam in his eyes, the cruelty and anticipation twisting his features.

He reached out and tucked a stray strand of hair behind her ear. "I feel I can tell you this. Only you and I understand this, don't we? Only you've been here this whole time. Only you."

She shuddered, her skin crawling.

Memories lanced through her, sharp and painful. Memories she'd repressed for years, buried somewhere so deep she'd forgotten they were even there.

That night on the road. The high beams in her rearview mirror. The sheer relief when she'd caught sight of him striding toward her, his breath steaming in crystalized white clouds.

The nametag she'd glimpsed sewn on the pocket of his uniform as he leaned into the driver's side window and shone his flashlight into her eyes.

His tall, sturdy form. His pleasant, unassuming face. A face she'd recognized.

"I know you," she whispered groggily.

He reeled back, like she'd surprised him. "What the hell did you say?"

"I remember," she said. "Your name . . . Pike."

His expression contorted. He seized her chin and yanked it up, forcing her to meet his furious gaze. "You little whore! That's all you are. All you've ever been. How could I have ever thought you were anything special? My mistake. And I'll correct that mistake tonight. You're pathetic. Pitiful. A waste of my time, just like that old blubbering hag. You should have heard her scream, Hannah. I wish you'd heard it."

Hannah stiffened. "No!"

"I visited her. The one you stayed with. What was her name? Oh, yes. CiCi."

Even in her stricken state, the horror of his words sank like claws into her brain. "You didn't—hurt her."

Pike's smile widened. "I did. I had to. I couldn't leave her thinking she'd done a good deed by aiding and abetting you. That's not how the world works. It's not how I work. And *I* decide, Hannah. Not you. NOT YOU."

A terrible buzzing sounded in her head. Her vision narrowing as dizziness lurched through her. Not CiCi. *Please, no.* Grief—and guilt —slammed into her.

The woman had done nothing but help. She'd shown kindness and mercy, and CiCi was dead now because of it. Because of Hannah.

She didn't want to see the images flashing behind her eyes, didn't want to imagine it, but she did. Every horrible thing Pike must have done to her.

She remembered CiCi's sharp gaze probing her own. *There are two kinds of fear . . .*

CiCi's gun. The Ruger .45. It was still in her pocket.

She fumbled for the pistol. Her stiff fingers closed over the grip. She struggled to pull it out. Something snagged on the seam of the pocket. She yanked it free and thrust the gun at him.

He looked like a normal person. Nothing special or different about him at all, nothing to betray what he really was.

Except for his eyes. Dark and liquid. Unblinking. Nothing behind them—nothing at all. He grinned at her. "Just what are you going to do with that?"

The muzzle trembled, wavered. She couldn't seem to keep it still. The pistol that had felt so feather-light before was suddenly heavy in her hand. The heaviest thing she'd ever held.

Pike laughed, cruel and malicious and ugly, like nails on a chalkboard.

She held it out, pointing shakily, her finger frozen on the trigger.

"Like you know how to use that. I've already broken you, or have you forgotten?"

The memories flooded in, freezing her blood in her veins, paralyzing her. The endless agony. The fear. The awful *crack* of her own bones splintering beneath her skin.

Pull the trigger. Her brain screamed at her body to obey. Nothing happened. The weapon remained inert. A lump of metal. Useless.

Pike lunged at her. He seized the gun and ripped it from her hand. He tossed it across the room. It skittered across the carpet, smacked the base of a bookshelf, and landed several yards away.

He spun and kicked her in the ribs. Sharp pain flared through her torso.

Instinctively, she curled into herself, arms crossed protectively over her belly, knees drawn up, chin lowered and tucked against her chest.

She was utterly worthless. Just a victim. Nothing more.

What had she thought? That she could do this? That she could defend herself against a psycho, against a madman? Against someone so much bigger and stronger and more lethal than she was or ever could be.

He kicked her again. "Look at me, you little—!"

Shouts and screams from outside. More gunshots.

She heard everything as if filtered from far away, from deep underwater.

Cold tears tracked down her cheeks, blurring her vision. Another world lay out there. A world she'd never see again because she was never leaving this building.

Pike drew a wicked-looking tactical knife. "It's your turn, Hannah," he said, eager anticipation mingled with the contempt in his voice. "Your turn."

54

LIAM
DAY EIGHT

Liam hesitated before the heavy steel exit door. Instead of shoving open the door and fleeing, he checked to make sure it was locked. It was.

He would end this threat. Then he would get Hannah.

He moved through the opened doorway directly to his left. Dim light flared through the window on the far wall. The strong chemical scents of industrial cleaners and bleach stung his nostrils.

It was a ten by ten supply room filled with shelves of spray bottles and white gallon jugs, boxes of hairnets and plastic gloves. A mop and large yellow bucket stood in one corner.

He shrugged off his go-bag and leaned it against the back shelf next to the mop bucket. He removed his coat and draped it over the bag.

It was freezing, but he needed a full range of movement. Exertion would warm him up soon enough.

If he went back to the library, they would pursue him, lead the danger straight back to Hannah. She would be safe so long as he kept them occupied.

As long as he ended the threat here and now.

The long dark hallway created the perfect choke point. He had a full magazine, plus two spares and the confiscated pistols bulging in his left coat pocket. A 1911 and a Smith & Wesson M&P 2.0, both fully loaded.

He did a quick system check on the Glock, took up a position against the wall on the opposite side of the door, and gripped his weapon low and ready.

Liam waited. Blood rushed in his ears, tension thrumming through him. He hated killing. He found no pleasure in it. The deaths would haunt him later, weighing his conscience. Just like all the others.

He hadn't asked for this fight, but he would win it. He would end it.

The shuffling noises drew nearer. The hostiles creeping quietly, hesitantly, not speaking. Liam strained his ears for every sound. Four sets of boots. Maybe five.

He diagrammed the bakery in his head, saw the dark shapes of the hostiles as they advanced in his mind's eye. They were confined to single file in the hall like cows in a slaughterhouse chute.

Come on, come on.

"He went out the back," someone whispered.

"Then go get him," a deeper voice retorted.

The voices were close. In the hall, headed toward him.

His pulse jumped. He crouched, readied himself.

A muzzle appeared. The first hostile emerged in front of the supply closet doorway, inching forward, weapon held straight out in front of him, his focus on the rear door.

Liam swung out and fired a double-tap into the hostile's chest.

The thunderous boom in the confined quarters exploded in his eardrums.

The man jittered and fell. His pistol clattered to the tile floor.

The man behind the first hostile had no time to react. Liam put two rounds into his head before he could scream or even blink. A spray of blood and he was down. Three hostiles left.

Liam stepped over the two dead bodies and aimed at his next target.

The third attacker had the presence of mind to duck. Liam's fifth shot slammed into the drywall above the fourth attacker's head. He missed.

Hostile four, crouched at the end of the hall, fired three rounds in rapid succession. Two pinged into the metal exit door behind Liam. One whined past his right ear and smashed into drywall, spraying him with dust.

Liam's ears rang from the concussive blasts. Sound went distant and tinny.

His next two shots didn't miss.

Number Four sagged, his legs buckling as he clutched at the puncture wounds in his chest, a streak of red painting the wall behind him.

Before Liam could lower his weapon and re-aim, the third thug charged him. Thick neck, brawny arms. A heavy brawler used to winning bar fights.

He barreled into Liam's gut headfirst and sent him sprawling backward. Pain erupted from his stomach, stole his breath.

Liam attempted to roll with the attack to absorb the impact. He fell over the body behind him, arm flailing. His gun hand struck the door frame, and the Glock was knocked from his grasp.

Gasping, his spine wrenching painfully, he managed to twist

away from the attack as he fell through the doorway of the supply room.

Liam hit the tile hard, his shoulder banging into the mop bucket, white pain like an electrical shock shooting up his spine. His lower back spasmed. Agony flared through his whole body.

He clambered to his feet, but not fast enough.

The brawler slammed into him again, slashing hard with a knife. Liam managed to spin away even as he crashed against the shelves, sponges, and paper towel rolls raining down on his head.

The wicked blade carved the air again. Liam turned into the knife attack, and using his left arm, he struck the knife-wielding hand with the edge of his palm to deflect the strike.

But Brawler came down on top of him, pummeling Liam's head and shoulders with his left fist, swinging with that deadly knife again with his right.

It was too dark. Hard to see the flash of the blade.

Liam slammed his head backward, smashing Brawler's face and crushing his nose. Blood sprayed everywhere. Brawler let out a pained grunt, lost his grip, and staggered back.

Liam climbed to his feet, slower this time, knocking into the mop bucket with his feet.

A scream. Muted, distant, and tinny. So low and soft he might have imagined it. But Liam knew it. Felt it like a punch to the gut.

Hannah.

Cold dark dread unfurled in his chest.

Urgency crackled through him. Hot anger underscored with panic.

Liam exploded into action. Seizing the mop, he whipped around and flipped it so the mop head faced him, wielding the handle like a martial artist's staff.

He lunged forward and drove the rounded end of the handle into

Brawler's Adam's apple. Brawler made a wet rasping sound, his eyes wide with shock. He dropped the knife and staggered back against the shelf.

The metal shelving rattled. Spray bottles of 409 and window cleaner thudded to the floor.

Grunting from the effort, from the pain, Liam rammed the handle into his throat a second time and kicked the man off his feet.

Brawler's skull bounced dully off the floor, and he went still, his jaw slack. Dead from a crushed windpipe.

Chest heaving, Liam strained to hear over the tinny ringing in his ears. His spine protested with sharp stabs of pain. The adrenaline dump left him shaky and lightheaded.

None of that mattered. Only one thought drove him. One purpose. He had to reach Hannah before it was too late.

Wincing but moving quickly, he returned to the supply room, stepping over bodies and sticky, pooling blood. So much blood. So much senseless death.

Liam shrugged into his coat and go-bag and retrieved his Glock, which had slid beneath one of the shelves. He unlocked the bakery's exit door and raced for the library.

55

HANNAH

DAY EIGHT

Hannah felt herself fading, her mind taking her far away. It was a relief. A gift. She'd disappear. Simply cease to exist. No more pain. No more cold. No more fear.

Milo, she thought dimly. *Milo.*

A fragment of a memory drifted into her disintegrating mind: her and Milo snuggled together in his bed, Milo's eyes growing sleepy, her fingers in his soft hair as she sang his favorite lullaby. *Blackbird, fly . . . You were only waiting for this moment to be free . . . to arise . . .*

She didn't want to die. She needed to fight, to fight with everything in her, to the bitter end. Until her broken body gave out on her, she would keep trying. She had to.

She kicked weakly, blindly, her boot connecting with Pike's shin. He growled in pain.

She rolled onto her side, her belly heavy and cumbersome, struggling to get to her hands and knees, to crawl away. She reached the first bookshelf, scrabbling, frantic, chest heaving.

Pain exploded across the back of her head. Stars spun across her darkening vision. Her stomach lurched with nausea as she collapsed.

Pike seized her hair. Roots tore from her scalp. He jerked her roughly onto her back. Confusion and desperation swamped her. The pain was blinding.

He knelt on top of her, an immense pressure on her chest, her belly. He leaned in close. His breath hot on her face. The sickening sweetness of clove strangling her throat.

She struck at him, flailing weakly, her battering fists nothing more than an irritation to him.

His knife flashed in the darkness. He would kill her now. He would cut—

A savage bark exploded through the library.

A blur of white bolted through one of the broken windows and streaked through the darkness. Hannah's heart stopped. *Ghost.*

Ghost was a flurry of fur, claws, and teeth. The huge Great Pyrenees barreled across the library and sprang at Pike, aiming straight for her attacker's throat.

Pike managed to half-turn, to get his arm up in defense.

Ghost didn't hesitate. He seized his left forearm in his jaws and shook fiercely.

Pike howled in agony. The knife clattered to the carpet.

Still gripping Pike's arm, Ghost dragged him backward and knocked him off Hannah.

The weight released from her chest. She could breathe again.

"Get off!" Pike shouted. He beat at the dog's head with his fist, smashing his snout and digging at his eyes until he released Pike's arm.

Ghost circled Pike, growling fiercely. A huge muscled beast, glowing white in the darkness like some phantom creature from the underworld.

Pike backed up with a curse and knocked into one of the study tables. A chair tangled Pike's legs and he nearly tripped. He seized the chair and hurled it at the dog.

Ghost darted easily aside. The chair struck a bookshelf, several books wobbling. He snarled, teeth bared, saliva glistening. Like a rabid wolf.

Ghost growled and snarled with a ferocity Hannah had never seen. Gone was the regal, serene animal who'd pressed against her to offer comfort and strength, who'd slept beside her, who'd gobbled beef jerky from her hand, gentle enough even in his hunger not to nip her fingers.

This Ghost was pure white devil. One hundred and forty pounds of brutal strength and teeth and fury. And every ounce of it aimed at his former owner.

"Down! Back!" Pike staggered to his feet, his wounded arm clutched to his chest. With his right hand, he fumbled for something at his side. "Obey, you stupid dog!"

Ghost didn't obey. He remembered, just like Hannah remembered.

With a flurry of fur and teeth, the Great Pyrenees charged.

Pike lurched backward and crashed into the bookshelf behind him. Books toppled and cascaded to the carpet.

Dog and man went down together.

Ghost leaped on top of Pike and pushed him flat on his back against the carpet. He lunged for the man's throat. His teeth gleamed white and razor-sharp, his lips peeled back.

Pike flung up his left arm to defend his neck. He held something in his hand. Something small and dark and metallic. Hannah's heart stopped beating. A gun.

They were a blur in the darkness. A white and dark shape battling to the death. Ghost growling and biting and Pike punching him in the head, the torso, the snout, beating at him with the gun and trying to aim it at the dog, to get off a shot.

Panic clutched at her, pulling her under, but she fought it, fought to remain present. Desperation congealed in her belly. She searched frantically for some way to help, to stop Pike.

She seized a heavy book from the floor and hurled it at their grappling bodies. It thudded into Pike's side but did nothing. She threw another one. It struck Pike's arm and threw off his aim.

A gunshot cracked the air.

She cringed, her ears ringing. Ghost snarled in outrage.

Before she could find another book to throw, a second gunshot fired. This one didn't miss.

Ghost faltered. He whimpered and dropped on top of Pike's chest. His massive body went limp.

Pike pushed the dog off himself and staggered to his feet. He turned back toward the dog. His left arm held tight to his chest, limp and useless. The pistol in his right hand.

The gun rising, aiming for Ghost. To finish him off. And then her.

Terror and helplessness jolted through her. "No!" she screamed.

"Hannah!" A shout. From somewhere outside, near the front entrance. It was Liam. He was coming for her.

Footsteps running toward them. But not fast enough. Not enough.

"Liam!" she cried, frantic. "In here!"

With a furious curse, Pike backed away, clutching at his wounded arm. His features contorted in an expression she'd never seen on his face—fear.

He spun and fled, weaving between the bookshelves as he sprinted for the wall of windows. He lunged onto the waist-high bookshelf and launched himself through the window and out into the night.

Hannah's only thought was for Ghost. She scrambled across the carpet, head spinning dizzily but she ignored it, collapsing to her knees at his side with a gut-wrenching sob.

The dog lay limp and unmoving on his side, long legs splayed, head tilted back. A line of black blood dribbled through his white fur from above his right eye, drenching his floppy ear and staining his snout.

More blood pooled along the top of his head. The bullet had skimmed his skull. Bloody glass shards glinted on his coat from his leap through the jagged window frame.

Horror and dread twisted her insides. She pressed her hands into his fur, feeling desperately for a sign of life.

His chest rose and fell beneath her fingers. A faint whimper escaped his jaws.

He was alive. She could have wept with joy.

Liam crashed through the entrance doors and sprinted to the stacks. He gripped a pistol in both hands, high and ready to shoot.

Even in the darkness, she could see the black smudges marring his face—blood. He looked like some vicious warlord or Viking fresh from battle. A killer.

Relief warred with her fear. She saw the man under the blood— the warrior who'd protected her. Relief won. "You—you're not dead."

"Where is he?" Liam cried.

She pointed at the windows. "That way. He ran out there."

"Stay here," Liam said. "I'm finishing this."

Before she could say anything, he was gone. A shadow among shadows as he plunged out the broken window after Pike.

56

LIAM
DAY EIGHT

Liam slogged through the darkness, searching for the sadistic psycho. The wind made his eyes water and his nose run. He'd taken the time to buckle on his snowshoes. It made him faster, even with the white-hot pain flaring through his lower back.

Drops of blood were splattered beside the deep prints from where the psycho had staggered through the snow. He was wounded. That made him easier to follow.

Righteous anger burned through his veins. An inexhaustible fury. He would kill the man without remorse, without mercy.

The scene in the library was seared into his mind: Hannah crouched desperately over the dog's body, fear and dread contorting her features, her drawn face a pale moon in the dark.

He'd almost lost her. He hoped Ghost was okay, but it was Hannah he'd sworn to keep alive. He'd promised himself and Jessa that he would save this woman.

And he meant to do it. Had to do it.

He dug his hand into his coat pocket and felt the scrap of gray and green knitting like a smoldering coal. The tiny knit hat.

Remorse and regret strangled him. He was a fool. Always had been.

It would make up for nothing. It would change nothing. The past was still the past.

He knew that. And yet.

He couldn't leave Hannah and the child in her belly.

Couldn't abandon them to this monster who stalked their every move, who seemed to know where they were headed even before they did, like some supernatural demon of myth and nightmare.

Liam didn't fear him. Anyone who preyed on women was a coward. Human garbage. That's why he'd fled. He was nothing more than a gutless cur who couldn't fight a man face-to-face but crouched and skulked in the shadows, preying on the weak and defenseless.

Liam's only thought was to kill the scumbag, to be done with this once and for all.

The soldier in him took over. He pushed out the pain and narrowed his complete focus to the task at hand. He scanned the road and buildings ahead of him and to either side, alert to any threat.

He edged around the Dollar General, pulse thudding in his ears, thighs burning from the exertion. Even in snowshoes, it was exhausting. The throbbing in his spine slowed him down even more. But he didn't stop. He would never stop.

Shouts and yells echoed from further down the street. He swerved behind a dentist's office, pressed his back against the wall, and peeked around the corner.

A group of about seven men and women were working their way up the street toward him, toward the library, their flashlight beams and loud voices betraying their presence. A quarter of a mile away at most.

They'd regrouped after Liam's attack. Their numbers had thinned significantly. They were slow, probably limping from injuries, but they were still coming.

Their shouting was angrier now, furious. It was personal. They wanted him dead for the half-dozen men he'd killed.

Hannah was a sitting duck. They'd find her and kill her just for being with him.

Dread slicked his insides. Fear sprouted deep in his gut and took hold. Not for himself. Never for himself.

For her, and the innocent baby she carried.

He let out a low curse. He had to go back.

He glanced behind him at the bloody trail and the prints leading between the bank and the dentist's office, headed northwest.

He could end this now. It would take time, precious time he didn't have.

Damn it! He hated leaving a threat out there, loathed it with every fiber of his soldier's being. But he refused to leave Hannah exposed again.

His chest tight with worry, Liam spun and hurried back toward the library. His spine throbbed. His heart hammered in his chest, his ears. He continually scanned his surroundings, searching for any movement among the shadows crouching between the buildings.

He circled around the library parking lot and reached the broken window. He slipped off his snowshoes and attached them to his pack with the paracord.

Using the brick ledge, he boosted himself over, careful of the jagged glass jutting from the frame. The electric shot of pain was punishing.

"Hannah!" he whispered.

She was crouched beside the dog in the center of the library, her face bone-white. She held a pistol in one trembling hand. She aimed it at him.

"Hannah, it's me."

She recognized him and lowered the weapon. Books were scattered across the carpet all around them, and several chairs from the nearest study table were knocked over.

Apprehensively, he lowered his gaze to the dog.

Ghost was bloody and lying on his side. With a pained whine, he lifted his head, blood drenching his muzzle, his ear, and the top of his skull.

He was hurt, but at least he was conscious.

Liam's heart nearly burst with relief. "We've got to go."

She didn't argue with him. She slipped the pistol into her coat pocket and stood shakily, her damaged hand pressed to her ribs. She winced.

His anxiety rising, he took in the state of her. "Are you hurt?"

"I'm fine."

She wasn't. Blood trickled from her hairline. Her long hair was a tangled mess. A purplish bruise was already forming around her left eye socket.

The psycho had hurt her, but she was on her feet. She was tougher than he'd realized. A survivor.

Still, she wouldn't last long. He could see that right off. Not as she was, bruised, and in pain and traumatized. Not with her pregnancy.

"Ghost saved me," she said.

He cursed himself again for taking so long with the thugs. If Ghost hadn't arrived in time . . .

He could kill a hundred enemies with ease with no fear for himself. His fear was for them. Fear that he couldn't protect them. That he would somehow fail again.

There was no time to think about the what-ifs and should-haves. That would come later. The guilt. The recrimination.

"We're getting out of here," he said.

"How?"

He recalled the two men standing guard beside the trucks, snow-mobiles, and ATVs. "The snowmobiles."

They needed to reach the vehicles before the mob. Every minute they remained here upped the threat tenfold.

57

LIAM
DAY EIGHT

"Let's go," Liam said.

"What about Ghost?" Hannah asked.

The dog clambered to his feet with a distressed whine. He swayed uncertainly.

Liam's heart contracted. Hopefully, the dog had it in him to make it, because Liam couldn't carry him and help Hannah. He liked dogs —liked this one a lot.

He'd do his best to save them both, but Hannah was his first priority. She had to be.

He felt guilty even saying the words. "He has to keep up. No other choice."

"He will," Hannah said. "My pack. The snowshoes—"

His brain cycled through the options at lightning speed. He still had his go-bag with his snowshoes attached. Hannah's bag was mostly food, her water, the tarp and sleeping bag. Important, but not essential.

She couldn't handle the extra weight. And he couldn't carry two packs, help her, and protect them.

But she needed her snowshoes to traverse the deep snow. They would be faster than their pursuers.

He left her and the dog and ran back through the stacks, grabbed the snowshoes, and raced back. He handed her the snowshoes. She clutched them to her chest.

Hannah took a step and stumbled. Liam snaked his free arm around her waist, his right still holding his Glock. It hurt him to hold her up, but he ignored it, pushed the pain down deep. "We have to go."

Together, they hobbled toward the entrance. Hannah flinched but didn't cry out or make a sound. The dog followed, slow and halting, his head down, an almost human look of hurt and confusion on his face.

Liam would administer first aid to them both once they'd reached safety. First, they had to get the hell out of here.

Distant shouts and yells carried on the wind. Another gunshot went off. Closer now. Much too close.

They skirted the study tables, the check-out counter, and the children's area. He pushed through the entrance doors, and they were out in the frigid night again, the wind stinging their faces.

They had a couple of minutes if they stayed out of sight of the mob. They took a few precious seconds to buckle into their snowshoes—Liam helping Hannah into hers.

Moving faster now, they circled behind the next building—a Rite-Aid with its windows busted in, trash and pill bottles scattered across the trampled parking lot. They passed two more offices and a restaurant.

Headlights glared just past the next building. Liam leaned

Hannah against the brick façade. She bent forward, rested her hands on her thighs, and breathed hard, exhaling white crystalized clouds.

He could see the whites of her eyes in the dim shadows. Her fear. But she was present, she was fighting her terror.

He saw her clearly in that instant—meek and damaged but also tough. She endured. It was who she was. He saw it shining bright and determined in her eyes.

She was like him. A survivor.

A fierce protectiveness flared in his chest. "Wait here," he said, his voice rough.

She nodded.

He inched forward and peeked around the corner, Glock up and ready. The wind kicked up white gusts, but the heavy snowfall had lightened considerably, increasing visibility.

Twenty yards away, he could just make out four old-model two-seater snowmobiles and five winterized ATVs parked in the middle of the street at the end of town.

The trucks were gone. The thugs must've packed their supplies already and sent the loaded vehicles back to wherever they came from.

The only reason they were still in town was to hunt Liam down.

One of the snowmobiles was already running, its engine chugging loud and ragged, headlights glaring. Glittering ice crystals swirled through the ghostly lights.

A waste of gas just for light, but it worked in their favor.

Two men stood guard. One leaned against the rear of a black and yellow Ski-Doo painted like a hornet, his rifle crooked in his arms while he shivered and blew into his gloved hands.

The second guard had laid his rifle crosswise across the front seat of a red and white Yamaha while he slumped sidesaddle, smoking a cigarette, cupping both hands to his face to shield it from the wind.

Neither of them acted alert or aware of their surroundings. They'd been waiting for hours and were freezing, miserable, and just trying to pass the time.

His nerves stretched taut. Steadying himself, Liam shut out everything else—the dog's heavy panting, the whistling wind, the sounds of the mob growing closer. His exhaustion, the pain pulsing through his spine.

He locked his elbow, brought his left hand up to brace his shot, and focused through the sights. He slowed his breathing, his heart rate, narrowed his focus to the target. Adjusted for the wind. Squinted against the swirling snow.

The man with the camouflaged hunting cap leaning against the yellow snowmobile had the weapon nearest at hand. Liam aimed at him, sighting center mass.

He curled his gloved finger around the trigger. His steady breathing crystalized in clouds around his face. Snow collected on his eyelashes, crystallized in his nostrils. Time stretched.

He squeezed the trigger twice.

Crack. Crack.

The man juddered and fell.

He'd hit his target. He needed to get the second one before he could reach for his rifle. The next target was already moving, reacting to the gunshots, but not fast enough.

Liam shifted slightly, aimed for the man's chest, and fired a double-tap.

Within two seconds, both targets were down.

He felt no guilt, no remorse. Not then, not in the heat of battle. He'd seen combat in warzones all over the world. He knew his enemy. The ones who stood between himself and his objective—to get Hannah to safety.

It was kill or die. And so he killed with skill and precision and efficiency. And he would continue killing for as long as he needed to do so, for as long as Hannah needed protecting.

Liam turned back for her. "Just a little further."

She stared at the dead bodies in the snow, gaping.

Behind them, the clamor of the mob grew louder. Ghost whipped toward the oncoming threat, half-whimpering, half-snarling.

Liam seized Hannah's arm. "Go!"

They ran for the snowmobiles.

58

HANNAH
DAY EIGHT

"Get on!" Liam ordered when they reached the nearest snowmobile—the hornet-colored Ski-Doo. The key was in the ignition, the engine rumbling, exhaust belching. Ready to go.

Hannah hesitated. The wind whipped her hair into her face. She couldn't feel her ears.

Fear clawed at her. Her brain screamed at her to escape, to run. But the dog had just saved her life. She wouldn't abandon him for anything.

She pointed back at the dog, who straggled several yards behind them. "I'm not leaving Ghost."

She expected Liam to argue with her, to throw her on the seat and drag her off against her will. He didn't. He went for the red Yamaha, reached for the key fob still in the ignition slot, and started the engine.

The Yamaha featured a large fiberglass trailer with slatted sides meant for pulling heavy loads. It was empty.

"Get the dog on the trailer," he said gruffly. "And for Pete's sake, stay down!"

Liam drew his tactical knife, and with a few efficient movements, he cut the starter power cords on the three other machines. The Yellow Ski-Doo died.

Behind them, someone shouted an alarm.

Snow erupted fifteen yards to the west. A rifle report followed right after. Another crack ruptured the air. And then another.

Hannah spun around and peered into the snowy darkness, her ears ringing. She could barely see their attackers but for the wavering flashlight beams, the muzzle flashes in the dark.

They couldn't see in the dark and falling snow either. Their shots were wild, but their next volley might not miss. The *rat-a-tat* of rifle fire exploded like a string of firecrackers.

Liam took up a defensive position behind the yellow Ski-Doo, steadied his arms across the seat, and returned fire. *Boom. Boom. Boom.*

Screams filtered their way. He'd hit one of them. Maybe more than one, judging by the shrieks and shouts of agony and outrage.

The thugs scrambled for cover. They threw themselves behind the bank and the Dollar General on either side of main street, both buildings a few hundred yards away.

"Now, Hannah!" Liam shouted.

She crouched as low as she could and shuffled to the rear of the red snowmobile. Her fingers were so stiff, it took her three tries to open the sled gate. She gestured to Ghost. "Inside, now! It's for your own good."

Ghost staggered, barely upright. He halted several feet away. He lowered his bloodied head and whined uneasily.

He loathed the idea of returning to anything resembling a cage, even one about to save his life. She didn't blame him.

"Hannah!" Liam cried.

More gunshots shattered the crisp air. Several rounds smashed into the looted grocery store across the street.

She stumbled through the snow and seized Ghost's scruff with her good hand. "You have to do this! Do it for me." She pulled him gently but insistently toward the trailer. "Trust me."

Ghost whined again but didn't balk. He allowed her to lead him onto the sled. If he'd refused to go, she couldn't have made him. The dog weighed more than she did, even pregnant.

She shut the clasp on the trailer with trembling, half-numb fingers. He'd be freezing in the wind and snow, but it was the best they could do. She slipped off her snowshoes and tossed them in the trailer beside him.

"Done!" she shouted to Liam.

Liam already had his snowshoes off. He pocketed his pistol, leaned down, and seized a rifle from one of the fallen men. He fired several more rounds of covering fire to give them a moment of breathing room. The rifle cracked again and again.

He helped her onto the front seat and squeezed in behind her, his chest against her back, his legs straddling hers. She yanked on the helmet while Liam pulled on another one sitting on the seat, not bothering to brush off the snow or buckle the strap.

Slinging the rifle over his shoulder, he reached around her for the handlebar grips.

"Hold on!" he shouted into her ear.

Liam throttled the engine. They burst forward in a cloud of blue smoke, spitting snow, and careened into a tight U-turn. The old machine was rough and loud—but still fast.

More rifle cracks. Rounds sprayed the snow a dozen yards to their right. Hannah's heart leapt into her throat.

Liam slewed sharply left. The Yamaha's backend fishtailed

precariously, sending up a wide arc of snow spray. She was thrown sideways against Liam's arm, nearly losing her seat. She had a difficult time holding on with only one good hand.

She dared a glance in the rearview mirror to check on Ghost. He was still there. She couldn't make out much more than a flurry of white fur.

Liam corrected the skid and they straightened out, bounded at high speed over unbroken fields of snow, bouncing and slamming, each jolt sending shudders through her body.

They headed south out of town, whizzing by trees, barns and fences, a few hunched buildings set back from the road.

Three of the ATVs were in pursuit, but they weren't close—their headlights distant stars in the Yamaha's mirrors.

She didn't hear any more gunshots, but that didn't mean there weren't any. The roar of the engine drowned out all other sounds.

As they fled into the night, Hannah kept her feet flat on the running boards, leaned into the turns, and held on for dear life.

59

PIKE
DAY EIGHT

Pike banged his shoulder against the unlocked rear door of Dot's Diner and stumbled inside. The door swung shut behind him. He blinked in the complete blackness and paused.

Fury boiled through his veins. He wanted nothing more than to murder the soldier boy who'd dared to come after him. He'd rip the man's phalanges from the bloody stumps of his fingers. Painstakingly slowly. One by one, until the soldier begged for his own death.

Pike was out his KA-BAR tactical knife and his Sig. He'd lost them both in the library to the mutinous white beast and the cowering mouse, Hannah Sheridan.

He had planned it perfectly. The ploy to distract Soldier Boy so Pike could sneak in and finish his prey. Only that damn dog had appeared out of nowhere, had the gall to attack *him*! He owned that disgusting mutt—had purchased him for a steep price too.

All Pike had to show for it was his throbbing left forearm. He felt with his right hand along the wall and fumbled deeper into the building. He rounded a corner and felt open space around him.

He pulled the flashlight from his pocket, flicked it on, and scanned the floor, keeping the beam low. He was in some kind of office or administrative room.

The only window opened to the restaurant's kitchen, dishwashing area, and wait station. He didn't have to worry about the flashlight betraying his location.

He sank into an office chair behind a cheap IKEA desk, propped up the flashlight, and examined himself. Several rips marred the sleeve of his coat. Blood stained the fabric and dribbled down his arm.

He pulled off his gloves with his teeth and eased out of his coat. Wincing, he rolled up his bloodied shirtsleeves. He gritted his teeth at the sight of the wound.

Teeth marks punctured his skin, deep enough to lacerate the muscle in a few places. It looked worse than it was. He was lucky the force of the dog's jaws hadn't shattered his forearm.

He'd managed to shoot the rabid animal before it could do serious damage. Without his thick coat and layers of clothing as protection, the dog would've torn his throat out in a matter of seconds.

Pike hoped he'd killed it.

Pain throbbed through his left arm from his wrist to his shoulder. He needed a damn cigarette.

With his uninjured hand, he withdrew the pack, fumbled with the Zippo one-handed, and finally managed to light up. He drew the smoke deep into his chilled lungs. Clove filled his nostrils, eased the tension thrumming through him.

He blew a cloud toward the ceiling. There was no fan, no vent, and the smoke hung in the air.

This was just a minor setback. He'd be back in the game by morning.

Hannah Sheridan was going home. Well, then. So was he.

Outrage coursed through him. At her. At all the people in Fall

Creek he loathed and bitterly resented. His mother. His brother. And especially Noah Sheridan.

He'd get his revenge on all of them. Wring every ounce of it out of her broken and shattered body.

He didn't know why he hadn't killed her years ago. Before and after that night, he'd been careful, never choosing prey that would be missed.

He chose druggies and whores and homeless street rats that no one cared about. And he rarely hunted too close to home.

But when he'd parked behind her Camry on that deserted road that Christmas Eve, he'd felt a thrill like he'd never felt before. He knew who she was before he'd even gotten out of his truck.

Noah Sheridan's wife. The cute little thing with those vivid green eyes, the pretty outsider with the fabulous voice that should've been showcased in Nashville or Hollywood but was instead going nowhere fast, trapped in a small town with a piss-poor husband and a whiny brat.

There was something about stealing something right out from under someone's nose. Something about working and eating and laughing with people who had no idea who you were, what you'd done.

It was intoxicating.

Somehow it had made living in that crappy town with all those insufferable people—including his own family—bearable.

They all knew Hannah Sheridan. They all believed she was dead and gone.

He reserved a special hatred for Noah Sheridan. Watching the man squirm under the microscope—suspect *numero uno* in the case for months—had been a particularly memorable and extraordinary pleasure.

Every time he laid eyes on the man or his brat of a son, a little thrill went through him. He would wave and call Noah over, engage in small talk with that hateful smile plastered to his face, all the while his hand in his pocket, holding the phone with the live video feed of Noah's wife.

But that part would end now. It would end when he cut his own flesh and blood out of her, and then finish her himself, the way he wanted. Not quickly or easily.

He had not lost control of this yet. He could still find her before she reached Fall Creek.

60

PIKE
DAY EIGHT

Pike smoked the cigarette down to the filter and tossed it on the floor. The ember flared and died. He didn't care if he burned the whole building down.

Gingerly, he rolled his sleeve down and eased into his coat with a pained hiss. He put his gloves on, stood, and grabbed the heavy flashlight.

He searched the commercial kitchen until he found something he could use. His flashlight beam swept across stainless-steel counters, cabinets, and an industrial-sized stove. The place stank of spoiling vegetables and faintly of burnt plastic.

The cone of light highlighted a hefty meat tenderizer mallet lying on the stainless-steel island in the center of the prep area. It would do.

When he tried to pick it up with his left hand, an electric shock of pain shot up his arm. He dropped it with a wince.

Furious, he gave the island a savage kick and cursed as the clang reverberated in the silence. He slammed the flashlight down, picked up the mallet with his unwounded hand, and shoved it through his belt loop beneath his coat.

Holding the flashlight low at his side, he exited the back of the diner with care, scanning the snowy darkness before stepping outside.

No one was around. Angry shouts and gunshots echoed from the direction of the library. Maybe the thugs had found the girl and Soldier Boy.

He doubted it. Soldier Boy would've hightailed it back to save the girl and execute their exit strategy. It was the only reason he'd backed off from pursuing Pike.

No matter. Pike could ambush them at any point along the way. He had the advantage here. Not them.

Just as soon as he took care of this arm. He needed a damn doctor to patch him up and provide a truckload of pain meds.

Lucky for him, he had an idea where to go.

His head lowered against the brutal wind, he skirted the diner's parking lot and found his way back to Main Street. He returned to the gas station up the street where his purple snowmobile still waited for him.

Two men remained at the gas station, both holding rifles and standing about ten yards apart. The first one faced south toward the library and the end of town.

The second man stood guard over a pile of dead bodies. Half a dozen, at least. Next to him, two old model snowmobiles towing large sleds were loaded with jerrycans full of gas.

The rifle he carried belonged to Pike.

Pike grimaced. A dark thrill raced up his spine. He'd need gas to get where he was going. He'd need his gun back too.

He hooked the flashlight to his belt and exchanged it for the mallet. He hefted it in his hand, relished the weight of it. It would work just fine.

He crept up behind the man, his boots not as silent as he wished, but the man was distracted by the shouting and gunfire past the library. The wind whistled and moaned, muffling his movements.

The poor sap never even saw Pike coming. He never saw the swing of the mallet either, but he certainly felt it slam into his head and splinter his skull.

The man dropped to the snow with a heavy thud.

Pain scoured Pike's left arm, his muscles screaming in protest. Pike gritted his teeth and let the mallet slip out of his hands.

He bent and picked up the rifle instead. *His* rifle. The scoped Winchester Model 70.

More pain flared up his forearm, but he endured it. He did a quick system check and found everything as he'd left it—the weapon in pristine condition and fully loaded.

The second guard swung around to check on his buddy with a bored expression.

Pike pointed the Winchester at his face.

"Hey, man—"

"Get your hands up. Drop your weapon."

The guard started to raise his weapon, then noticed his friend's body behind Pike, already growing cold in the snow. Wisely, he changed his mind.

He unslung the rifle, dropped it a few feet away, and raised his hands. "Don't shoot me, man. I'll tell you whatever you want to know."

"You find a doctor when you ransacked this town?"

The man shifted nervously from foot to foot. "Hank said he got a good stash of oxy from the clinic. There was a doctor there. A few patients we sent packing. Maybe he was a pediatrician? I don't know. I did what you asked, okay? Don't kill me, man."

"That'll do." Pike gestured with the rifle. He'd leave this idiot alive long enough to take him to this doctor. Then he'd put him down like the maggot deserved. "Take me to him."

61

HANNAH
DAY EIGHT

Hannah was so tired, she kept falling asleep, slumping in her seat, and jerking herself back awake. Her back, shoulders, and hips hurt, her muscles cramping.

Cold needled her extremities. Her feet were blocks of ice, her nostrils raw from inhaling the frigid air. Her eyelids were nearly glued shut from squinting against the icy wind.

They'd been riding hard for what felt like days but was less than two hours.

They'd lost the pursuing ATVs quickly enough. They couldn't go nearly as fast as the Yamaha, rickety as it was.

They skirted town after town and kept going. On every side lay forests interspersed with bleak and wintry farmland. The endless white pockmarked by an occasional dark smudge of a dilapidated barn or shed or house.

It was sometime in the early morning on New Year's Eve. Nothing moved. No cars or trucks on the road. No planes arcing across the black sky.

They might have been the only living creatures in the universe.

Finally, Liam slowed to a stop and switched off the engine. He pulled off his helmet. "We just exited Manistee National Forest. We're outside of Newaygo."

They were parked on the shoulder of an empty road lined with pine forests. To their right sat a three-story ramshackle farmhouse on a small hill set far back from the road. No other houses or buildings were in sight.

"Stay here," Liam said.

Hannah was too exhausted to argue. She just wanted to get off the stupid snowmobile and find somewhere safe to rest—and to pee. And she was desperately worried about Ghost.

Liam retrieved his pistol, slid off the snowmobile, and slipped on his snowshoes. He moved cautiously toward the tree line. Within a few moments, his stealthy form had disappeared into the dark.

He didn't use his flashlight or approach the property head-on like most people. He was sneaky. An invisible threat.

She shuddered, once again grateful he was on her side.

Hannah managed to get her helmet off and let it drop into the snow. She clambered awkwardly off the Yamaha and sagged against it, hugging her arms to her chest and shivering.

Her legs were blocks of ice. She could barely stand, let alone walk back to check on her dog.

The wind had stilled. The night was pitch black and utterly still. Miles and miles of endless snow.

Everything sounded different in the freezing cold. Sharp-edged and brittle. The hiss of the wind skimmed over the ice and hard-packed snow and through the bare stiff branches of oak and maple and birch. Pine boughs rustled.

Her mind was sluggish. It felt like her brain cells were freezing.

Her mind drifted. She didn't even hear Liam returning until he was at her side.

He held the pistol low at his thigh. "The house is empty. And the barn. No one's been there for at least a week."

"G-Ghost," she said through chattering teeth. "What about Ghost?"

Liam knelt next to the sled and checked on Ghost. He was conscious but sluggish and barely alert. His whole body was shivering violently. Snow and ice crusted his coat.

The poor dog had been exposed to the elements the entire trip. If only they'd had a blanket or something to shield him from the wind and cold. Hopefully, his thick fur was enough to protect him.

Hannah's heart constricted. If anything happened to him, she didn't think she could bear it. Not after everything she'd already been through. Not after everything she'd endured.

One more loss might break her, shatter her into a thousand pieces.

It didn't matter that she'd only known this dog for a week. They were the same. He was hers, and she was his. Her past and future entwined with his in ways she couldn't articulate.

She needed him. She needed him to be okay.

"Is it safe to stop?" She hoped desperately that Liam would say yes. Ghost needed rest, and so did she. "Can we stay here?"

Liam stood, scanned their surroundings again before answering. "He's still out there."

"H-he won't give up. He'll come after us. But I don't think he'll come tonight." She angled her chin at the dog. "Ghost did a job on his arm."

Liam gave a tight nod. "He did good."

"He's hurt. He needs a veterinarian."

"Don't know where we'll find one."

"We have to look. Not every town will be like Branch. Some will still be holding up okay."

"It's a risk to stay here."

She licked her chapped lips. Liam wasn't wrong. But Ghost was wounded. He needed medical attention. Maybe he'd be okay and heal on his own, or maybe his brain was swelling dangerously or he'd sustained some other traumatic injury they couldn't see.

"Ghost saved me. We can't just leave him like this." She raised her chin. "I won't."

"Fine." Liam shook his head in resignation. "At dawn, we'll look for a doctor. We'll stay here for a few hours to rest and get warm. That's it. Not a minute longer."

"In the farmhouse?"

Liam pointed to a large red barn behind the farmhouse. "It's safer to stay there. Less of a chance of someone breaking in looking for food. The hay will insulate us from the cold."

She nodded. He was right. She didn't want to be anywhere near other people.

They were both skittish and edgy, their nerves raw.

Liam pulled a penlight from his pack and handed it to her. "Keep it aimed low."

He dropped Hannah off at the barn, used a lock pick to open the old padlock barring the doors, and shoved one open.

Hannah trudged into the barn, kicking snow off her boots, and breathed in the musty scents of hay and manure and grease.

A couple of old tractors hulked in the shadows on the far end. Piles of hay. Four stalls and a tack room. Large rusty tools she didn't know the names of hung along one wall.

Liam parked the snowmobile behind the barn, out of sight of the road and the farmhouse. Hannah took the opportunity to relieve herself. It was as awful as it always was—the bone-rattling cold, her teeth chattering, fingers so stiff she could barely get her pants back up.

After she'd finished, Liam reappeared, cradling Ghost in his arms like a child. She aimed the light at the ground and held the barn door open as Liam carried Ghost inside.

He gently laid the dog on a pile of hay next to an empty horse stall. He searched the tack room and returned with several moth-eaten saddle blankets.

He knelt beside Ghost and rubbed the snow from his coat and wiped down his legs and tail. He draped the blankets across his torso. Unslinging his backpack from his shoulders, he tugged out a first aid kit and daubed at the bloody fur of Ghost's head and throat with blood-clotting gauze.

After so callously dispatching multiple human beings, Liam treated the animal with more tenderness than Hannah would've expected.

She still wasn't sure how she felt about that. But right now, she was too tired to object to anything, certainly not rest and warmth.

When Liam was finished with Ghost, he turned to Hannah. "Where are you hurt?"

Gingerly, she grazed her ribs with her fingers. They were sore and tender, but hopefully not broken. Her scalp stung. She pushed up her hat and felt dried blood crusted at her hairline.

The memories rushed in—*his* face looming over her, that red slash of a mouth, the awful scent of cloves clogging her throat, the terror.

She closed her eyes, forced them open. Pike wasn't here. She was safe. "He kicked me. Punched me. Ghost got there before he . . . before anything happened."

Liam's mouth tightened. His eyes went hard. "I'd say plenty happened."

Her hand strayed unbidden to her stomach. She felt movement, like a fish flopping, an alien creature sliding around inside her.

She didn't care. Told herself she didn't want it. Loathed the idea of *his* spawn growing inside her. And yet . . . The barest glimmer of relief flickered through her.

"I'm fine," she said. "Everything's okay."

"You're not fine, Hannah," he said gruffly. "Let me help you."

She stiffened but allowed him to clean the cut on her forehead, apply a topical antibiotic and butterfly bandage, and give her Tylenol for her sore ribs. His fingers were calloused but gentle.

Her stomach knotted with a tangle of competing emotions. To be touched in kindness rather than cruelty was both incredibly unnerving and a comfort at the same time.

Her eyes were suddenly wet. She could have wept right then and there.

Liam was certainly dangerous, but he wasn't a danger to her. He'd proved that again and again tonight. He was on her side.

It was her own fear she needed to conquer.

He drank from his water bottle and handed the spare one to her. It was still full.

She drank deeply and wiped her mouth. "Thank you, Liam."

He only grunted.

She handed Liam the penlight and collapsed into the pile of hay next to Ghost. His chest rose and fell—barely. He smelled like wet fur and dog breath and comfort. She snuggled against him, his furry back against her belly, his fur tickling her cheek. He whimpered softly.

"What time is it?" she asked Liam.

"Two twenty-five a.m."

"It's New Year's Eve," she said, hardly able to believe it. "Today."

Liam only grunted. He brought her two extra saddle blankets.

"It's just a day like any other. Cover yourself with hay and drape the blankets over you."

Her bones ached with exhaustion. Her lower back hurt, along with her ribs in several places. She winced as she drew the blankets over her legs.

Instead of joining them in the hay, Liam stationed himself on an overturned five-gallon bucket near the barn door, the AR-15 rifle he'd stolen in his lap. Standing guard. Still watching over them, even though he had to be as weary as she was.

He set the two pistols he'd confiscated from the thugs beside him on the barn floor, pulled out an emergency thermal blanket from his go-bag, and draped it across his shoulders.

"Aren't you going to sleep?"

"Not tired."

She didn't believe that. Looking at him again, she realized how weary he truly was. How he moved gingerly, pain shadowing his eyes. He was hurting. Physically, but also, more than that.

He'd saved her tonight, her and Ghost both. And it had cost him to do so.

62

HANNAH
DAY EIGHT

Brittle cold fingered through the cracks in the barn walls. Hannah burrowed deeper into the hay. The heat from Ghost's body radiated into her own. If she wasn't warm, at least she wasn't freezing.

Liam took off his hat, raked his hand through his chestnut hair, and pulled it low over his ears. He glanced at her, his expression tense. Dark shadows ringed his eyes. His jaw worked like he had something to say but was restraining himself.

"What is it?" she asked, even though she already knew what was coming.

Liam watched her steadily, his gaze unrelenting. "What does he want?"

Her cheeks heated. She wanted to look away. To run and hide. But she couldn't. It was time to have this conversation. Liam Coleman more than anyone deserved an explanation. The truth.

"He wants me. He wants this." She gestured at her belly. "He's going to cut it out, and then he's going to kill me. He can't let me live.

It's like—like as long as I'm alive, he loses. And he can't bear losing control of anything."

"Then we make sure he doesn't find you."

"He—" she swallowed. "He knows where I'm going."

A muscle in his jaw twitched. "What do you mean?"

"I mean, not which small towns we'll stop at on the way or our direct route. But he knows the destination. He knows where home is."

She closed her eyes, sucked in several deep breaths, opened them.

The darkness pushed in, but she pushed back. Counted the wooden planks of the barn wall, the colored threads of the saddle blanket, the strands of straw.

She willed herself to stay present, to remain centered. It was easier this time. "Because I know him. I'd . . . forgotten. But I remember now. Who he is."

Hannah saw the scene unraveling in her mind's eye as vivid and visceral as if it were happening here and now. The chilly winter night. The busted tire. The shoulder of the empty, isolated road.

Snow crunching beneath her boots, icy crystalized clouds billowing from her mouth with every breath as she cursed herself for not having a spare tire. She'd gotten a flat a month ago and never got around to replacing the spare.

Yet another fight between her and Noah. She wanted to replace the spare; he said they couldn't afford it. Not with her looming tuition and the enormous daycare bills for three-year-old Milo.

Because she wanted to go back to school and finish her degree, and Noah wanted her to stay home. Not because he was sexist, but he wanted Milo to have what he hadn't—two present, engaged parents.

Hannah had Milo at eighteen. A surprise, not a mistake. She loved him with her whole heart. She'd never call him a mistake.

Still, her pregnancy had changed the trajectory of her life in unexpected ways.

Twenty-two-year-old Noah Sheridan had proposed after only five months of long-distance dating. *I want to be a father,* he'd begged her. *I want to make a go at this.*

Hannah had always been one for adventure, jumping feet-first into the unknown. She'd dropped out of her music theory and music education dual degree program at the University of Michigan, packed up her meager campus-housing belongings, and moved in with Noah in his hometown of Fall Creek.

And just like that, she was a cop's wife, about to be a mother, stranded in a tiny backwoods township in southwest Michigan—cut off entirely from the life and dreams she'd known.

It hadn't been easy for either of them. They were young, selfish, and immature.

Noah was used to a bachelor's life. He was loyal to the friends he'd known all his life. Too loyal. Hannah was the outsider. The one who didn't belong.

After three tense and miserable years, she was done trying. Done with feeling so lonely and isolated, so angry and resentful.

She sat in the Camry's driver's seat, ruminating on her failing marriage, getting angrier and angrier at him, at herself, at this ridiculous situation, her gloved fingers restlessly drumming the steering wheel.

The heat and the radio were both cranked to max. She angry-sang along to "All I Want for Christmas is You." Guilt stabbed her. She would be gone on Christmas, wouldn't be home for presents and pancakes smothered in peanut butter and whipped cream, Milo's favorite.

She'd make it up to Milo, she swore to herself. Earlier that day, they'd tried to be a family for him, spending the afternoon at a ski resort, showing him the ropes with the tiny new skis her parents had shipped as an early Christmas gift.

They had always made it work when he was present. They both loved him. It just wasn't enough.

She picked up her phone again and stared at it, simultaneously guilty, furious, and heart-broken. The stupid battery was dead. The charger she usually kept in the Camry was gone. Noah had used it for something and forgot to put it back.

She hurled the phone on the passenger seat and wiped fiercely at her face.

Shivering, she peered through the frosted windshield at the scarecrow trees on either side of the road. A few ragged clouds drifted across the moon. Darkness loomed just beyond her headlights, suddenly seeming sinister and alive.

Unease sprouted in her gut. She'd planned to drive ninety miles north to her best friend's house in Grand Rapids. Not her wisest decision at eleven o'clock at night on Christmas Eve, but it was too late to change her mind now.

She hugged herself, rubbed her arms, suddenly chilled from more than the cold. No one knew she was out here.

She glanced at the gas needle. Still three-quarters of a tank. The heat would last for a while.

What if no one drove by all night? What if no one stopped? What if—

The rumble of an engine broke through the music on the radio. Headlights washed over her and filled the interior of the car.

A black Ford F350 with a shiny grille, bull bar, and hunting spotlights set atop the roof pulled onto the shoulder behind her Camry.

Relief flared through her veins, followed by a twinge of apprehension. A woman alone had reason to worry.

In her rearview mirror, she watched a broad, shadowed shape

climb out of the truck and shut the door, engine still running. He strode through the snow toward her. He wore a uniform beneath his coat. Like a police officer, but not quite.

Hannah! That disarming smile. An unassuming guy, medium height, medium build. Buzzed dirty-blond hair, pleasant features. Brown eyes so dark they were almost black. *Hannah Sheridan. What are you doing so far from home?*

At first, she'd just stared at him blankly. Then she'd recognized him. He lived in Fall Creek on the other side of town. He was some kind of law enforcement officer.

She'd seen him a few dozen times before—at the gas station and grocery store, the bar with friends a couple of times, a New Year's bash one of Noah's cop buddies had thrown.

An acquaintance. He was the brother of her husband's best friend. Both of them cops. She thought he was a deputy, but she wasn't sure.

She'd never really liked him, but that didn't matter now, did it?

The man lifted his coat slightly, revealed the badge clipped to his belt. Smiled wider. *How's Noah doing? He playing any football lately, or is that tennis elbow still giving him problems?*

He was a known entity. A friend, or close enough. The tension in her shoulders eased. She smiled back at him.

You're out awfully late, Hannah. Anyone know where you are? A question laced with hidden minefields. She hadn't seen the danger, hadn't known to watch her step.

With her phone dead, she hadn't had a chance to check in with her best friend, Carly. Carly would give her the spare room in a heartbeat, no questions asked. Hannah hadn't needed to ask ahead of time. That was the kind of sister-bond friendship they shared.

As for her husband . . . no. She hadn't said a word to him as she'd furiously packed an overnight bag and stormed from the house, slamming the door for good measure.

You're shivering! You need to get out of the cold. Sorry I don't have a spare, but I'm happy to give you a ride home. I was just on my way to visit my mother. It's hardly even out of the way.

She'd had no reason not to trust him.

Until she did. And then it was too late.

63

HANNAH
DAY EIGHT

"Gavin Pike," Hannah said, the words like barbed wire on her tongue. "That's his name."

She felt Liam's eyes on her. Piercing straight through to her core.

"He knows who I am." Her heart clenched like a fist. She thought of Milo. Of Noah. Of Pike hurting them. "He knows my . . . my family. He lives in Fall Creek too. He knows exactly where to go."

Liam didn't say anything. His expression was stony, unreadable.

"He . . . he killed CiCi."

Liam cursed.

"She was a good person." Fresh tears strangled the back of her throat. "She didn't deserve what happened to her."

"The good ones never do."

"She helped us. She didn't have to, but she did."

"I know," Liam said. Steel in his voice. Resolve. "I'm going to kill him. I promise you that."

"Thank you," she said simply. "For everything."

It was all she had. She couldn't pay him, couldn't offer him anything but her gratitude. She hoped it was enough.

He didn't speak for a long time. He stared at the barn doors, jaw tensed, his gun gripped in both hands. Like he wished Pike would come walking through those doors right now.

Absently, she rubbed her ruined hand. The swollen, twisted joints ached in the cold. Her fingers were deformed and ugly. She could barely move them, only with great effort. And pain.

Would Noah even want her back now? After what Pike had done to her? That night, she'd been so angry and resentful, but now she wondered why they'd fought at all.

It seemed so pointless, so meaningless. They'd loved each other. They'd had Milo.

They'd had everything and they didn't even know it.

Liam cleared his throat and glanced back at her. "Let me see the gun."

She went still. "What gun?"

He just stared at her.

Of course he knew about the pistol. She'd pointed it at him in the library. As if she could've done anything with it anyway. In her hands, it was as useless as a squirt gun.

"CiCi gave it to me," she said, chagrined. "I should have told you."

"Yes, you should have."

She dropped her gaze, unable to meet his penetrating gray-blue eyes. Shame washed through her. "I'm useless with it anyway. I—I couldn't even pull the trigger."

He held out his hand, palm up. "Let me see it."

She fished the .45 out of her pocket and gave it to him.

He turned it over in his hands, examining it. "It's a good choice for you. Small and light. Reduced recoil. Well-balanced."

He ejected the magazine, then pressed the slide back slightly to open the action and check the chamber. He frowned. "This weapon is loaded. Did you disengage the safety?"

"What?"

He slapped the magazine back in and pointed to a small slide-mounted lever. "You see this here? It's the safety. Even when you squeeze the trigger, if the safety's on, the gun won't fire."

Her cheeks grew hot. Her family had always used Glocks with a trigger safety. Forgetting the Ruger's safety switch was a stupid mistake. In her panic, that knowledge had abandoned her, her mind retreating to what she'd always known.

"I'm sorry," she said, feeling incredibly foolish.

He handed the weapon back to her, safety still on. "Do better next time."

Relief mingled with her embarrassment. She *had* squeezed the trigger after all.

She'd had the guts to do it. To shoot him.

That's what mattered. When the time came, she could do it again. She would do it again.

Liam zipped his pack and switched off the penlight. "Get some sleep. Dawn will come early."

She placed the gun carefully in her pocket and laid back in the prickly straw. Ghost was sleeping. She rolled toward him and buried her fingers in his coat, inhaled the dank scent of him. Pressed her cheek against his soft fur and let her weary eyelids close.

But sleep didn't come, no matter how exhausted she was. The night's events wouldn't stop circling inside her head, again and again. And every time, it ended the same—with Hannah paralyzed, impotent. Powerless.

Even with a weapon, she hadn't been able to defend herself. Or Ghost.

Liam was here now, but he wouldn't always be here. Ghost wouldn't always be able to protect her. She would have to do some of the protecting too.

She didn't want to be helpless. Didn't want to be afraid. And she didn't want to be a victim. Not anymore.

Pike had done that to her. He'd changed her, molded her into the meek and cowering creature that he demanded. But she hadn't always been that way.

Once, she'd been strong, opinionated, stubborn. Confident.

But then that terrible Christmas Eve happened. And everything that came after.

She didn't have to be that girl anymore. The girl stolen from her own life. The girl locked in a cage.

Hannah Sheridan got to decide who she was, who she could become. It started right now.

She sat up. "Liam."

He turned toward her. She couldn't see his rugged features in the dark, only the solid shape of him, a shadow deeper and darker than the other shadows.

"You know how to fight," she said. "How to defend yourself."

He didn't answer.

"You know how to use a gun."

Still he said nothing, waiting.

"You can teach people what you know."

"Is that a question?"

Her mouth twitched in the dark. Not a smile. Not yet. "Will you teach me?"

"Yes," Liam said, "I will."

The End

AUTHOR'S NOTE

I hope you enjoyed *Edge of Collapse*! When I set out to write an EMP survival thriller, I knew I wanted to do something different. I had this idea—could the grid going down be a positive thing for anyone?

I had this image of a locked door opening in my head. Who was behind that locked door? Why was she there? What could an unlocked door mean to her? Freedom? Salvation? And that, my friends, is how the character of Hannah was born.

In researching EMPs, I discovered a lot of conflicting information. The truth is, we have a lot of theories and ideas, but we don't know for certain exactly how devastating an EMP would be. A lot depends on the size, strength, and height of the detonation. Would it be strong enough to take out phones? Radios? The electronic systems in our cars?

While I tried to be as accurate as possible, a little creative license is part of the fun of fiction. We get to imagine a world, put our characters inside it, and see what happens.

A little note on pregnancy. Every woman experiences it differently. I carried small and was active up until the week I was due. My best friend threw up the entire nine months. My cousin never had cravings. I couldn't stop eating chocolate. Some of my friends glowed with energy through most of their pregnancies, others struggled to just get through each day. Hannah's struggles are uniquely hers, just as every pregnancy is unique.

I hope you'll continue to follow Hannah, Liam, and Ghost on their journey throughout the *Edge of Collapse* series.

Thank you for reading!

ALSO BY KYLA STONE

The *Edge of Collapse* Post-Apocalyptic Series (EMP):

Chaos Rising: The Prequel

Edge of Collapse

Edge of Mayhem

Edge of Darkness

Edge of Defiance

Edge of Survival

Edge of Valor

The *Nuclear Dawn* Post-Apocalyptic Series (Nuclear Terrorism):

Point of Impact

Fear the Fallout

From the Ashes

Into the Fire

Darkest Night

The *Last Sanctuary* Post-Apocalyptic Series (Pandemic):

Rising Storm

Burning Skies

Raging Light

No Safe Haven (A post-apocalyptic stand-alone novel):

No Safe Haven

Historical Fantasy:

Labyrinth of Shadows

Contemporary YA:

Beneath the Skin

Before You Break

ACKNOWLEDGMENTS

Thank you as always to my awesome beta readers. Your thoughtful critiques and enthusiasm are invaluable. As I embark on a brand new series, your support and encouragement meant everything to me

Thank you so much to Fred Oelrich, Melva Metivier, Wmh Cheryl, Annette Cairl, Jessica Burland, Sally Shupe, Becca and Brendan Cross, Robert Odell, and to George Hall for his keen eye and military expertise.

To Michelle Browne for her line editing skills and Nadene Seiters for proofreading.

And a special thank you to Jenny Avery for catching those last pesky errors and for her genius with maps and geography.

Another special thank you goes to Rhonda Stapleton for the suggestion of CiCi as an elderly but tough gun-toting broad with a soft heart for a specific few. This idea inspired a memorable minor character who I ended up loving to pieces. May CiCi live on in our hearts forever.

And to my husband, who takes care of the house, the kids, and the cooking when I'm under the gun with a writing deadline. To my kids, who show me the true meaning of love every day and continually inspire me.

Thanks to God for His many blessings.

And to my loyal readers, whose support and encouragement mean everything to me. Thank you.

ABOUT THE AUTHOR

I spend my days writing apocalyptic and dystopian fiction novels, exploring all the different ways the world might end.

I love writing stories exploring how ordinary people cope with extraordinary circumstances, especially situations where the normal comforts, conveniences, and rules are stripped away.

My favorite stories to read and write deal with characters struggling with inner demons who learn to face and overcome their fears, launching their transformation into the strong, brave warrior they were meant to become.

Some of my favorite books include *The Road*, *The Passage*, *Hunger Games*, and *Ready Player One*. My favorite movies are *The Lord of the Rings* and *Gladiator*.

Give me a good story in any form and I'm happy.

Oh, and add in a cool fall evening in front of a crackling fire, nestled on the couch with a fuzzy blanket, a book in one hand and a hot mocha latte in the other (or dark chocolate!): that's my heaven.

I mean, I won't say no to hiking to mountain waterfalls, traveling to far-flung locations, or jumping out of a plane (parachute included) either.

I love to hear from my readers! Find my books and chat with me via any of the channels below:

www.KylaStone.com

www.Facebook.com/KylaStoneAuthor
www.Amazon.com/author/KylaStone
Email me at KylaStone@yahoo.com